DOUBLE TROUBLE

STEPHANIE HARTE

Boldwood

First published in Great Britain in 2024 by Boldwood Books Ltd.

Copyright © Stephanie Harte, 2024

Cover Design by Colin Thomas

Cover Photography: Colin Thomas

A CIP catalogue record for this book is available from the British Library.

Paperback ISBN 978-1-83533-182-8

Large Print ISBN 978-1-83533-178-1

Hardback ISBN 978-1-83533-177-4

Ebook ISBN 978-1-83533-175-0

Kindle ISBN 978-1-83533-176-7

Audio CD ISBN 978-1-83533-183-5

MP3 CD ISBN 978-1-83533-180-4

Digital audio download ISBN 978-1-83533-174-3

Boldwood Books Ltd
23 Bowerdean Street
London SW6 3TN
www.boldwoodbooks.com

In loving memory of my Cairn Terrier, Ruby
You were by my side for fifteen wonderful years
I miss you more than words can say
Rest in peace, little one

1

DAISY

Tuesday 30 December

'I'm going for a smoke,' I said, picking up my pack of Marlboros and disposable lighter.

With a mascara-coated cotton wool ball gripped in her finger-tips, Lily tore her attention away from the light-up mirror. She swivelled around on the stool, making a point of looking up at the clock and letting out a sigh before she replied.

'Don't be too long; my bed's calling.'

Lily took her position as the self-appointed designated driver very seriously. It made perfect sense to me, as she didn't drink or do drugs. But she liked to try and hold me to ransom over it. I didn't give a flying fuck whether she gave me a lift or not. She was my twin, older by a mere fifteen minutes, but that didn't give her the right to call the shots. She wasn't my keeper.

'You don't need to wait for me. I'll get a cab,' I said over my shoulder.

I hadn't tried to hide the irritation in my voice. Why bother? She knew I despised her. She always had something to complain about and could suck the joy right out of the room just by opening her mouth. I was in a bad enough mood because of MacKenzie and the last thing I needed was Lily winding me up. I was fit to blow my top.

I pushed open the backstage dressing room door with more force than necessary and stepped into the hallway, which led to the alleyway. The familiar scent of stale urine wafted up my nostrils when I emerged outside. Despite the management's best efforts to keep the side entrance to Eden's clean, the dimly lit passage was a magnet to a person with a full bladder. During the day, people wouldn't have dreamt of pissing here, but that all went out the window once booze was involved. When nature called to a drunk, they didn't care where they relieved themselves.

Flipping the lid of the pack, I took out a cigarette, pausing momentarily to light it before walking towards the end of the building so that I could people-watch. But the London street was deserted. When I leaned against the brickwork, I could feel the rough, scratchy surface through the fabric of my coat.

I closed my eyes and took a long drag, hoping to banish thoughts of my sister from my head. I was still drawing the smoke into my lungs when I heard a car stop abruptly in front of Eden's. My eyes snapped open. Keeping my body close to the wall, I extended my neck so that I could see around the corner. A huge SUV with blacked out windows far too big for city driving had pulled up at the kerb.

The driver stayed inside while the other doors opened. Three bear-sized men climbed out, and my pulse rate spiked in response. My thoughts turned to MacKenzie, cashing up the night's takings inside, and my blood ran cold. Even though we weren't on the best of terms, the idea that something bad was about to happen to him made the contents of my stomach flip, but my feet remained rooted to the spot. There was nothing I could do to help him.

The sound of the men's footsteps echoed across the empty street. As the vibrations bounced around above me, it made the narrow passage feel eerie. The hairs on the back of my neck suddenly stood up, and my breathing became erratic. I knew this alleyway, so I had no reason to react like this, but the walls felt like they were closing in on me.

Worried that the smoke might give away my hiding place, I dropped my cigarette onto the floor and ground it out with the toe of my shoe. I held my breath as I watched the three men approaching the half-pulled-down shutter of the club entrance. They walked with purpose, shoulders back, standing tall. Most of the door staff had clocked off for the night safe in the knowledge that it was well past last orders. Only skeleton staff remained.

I could see Igor, the head doorman, standing guard at the entrance, waiting to pounce on anyone stupid enough to try and step over the threshold of his domain after closing hours. It always amazed me what lengths people would go to to get another drink when they'd already had enough to pickle their livers. But then again, we were all guilty of not wanting a good night out to come to an end, weren't we?

The men's footsteps ceased, and I saw them exchange a few words with Igor, but their voices were so low I couldn't make out what they were saying. My heart skipped a beat when I heard the distinctive sound of the metal shutter moving. I knew he must have let them in.

2

LILY

'You were quick. I wasn't expecting you back so soon,' I said.

I'd been reaching under the dressing table for a fresh cotton wool pad when I heard the door to the dressing room open. Taking my make-up off was my top priority. I didn't want to wake up with mascara and lipstick smeared all over my pillow, so I was determined to remove every last trace. As I looked into the mirror, I jumped, startled by the presence of three guys wearing dark suits and ties staring back at me. I'd never seen them before. I wasn't sure what they were doing at the club after closing time, but I wondered if they were looking for Samson Fox, the owner. Judging by the way they were dressed, they might be going to a business meeting, and I'd been told it wasn't unusual for Samson to entertain clients in the early hours of the morning.

'Can I help you?' I asked, turning around on the stool to face them. 'Are you looking for Samson?'

I tilted my head to one side while I waited for a reply. But it didn't come. As a performer, I was used to controlling my nerves, but all of that went out of the window when one of the men closed the distance between us, reached forward and grasped both my hands in his. I dropped the cotton wool pad I was holding as he dragged me out of my chair, hauling me to my feet. The speed at which it happened blew my mind.

'What's going on? Get your hands off me!'

I was desperately trying to break free of his grasp, but his hold on me was too strong.

'Igor, Igor, I need some help in here,' I yelled at the top of my lungs.

The man clamped the fingers of one of his hands over my mouth while holding both of my wrists with the other. I tried to sink my teeth into his flesh, but I couldn't seem to latch on because his hand was cupped.

A million thoughts started bombarding my brain. How had they got in? Igor was on the door, and nothing usually got past him. Where the hell was he? He was a huge guy and was well used to manhandling lumps like this. Even though he'd have been outnumbered, he was an expert in control and restraint. He could fell the biggest opponent without breaking into a sweat, using pressure points to bring the person to their knees and have them begging for mercy. A horrifying thought crashed into my brain. Something must have happened to Igor. Otherwise, he'd have come when I called.

The only other person on the premises was MacKenzie, who was cashing up the takings in the bar on the floor above. He was a bit on the scrawny side, but beggars couldn't be choosers. The minutes were ticking by, and I was still alone in the basement, praying Daisy would hurry up and finish her cigarette. I'd always loved the peace and quiet of our dressing room and the fact that you felt cut off from the hustle and bustle of the rest of the club, but not any more. I felt isolated; out on a limb and totally at the mercy of the men who had barged into my private space.

Nobody was coming to help. I had to fight back. But I was slight and not physically strong, so I knew I was no match for the man holding me. Then, a sudden burst of determination flooded through my veins, and I started twisting my arms around, trying to break out of the man's grip. When he laughed at my efforts, it riled me up more. I managed to get one of my wrists free, so I clawed at his hand with my long nails, hoping to pull his fingers off of my mouth. As he let go, I screamed blue murder, but my cry for help was short-lived. One of the other men shoved a gag into my mouth with such force that when it hit the back of my throat, I thought I was going to vomit. The reflex was so strong I felt myself retch. He covered my mouth with silver duct tape, and I felt my nostrils flare as I dragged air into my lungs while battling to control my breathing.

The man pulled out a set of plastic restraints and cuffed my wrists behind my back. As he tightened the strap, he caught my skin. The pinch stung, which made me yelp. I'd never felt so helpless; tears stabbed at the back of my eyes, but I wouldn't give these men the satisfaction of seeing me cry. The man who wasn't involved with tying me up opened the dressing room door, and the other two linked their arms through the crooks of my elbows and started leading me out of the room. I immediately dug my heels into the floor, bent my knees to concentrate my body weight and leaned backwards, trying to make myself as heavy as possible. But it made no difference. They were able to move me without any physical effort.

As we left the dressing room, I hoped they would turn right and follow the corridor out to the alley where Daisy had gone for a smoke. I knew she wouldn't be able to fight off the men either, but at least she could raise the alarm. But they went the opposite way, dragging me up the flight of stairs. The sound of our shoes echoed against the stone, and I hoped Igor would hear us and come to investigate, but he didn't appear. Once we'd climbed to the top, they pulled me along the carpeted hallway. My eyes darted left and right. I was hoping I'd catch sight of MacKenzie or Igor, but there was no sign of anybody. Eden's seemed unnaturally quiet even at this unearthly hour of the morning.

When we walked out of the club, my heartbeat went into overdrive. I could feel my pulse throbbing at the side of my neck. Time was running out for me. I had no idea why these men were spiriting me away in the middle of the night. But they were going to get away with it. The street was deserted, so there were no witnesses to the crime they were committing. Hopelessness rose within me when the man who wasn't linking my arms strode ahead of us and opened the back passenger door of a large dark car. I started wriggling and bucking, trying my best to break away while I still had the chance, as all the while, the car's interior grew closer. I twisted my head from side to side, hoping to catch the eye of a passer-by, but it was useless. Eden's warren-like interior was spread between two arches beneath Denmark Hill Station. Although it was far too late for any commuters to be milling about, this area of Camberwell was normally a hive of activity around the clock. Not tonight, though.

Just as I was about to be bundled into the back seat of the car, I turned my head to one side when I saw a flash of red out of the corner of my eye. My breath caught in my throat as I realised it was Daisy. She was standing at the junction of the main road and the alleyway that led to the side entrance of the club. I wasn't sure if she'd seen me, so I tried to scream to get her attention, but the sound was muffled by the gag and the tape, so nothing came out.

Despite my best efforts to hold them back, tears began streaming down my cheeks. There was nothing more terrifying than being overpowered and forcefully taken by strangers. My anxiety was going through the roof. Hysteria simmered inside me. I'd never known fear like this. It was paralysing.

The car's engine started, and moments later, it pulled away from the kerb. God only knew where they were taking me and what they were going to do to me. I'd been thrown into a nightmare there was no waking up from.

3

DAISY

I'd glued myself to the wall, gripping the brickwork for stability, hoping I was invisible to passers-by while I'd waited for the guys to re-emerge from Eden's. It felt like it had taken an eternity, but in reality, probably only five minutes had passed.

When I saw one of the men striding towards the car, I peered into the darkness, craning my neck to get a better look. He opened the back passenger door closest to the kerb before walking around the boot of the car and climbing in the other side. My breath caught in my throat when Lily came into view. Her hands were cuffed behind her back, and she was flanked on either side by the other two men, wriggling like a fish caught on a line trying her best to break free. I edged forward to get a better look. She couldn't call for help. Her mouth was taped shut. The look of sheer terror on her face said it all. I could hear my heartbeat pounding in my ears. There was too much to take in. I couldn't process what was happening. My head felt like it was about to explode.

Her eyes were bulging with fear as they towed her towards the SUV. When she reached the car, she started thrashing about in a last-ditch attempt to escape. What the fuck was going on? Where were those guys taking Lily? And more importantly, why were they bundling my sister into the back of a car in the early hours of the morning? What could they want with Lily? There was no way she'd have got herself mixed up in any trouble. She was the straightest person you could ever meet. She wouldn't even park on a yellow line for fear of getting a ticket, not even for a split second.

Just before they pushed her onto the back seat, Lily turned her head in my direction. I wasn't sure if she'd spotted me before I sank back into the shadows. I couldn't let her blow my cover. I knew that was cowardly behaviour, but I didn't want to get mixed up in whatever it was she was involved in.

As the last man went to get into the car, he glanced towards the alley, training his eyes on my hiding place. I'd been trying to stay still, but maybe he'd noticed a slight shift in the shadows. Trust me to be wearing red. Only time would tell if he'd caught sight of me.

After what seemed like an endless pause, he climbed in next to Lily and closed the back door. As the SUV pulled away, I tried to get a look at the number plate, but I couldn't make it out from where I was standing, and I wasn't about to step away from the wall and risk being seen.

Once the car had faded into the distance, I knew I had to raise the alarm. I charged down the alley, relief flooding my body as I stepped inside the safety of the club. After making sure I'd bolted the door behind me, I ran along the corridor as fast as I could, but it wasn't easy in heels. The sound of my stilettos connecting with the concrete floor filled the space in the basement around me. I bounded up the steps and only stopped to catch my breath for a split second when I reached the top. A moment later, I ran along the hallway, past the first door on the right, which led to the stage where Lily and I sang on a Tuesday night. Although the venue only held five hundred people, it seemed to take an age to reach the second door, MacKenzie's office, which separated the bar from the live-acts venue. He looked up from a pile of twenty-pound notes when I burst into the room.

'What's up?' he asked.

'Lily's just been bundled into the back of a car by three heavies.'

I wasn't used to exercise like this, so I was breathless from the exertion. My chest was heaving from running.

'She's what?' he quizzed with a look of confusion plastered across his features.

'She's been kidnapped. I don't know what to do,' I threw the palms of my hands up. 'I'd better call the police.'

'No way. Samson will go nuts if the Old Bill starts sniffing around his club,' MacKenzie replied.

I'd been expecting a bit more of a reaction from him. It wasn't normal for a young woman to be snatched, but the way he was carrying on, you'd swear this sort of thing happened every day of the week.

'So what should I do?' I put my hands on my hips and stared at him, frustrated by the lack of help he was offering me.

MacKenzie shrugged his bony shoulders. 'Go and ask Igor. Maybe he knows something.'

'Where is he?'

'Not sure; he's probably still on the door,' MacKenzie said before casting his eyes back to the wad of notes he was holding.

It went without saying that most doormen were big individuals, and Igor was no exception. I could see the huge shadow of his sizable frame as I got closer to the shutter. It was dark in the foyer, but the street lights outside were casting a hazy glow into the open space. Igor was leaning against the wall, scrolling through his phone. He turned around to look at me as I approached.

'Lily's been taken.'

Igor's white-blond eyebrows knitted into a frown.

'Taken?' he questioned.

I nodded. 'Do you know what happened?'

'No.'

'You didn't see anything?'

Igor shook his clean-shaven head.

'Are you sure? I was in the alley having a smoke, and I saw three men leave with her a few minutes ago.'

'I'm sure,' Igor nodded.

I'd seen him let them in. Then a little while later, they'd walked right out of the entrance in front of where Igor was standing. He noticed things other people didn't. He was constantly alert, always on the lookout for potentially risky situations. It went with the territory. So how could he have missed them?

I could tell he knew more than he was letting on, by the way his eyes darted from side to side and the fact that he seemed reluctant to look at me. He'd tried to bat away my suspicion, but he hadn't quite managed to. I knew full well I was embarking on dangerous ground, but I carried on regardless. I had to know what was going on.

'Have you been here the whole time?' I quizzed.

'Yes.'

That was either a blatant lie, or Igor had turned a blind eye when the men took Lily against her will out of the club. If he knew something, Igor's lips were sealed. I wasn't sure what I'd been expecting him to say. But I supposed he wasn't likely to blurt out, 'Oh yeah, now that you've asked, you might be interested to know, I stood by and watched your sister being manhandled out of the club.' He was bound to deny having any knowledge of what had happened. I wanted to call him out on it, but what was the point? He wasn't going to tell me the truth. It didn't make any sense.

The guys who took Lily were heavy-duty, so he could have been scared to get involved. Perhaps they'd threatened him. I didn't know the answer. Lily and I had always got on well with Igor, so I wanted to give him the benefit of the doubt. Maybe he wasn't lying. He might not have seen the men take Lily. He could have sloped off into the bar to help himself to a couple of free vodkas while he was waiting for us to finish up. If he'd admitted that he'd been away from his post, it would land him in hot water with Samson. If that was the case, I couldn't blame him for covering up. Being the head doorman was a tough job. Dealing with the drunk and disorderly could be dangerous and tedious. Samson expected a lot from him, so he deserved to have a drink on the house if he got the opportunity.

Oh, who was I trying to kid? I'd seen Igor standing at the entrance when the men approached. I knew he was lying to me. But why?

'You've got to help me. Lily's in trouble, and I don't know what to do.'

I'd never had a close relationship with my sister. We didn't see eye to eye on most things, but she was my twin, and whether I liked it or not, we shared an unbreakable bond. I couldn't just stand by and do nothing.

'I've already told you, I didn't see anything. It's getting late; I need to lock up,' Igor replied, washing his hands of the situation.

* * *

MacKenzie was slumped in his chair with his head in his hands, looking like a man with the weight of the world on his shoulders. He straightened his posture when I walked back into the office. My eyes were drawn to the traces of white powder visible around his nostrils.

'All right, babe?' he said as I came into view, replacing his scowl with a bright smile.

'Don't call me babe. Of course I'm not all right; Lily's missing,' I snapped, irritated by his stupid question.

'So, did the big Pole manage to shed any light on the matter?'

MacKenzie ran his forefinger backwards and forwards under his nose, dislodging the coke residue.

'No, he reckons he didn't see anything, but those guys came right out the front entrance next to where he should have been standing.'

'Maybe he'd gone for a shit or sloped off for a sly drink,' MacKenzie suggested.

'Or maybe he's involved,' I added.

'Listen, Daisy, don't go jumping to conclusions.'

That was easier said than done. I was really starting to worry now. I couldn't shake off the uneasy feeling creeping up inside me. A team of four security staff manned the door, but Igor had been the only one on duty when Lily was taken, so there weren't any other potential witnesses.

MacKenzie pushed his chair back, stood up and then walked over to where I was standing. As he went to wrap his arms around me in an attempt to comfort me, I moved out of his reach. He looked hurt at being shunned, but his feelings were the least of my concerns. His display of affection was too little, too late. He'd missed his chance with me. That ship had sailed.

'What am I supposed to think? My gut feeling is that Lily's in real danger.'

'Have you considered the possibility that Lily isn't as squeaky clean as you think she is,' MacKenzie said, throwing a different scenario into the mix.

I didn't even bother holding in the laugh that escaped from my lips. 'You're joking, right? You have met my sister before, haven't you?' I tilted my head to one side, waiting for his response. The cocaine MacKenzie had snorted was clearly affecting his judgement.

'You can laugh all you want, but it's human nature to suspect the dodgy-looking guy, not the fairytale princess.'

'I get what you're saying, but you know what Lily's like. She isn't one of life's risk-takers. She does everything by the book and doesn't have a daring bone in her body.'

'To the outside world,' MacKenzie said, determined not to let go of his theory.

I looked at him warily. I wasn't buying it. He'd only known Lily for about a month. I'd shared a womb with her, so I was better qualified to judge her character. Then again, maybe he was right. Maybe Lily wasn't as dull and dutiful as she led everyone to believe. Perhaps she had a wild streak after all. Anything was possible, but I found that idea hard to swallow. It was far more likely she'd been in the wrong place at the wrong time and she'd been snatched by mistake.

'Lily wouldn't have the nerve to stray off the straight path.'

'I wouldn't be so sure about that; it's always the quiet ones…' MacKenzie let his sentence trail off.

'As you appear to be such an expert, what do you think Lily's got herself mixed up in?'

'It's hard to say; it could be drugs, or she might owe somebody money, who knows? Your guess is as good as mine,' MacKenzie replied noncommittally.

'Drugs? She doesn't even drink. Lily's idea of letting her hair down is treating herself to a selection box at Christmas.' I shook my head. We were getting nowhere with this. 'If I can't call the police, what am I supposed to do?'

'Sit tight and see how things pan out, babe.'

'How many times do I have to ask you not to call me babe?'

I spoke through gritted teeth and fixed him with a glare.

'Oops,' MacKenzie replied.

'Mum and Dad are due back in a couple of days, and if she hasn't turned up by then, Dad will lose his shit.'

My parents had gone to York with a group of friends to see in the New Year. There was no way I wanted to phone them to tell them Lily had been snatched. They'd be on the first train home if they knew their precious daughter was missing.

'She'll be back by then.'

'You seem pretty sure about that.'

I locked eyes with MacKenzie, and he flashed me one of his winning smiles, but it was lost on me. I had a feeling in the pit of my stomach that he was hiding something from me.

'Call it intuition. The best thing to do is sleep on it. Things always look different in the morning.'

MacKenzie attempted to swipe away my concerns, but a growing sense of unease was building up inside me. How was I supposed to sleep when a vision of my sister, handcuffed and gagged, being bundled into the back of the car, was etched into my brain?

'If you know what's good for you, you won't start digging too deep into this.'

'What's that supposed to mean?'

What was MacKenzie implying? Was he threatening me? The palms of my hands began to sweat. I suddenly felt scared for my own safety.

MacKenzie jumped out of his skin when his mobile began to ring, sparing him the trouble of answering my question.

'Aren't you going to get that?' I asked when the phone kept ringing.

MacKenzie shrugged.

'It must be important if somebody's calling you at this time.'

'Give me a minute, will you,' he said as he picked up the handset.

He gestured with a flick of his head for me to leave the office. I stepped out of the door, but I made sure I stayed within earshot.

'Hello,' MacKenzie said.

I couldn't hear what the caller was saying, but judging by his response, they weren't exchanging pleasantries.

'I know you did, and I'm really sorry, but I need more time. I can't raise that kind of money in a couple of days...'

Something told me if I could untangle the connection between MacKenzie and whoever he was talking to, it would lead me to Lily. I'd be amazed if he didn't know more about my sister's disappearance than he was letting on.

4

MACKENZIE

One month earlier

'Hey, Mac, I thought you should know, Arben just sent two of his thugs over,' Leroy said.

I'd been restocking the bar, but this could wait. If Arben Hasani's guys were sniffing around, it top trumped anything I'd been previously doing. He was a cheeky fucker and should know better than to wander onto our turf without an invitation.

'What did they have to say for themselves?'

'Nothing. They didn't get out of the car. They just cruised past in a matte black BMW a couple of times before parking outside the entrance. They stayed there for a bit to make sure we'd seen them,' Leroy said.

Something was up. You didn't need to be a brain surgeon to realise that. London was subdivided by invisible borders drawn by organised crime gangs, and straying onto somebody else's patch didn't happen by accident. Samson wouldn't be happy to hear that Hasani, a drug lord from Has in north-eastern Albania, was trespassing on his territory.

'We've just had some unwanted visitors,' I said when Samson answered the phone.

'Not the Old Bill again. What the fuck did they want this time?'

Samson was fuming and he wouldn't be any happier when I told him who the mystery guests were.

'It wasn't the cops. Leroy spotted two of Arben Hasani's guys cruising past the front of Eden's,' I replied.

'And?' Samson's tone was dismissive.

'They parked outside the entrance for a while to make sure they'd been seen.'

'Tell Igor and the guys to keep their eyes peeled and phone me if anything goes down. I'll be in later on,' Samson said before he ended the call.

5

DAISY

Our practice space was truly a depressing sight. There was nothing luxurious about bare breeze block walls, a concrete floor and dusty, fly-covered cobwebs. We'd been out here for hours already and my fingers and toes were numb from the cold, and I was losing the will to live. But it would take more than my untimely death to derail Dad from his mission. He wouldn't rest until his girls hit the big time.

'OK, let's take it from the top,' Dad said, starting the backing track of 'Time After Time'.

'Oh, God, not again.' My voice came out in a whiney moan as my shoulders slumped, defeated.

Dad's head snapped around, and he glared at me with his bright blue eyes.

'Maybe if you put a bit of effort in, we wouldn't have to keep going over the same song.'

I could see Dad grinding his teeth while he waited for me to respond. Any words I uttered would go in one ear and out the other. I gave him a large sigh and an eye roll instead so he wouldn't misinterpret the way I felt.

'Well, maybe if you'd picked a song that had more backing vocals, I might be more engaged.'

I threw Dad a dirty look. I'd been trying to concentrate, but Lily sang for over a minute before it got around to my part, so I kept drifting off.

Dad stopped the backing track, and the cavernous space fell silent.

'It doesn't matter which song I choose; you always mess up your part.'

'Thanks for the vote of confidence; that really makes me want to put my heart and soul into this.'

I felt a scowl settle on my face.

'If you did, we wouldn't have to keep going over and over the same part,' Dad fired back at me.

I pitied the neighbours. They must be tearing their hair out listening to our eighties cover versions rotating on a loop. I kept hoping and praying that one of them would complain to the council about the noise so they'd ban us from practising in the garage – a space most normal people used for housing their car or storing junk. But unfortunately, everyone in our street was extremely tolerant.

'Just take a step back. Arguing is getting us nowhere,' Lily said.

Such wise words spoken by my perfect sister. If only I could be more like her. Lily was faultless. Flawless. Exemplary. Being a mere mortal, I was too busy marvelling at her superiority to notice Dad switching the backing track on. When it registered, it made my heart sink.

6

MACKENZIE

'Is this MacKenzie Cartwright?'

'The one and only,' I replied when I answered my encrypted handset.

'I have a message from Miguel Castro...'

I felt like somebody had just punched me in the gut. Even before the guy with the Spanish accent continued to speak, I knew bad news was coming.

'The ship carrying your cargo set sail from Ecuador twenty-nine days ago. It's currently out in the Atlantic Ocean, but we've just been notified it's run into trouble...'

That wasn't what I wanted to hear. There was still a long way to go. It usually took around thirty-two days to reach Rotterdam from the port of Guayaquil.

'What kind of trouble?'

I wasn't sure I wanted to know the answer to my question.

'There's a storm raging in the Atlantic, and forecasters are predicting the wind will get stronger before it dies down. Gusts of sixty miles per hour with seas as high as sixteen feet are expected.'

I rubbed my head with my free hand. Samson was going to go

batshit when he found out. We were running low on stock, so we needed this shipment asap.

'If the conditions get too bad, the proposed course can't be taken.'

'You're not serious.' I could feel my blood pressure spike.

'It's to be expected. We're in the middle of the winter season.'

The Spanish guy's words had an arsey tone to them. I didn't like his attitude, but I wasn't in a position to bite back. I took a deep breath to calm myself down before I continued our conversation.

'But I thought modern ships were designed to sail through bad weather.'

'They are, but the conditions are extreme. The captain may have to change course to avoid the worst of the storm.'

This had never happened to us before, so I wasn't sure what the significance of changing course meant. I was about to ask the question when Miguel's guy started to speak again.

'If that happens, there's likely to be a delay to the scheduled arrival date.'

'Oh, for fuck's sake,' I said under my breath, knowing exactly how that news would go down with Samson. His words raced around in my head for a few moments before I replied.

'How long are we talking?' I asked, getting straight to the point.

'It's impossible to say at this stage until we know what kind of detour the captain will have to make.'

'Keep me posted, will you? You can phone me any time, day or night.'

After I ended the call, I let the phone drop from my hand onto my desk. None of this was my fault, but Samson had a habit of shooting the messenger. I leaned back in my chair, trying to find the right words before I rang my boss, when a thought popped into my head. I didn't know for certain, but I was suddenly fairly sure I knew why Arben Hasani's crew were checking out our patch.

When the Albanians became key players in Britain's cocaine market, they had formed an alliance directly with the Latin American drug cartels producing the product. They'd muscled in and taken over established trafficking networks, and because Arben had men stationed in Ecuador, he didn't need to wait for news to reach him like we did. He heard it straight from the horse's mouth, which gave him a valuable head start.

If we ran out of gear before the shipment arrived, Arben was primed and ready to pounce. He'd been battling for supremacy since he'd appeared on the scene and wouldn't miss a golden opportunity like this. But Samson wouldn't give up control of his territory that easily.

Over the years, Samson had developed a thriving business selling party drugs to clubbers. As a teenager, he'd started off small, buying just enough to be able to negotiate a better price from his dealer, then he sold it onto people he ran into on a night out. When the money began rolling in, he upped his game. But it wasn't all plain sailing. As I knew only too well, supply and demand sometimes didn't tally. His Italian supplier had run into trouble and couldn't keep up with the orders. Samson had taken the bold move and changed to a Mexican middleman, which had pissed off his now redundant source. Although he made a small fortune selling gear, he wasn't big enough to branch out on his own like the Albanians had. Samson's empire was in serious danger of toppling, and if it did, it would take him with it.

I picked up my mobile, selected Samson's name and hit call. The sooner I got this over with, the better.

'I think I know why the Albanians have been sniffing around Eden's,' I said.

'Feel free to enlighten me,' Samson replied.

'One of Miguel's guys just phoned to say the ship carrying our gear is caught in a storm, and the captain might have to change course.' The words came spilling out of my mouth like coins from a slot machine.

'Let me guess; there's going to be a delay.' Samson didn't sound impressed.

'Possibly, but they haven't confirmed that yet.'

'Maybe not, but they will. Global warming has a lot to answer for.'

I didn't have Samson down as an environmentalist, but anything that disrupted his supply schedule would give him sleepless nights.

'Ring me as soon as you've got news. Have you sorted out the line-up for the auditions yet?' Samson's pause lasted the length of a heartbeat. 'I didn't think so,' he continued without giving me a chance to reply. 'For fuck's sake, MacKenzie. I'm sure I don't need to remind you that Eden's future is hanging in the balance. You know we're haemorrhaging money. We need to find a new act to pull in the punters asap. Get it sorted.'

'Consider it done,' I replied.

By keeping me in a state of chronic fear, Samson didn't need to use physical violence. The threat hanging over me was enough to ensure I obeyed orders.

I blew out a breath and put the mobile down on my desk before pulling out the bottom drawer. The fingers of my right hand curled around the neck of the bottle as I lifted it up. I unscrewed the top of the Havana Club and poured a generous measure of the Cuban rum into my empty coffee mug. I closed my eyes as the amber liquid flowed down my throat. It was going to be a long night, and I still had to play the dreaded demos.

I needed another drink. Wading through the list of hopefuls all wanting to perform at Eden's was painful at the best of times, but I really couldn't be arsed with this today. I didn't have unlimited time to spend listening to the hundreds of unsolicited submissions singers sent in. My inbox was bursting at the seams. As Samson wasn't here to see what I was up to, I'd play the ten most recent and delete the rest. He'd never know the difference as long as I produced a line-up. If I wasn't sold in the first thirty seconds, I'd give them the chop. There'd be at least fifty more emails tomorrow to replace the stuff I'd culled.

7

DAISY

'About time, too,' Dad said when I walked into the kitchen of our semi-detached house in Camberwell.

He was sitting in his usual spot at the head of the pine table, grinning from ear to ear, looking like a man whose numbers had just come up on the lottery. Mum and Lily were positioned beside Dad, opposite each other, beaming their heads off, too.

'What's going on?' I asked, eyeing them suspiciously.

'All that hard work has paid off. I've got you girls an audition at Eden's.'

'Eden's?' I questioned.

'You must know it?' Dad looked taken aback. 'It's a live music venue built under the railway arches at Denmark Hill Station.'

'Doesn't ring a bell,' I replied with disinterest coating my words.

'It's the only place like it in south London.'

Dad paused to allow time for the penny to drop, but I just stared at him with a blank expression on my face.

'Well, anyway, they're looking for a new act to be part of the regular line-up. For the past twenty years, Eden's has hosted live music every night of the week. Both established artists and new talent from rock, pop, metal, and blues play there. It only has a capacity of five hundred, so it's small. But it's a start. Loads of famous bands performed live there before they hit the big time,' Dad grinned at me with stars and pound signs in his eyes.

Nothing was going to dampen Dad's enthusiasm. He'd been waiting his whole life for an opportunity like this. The fact that I didn't feel the same way was of no concern to him. I'd love to break away from my family and carve out my own life right now. But my dad was never going to allow that to happen. Lily and I were his meal ticket, so he wasn't going to let us out of his clutches any time soon.

'It's fantastic news, isn't it?' Lily gushed.

Stupid bitch. My sister was gutless and always followed the path of least resistance where my dad was concerned. I fixed her with a death stare, so she quickly turned her attention away from me and smiled adoringly at Dad. She looked like she was going to burst with excitement. The display was sickening, and I had to stop myself from letting out an involuntary groan.

It was one thing belting out a few songs in the makeshift studio Dad had set up in the garage a couple of times a week just to keep the peace at home, but singing in front of a live audience was a different ball game.

'You should be over the moon, but you've got a face like a slapped arse,' Dad said.

'That's because I don't want to audition.' My tone was flat.

Lily and Dad exchanged a look of horror.

I was making a stand, but I knew I didn't have a choice in the matter. My dad was a control freak. More than that, he was a bully. A tormentor. And he could be handy with his fists if the mood took him. Something I knew only too well.

'You've got to be kidding,' Mum piped up. 'An aspiring singer would give their right arm for an opportunity like this.'

I felt the weight of her stare as her dark brown eyes bored into mine. But I wasn't an aspiring singer. She knew that. That was her dream, not mine. I'd tried to hammer home how I felt about performing repeatedly, but my objections always fell on deaf ears.

'Maybe you'd like to take my place then.'

I couldn't hold it in. My frustration made an appearance.

'Believe me, I wish I could,' Mum spat back at me. She tossed her dark brown curls over her shoulder before muttering, 'Ungrateful little cow,' just loud enough for me to hear.

Mum used to be a singer in her younger days. She'd met my dad when they were both part of the entertainment team at a holiday park on the Norfolk coast. They'd dreamed of hitting the big time, but they'd fallen a long way short.

'What's the problem?' Dad's face had turned red.

The atmosphere in the room was charged, so I'd have to tread carefully.

'I know you're excited, and I'm sorry to let the side down, but I don't think I can do it,' I said, trying my best to be diplomatic.

'Why not?' Dad threw his hands in the air. 'You've performed loads of times before.'

That was true, but there was a big difference between auditioning at Eden's and singing in the school play or to a handful of people in our local pub at open mic events who were more interested in pouring booze down their necks than listening to Lily and me belting out an old classic.

'It'll be fun, Daisy,' Lily said, her eyes shining.

'For you, maybe.' I let out a loud sigh before I continued with my protest. 'Why can't Lily audition on her own?'

When Lily's blue eyes filled with tears, I turned to face my dad. I knew how he was going to respond, but I'd asked the question anyway, unable to help myself. Even though I sometimes came off worse, I got a kick out of pushing his buttons. He pulled his hands into fists and flashed me a look of fury. I was about to witness his lecture in full-colour high definition. Should I pass the popcorn around or take cover?

'You know full well that part of your appeal is the fact that you're identical twins. People are as interested in the two of you as the sound of your voices. I'm not saying you haven't both got a great set of pipes, but even if you were tone-deaf, I reckon people would still pay money to watch you perform.'

I wasn't about to agree with him, but Dad was right; people did have a weird fascination with twins. Sometimes, I felt like Lily and I were part of a freak show, the way random strangers gawped at us. Old ladies were the worst offenders when we were little, but they'd been pushed to one side by horny teenage boys and labourers on building sites. If I had a pound every time Lily and I had been asked for a threesome, I wouldn't have to work for the rest of my life. Mum and Dad were also guilty of exploiting the situation.

The chair legs scraped across the tiles when Dad suddenly pushed himself back and stood up. He gripped the table with his fingertips, glaring at me while collecting his thoughts.

'You've got a very short memory, Daisy. Your mum and I sacrificed so much for you girls to make sure you had the best of everything, the opportunities we never had, and you can't do this one little thing for us.'

I bit down on the tip of my tongue, allowing myself to engage my brain before I replied in case I said something I might regret. But we were going over old ground. Any time I pushed back about being part of the act, Dad tried to guilt trip me. Before I had a chance to speak, his monologue carried on.

'Your attitude stinks. All the money we spent on your performing arts classes... money that we didn't have, and the countless hours we spent sitting on plastic chairs in church halls watching you practising routines was for nothing. I wished I'd blown the lot down the pub.' Dad's face had now turned purple.

I'd heard this speech a thousand times before, but Dad was really putting his heart and soul into it today. Trying to guilt trip me. My parents were in debt up to their eyeballs. A debt my dad decided should be shared by the whole family. How was that fair? But that was him all over. The pressure was suffocating.

'Don't upset yourself, Des. It's not good for your blood pressure,' Mum said as she got up from her chair.

She walked over to the kettle and flipped the switch. A moment later, it sprung to life. The sound of the water heating up filled the silence in the room.

'Who wants tea?' Mum asked.

I stood up and headed for the door.

'Where do you think you're going?' Dad called after me.

I didn't bother to answer and let his question hang in the air.

8

DES

My temples started to throb as my blood pressure climbed higher.

'That went well,' Tara said before letting out a long sigh.

She'd taken our daughter's desertion better than I had, which wasn't that surprising. I'd always had a quick temper, and Daisy knew just how to get under my skin.

'I can't believe she was so underwhelmed. This is the opportunity of a lifetime,' Lily said.

'I know it is. I've been trying to get you girls a break like this for years.'

Truth be told, I'd been trying to get myself a break like this my whole adult life. I'd left home at eighteen in search of fame and fortune. And although I was hugely ambitious, I'd never managed to hit the big time. Chasing fame and glory had almost cost me my home and my family. Kids today didn't know how lucky they were. We lived in a world where young men and women could make millions on OnlyFans by showing a bit of flesh. In my day, blood, sweat and tears were required to earn a living. I couldn't get my head around Daisy's attitude. I didn't know what to think. Being in the spotlight was a lucrative career path. Why didn't she understand that? I could almost taste the money. It was on the tip of my tongue, so I wasn't going to let my difficult daughter ruin our chance for success.

Lily reached over the table and ran her soft fingertips over my clenched knuckles, snapping me back to reality.

'I know how hard you've worked to get us an opportunity like this. It doesn't matter what Daisy thinks, I'm over the moon about the audition.'

'Thanks, darling. That's good to hear.' I smiled at Lily, touched by her show of support.

'Daisy can be an ungrateful little bitch sometimes,' Tara said as she poured boiling water into a pale blue ceramic mug.

That was an understatement if ever I heard one.

For several moments, the only sound in the room was the metal spoon intermittently clinking off the side of the cup as Tara swirled the tea bag around while she waited for it to brew.

'Don't let her wind you up, Des. You know what she's like. She loves nothing more than getting a rise out of you.'

'You don't have to tell me that! But how am I supposed to react?'

'Say your piece and then switch off.' Tara brought the mug to her lips but lowered it again without taking a sip. The tea was still too hot to drink.

'That's easier said than done. She does my nut in; I don't know how you do it.'

'I've had years of practice,' Tara replied, giving me a knowing smile.

Lily and Daisy had the same shade of blonde hair and blue eyes and were completely identical in appearance with no distinguishing features. But that was where the similarities ended. They were poles apart in personality.

Daisy had been much harder work than Lily from day one. She was naturally more high maintenance and incredibly stubborn. As a toddler, she used to hit Lily and push her over all the time. She was destructive with the presents they were given and always wanted whatever Lily was playing with. She demanded most of Tara's time and couldn't be reasoned with, so the health visitor told her early on to ignore Daisy's bad behaviour. She warned her not to give our daughter any attention or eye contact until she settled down. That advice stayed with her to this day. I found it impossible to follow. I ruled my household with an iron fist. While you were under my roof and all that. It was my way or the highway. Like it, or lump it. Thank God Lily was so eager to please; I'd have lost the plot years ago if she'd been defiant like Daisy.

9

LILY

'Are you OK?' Dad asked. 'You look like you've got the weight of the world on your shoulders.'

'What am I going to do if Daisy refuses to sing?'

'She'll come around when she's had a chance to get used to the idea. Daisy loves the drama. She likes making a fuss and gets a kick out of causing trouble,' Tara replied.

'Never has a truer statement been said about my daughter. If I had to use one word to sum her up, it would be trouble with a capital T,' Dad agreed.

Daisy could do nothing right in my dad's eyes, which caused her to rebel at every opportunity.

'I'm not trying to be nasty, but your sister was born awkward, and she hasn't mellowed as she's got older. She likes being difficult just for the sake of it,' Dad continued.

I sometimes felt Mum and Dad were too hard on Daisy. I'd frequently asked myself if she would have turned out differently if my parents had treated us equally instead of favouring me all the time. It must be horrible for her. Their one-sidedness made me feel uncomfortable, and it had driven a wedge between us. Daisy resented me for being The Golden Child, but it wasn't my fault.

Parents should never have favourites, or if they did, they should make sure they kept it a closely guarded secret and not make it so obvious. I didn't know how I'd feel if I were in her shoes. Even though I was only older by minutes, she was my little sister, so I was naturally protective towards her.

'I've been thinking about what Daisy said about the backing vocals.'

'What about them?' Dad narrowed his eyes, and I felt the weight of his stare.

I could feel myself begin to crumble as Dad's glare eroded my confidence. It was dissipating with every second that passed. I willed myself to keep going but a ball of nerves began rolling around in my stomach as I battled to find the courage to speak up. I was scared to challenge my dad for fear of unleashing his anger on me, but our family's future was riding on this audition so I had to force myself to dig deep.

'Daisy has such a small part in most of the songs we sing.'

'That's because she keeps messing up the harmonies.'

'I know she does, but it must be really boring for her. If you let her sing the lead on some of the songs, she might be more interested in auditioning. She knows all the words, and she's got a great voice—'

Dad put his hand up, stopping my sentence mid-flow. 'You're the lead singer. That's non-negotiable.'

Dad looked furious. A curly vein had begun pulsating in his temple, so I knew not to push it any further. His mind was made up. He wasn't about to change it, but it was a shame he wouldn't allow Daisy to showcase her talent.

'I get where Lily's coming from. That's not a bad idea, Des,'

Mum said in an unexpected show of support. 'You could always give it a go and see how she gets on.'

'No way.' Dad shook his head. 'We can't risk her messing up the audition. She might try to sabotage it just to make a point.'

'I suppose you're right,' Mum conceded without much of a fight. 'I wouldn't put it past her to try and ruin things for you. You know how jealous she is of you, Lily.'

'I'd be jealous of her too if she got to do all the singing while I chipped in with the chorus,' I said in my sister's defence.

'You're the one who puts in all the hard work, so you should be the one who gets rewarded,' Dad said.

He was our manager, so he made the executive decisions. I'd tried to fight Daisy's corner, but there was no point continuing the discussion. Dad wasn't coming around to my way of thinking. And I could see he was getting angrier by the minute, which made me retreat into my shell. Meekness was my weakness.

10

MACKENZIE

'Is this MacKenzie Cartwright?'

My stomach flipped as my brain registered the familiar voice calling my encrypted mobile. It was the man with the Spanish accent.

'Yes.'

'I have news regarding your shipment...'

'Has the storm died down?'

'I'm afraid not. The vessel is still in a dangerous situation. Waves have been battering the ship day and night.'

'Jesus. Is it going to sink?'

'A ship can survive conditions like this as long as the captain treats the storm with respect. Otherwise, it has the power to kill everyone on board,' the man replied without answering my question.

'So what's going to happen?'

'The storm has become too heavy to ride out, so the captain's going to divert three hundred miles south to avoid the worst of it.'

'Three hundred miles! Oh, for fuck's sake.'

I shook my head as his words sank into my brain. Samson was going to go mental when he found out.

'I know you're not happy about the diversion, but storms are an unavoidable part of life at sea. What can I say? It's not my fault. I don't control the weather. There's nothing I can do about it,' he said abruptly, then hung up.

I now had the unenviable task of passing the news onto my boss. He liked to portray himself as a successful, smooth-talking businessman but you'd be hard pushed to find a bigger villain if you tried. He was a nasty piece of work to put it mildly. Thanks to his dad having done time, Samson had connections to London's old school crime network and he wasn't afraid to use them. If I wasn't careful, I was going to end up dead. Samson would be looking for somebody to blame and I was right in the firing line. Don't shoot the messenger would be lost on him.

11

DAISY

I sat in the back of the car with my arms folded across my chest and a scowl pasted on my face. My mood was as black as the clouds gathering swiftly above us. I wondered if the universe was sending me a sign, warning me of impending doom. The light was fading fast, too fast, even for a day in early December. Rain was coming. That was a certainty. With any luck, it would be of biblical proportions, the like we'd never seen before in south London. I'd do anything to get out of going to the audition. Being swept away by a deluge seemed as good an option as any. I found myself crossing the fingers of both of my hands wedged under the armpits of my puffa jacket.

I peered through the steamed-up window as we passed the massive branch of Asda, looking for animals walking two by two. There was no sign of any elephants or kangaroos. Only a cross-section of the general public were milling around the huge frontage, pushing trolleys to and from the store. The thought of Noah loading the ark in the supermarket car park brought me some light relief and made the corners of my mouth rise.

Dad had given me the 'while you're under my roof, young lady, you'll toe the line' speech. He treated me to it on a regular basis, so I knew it word for word. I was well used to his heavy-handed approach to fatherhood. The man had serious anger management issues. I'd felt the full force of his rage more times than I cared to remember. He was unsupportive and controlling and had his fair share of toxic parent traits. Verbal and emotional abuse were two of his specialities. I tried not to let it faze me. But sometimes, it was impossible to ignore.

I was twenty-three, and he still treated me like I was five. The day I packed my bags and moved out couldn't come soon enough for my liking, but I couldn't afford it right now. The rental prices in London were sky high, and the money I earned waitressing at Nando's barely funded my social life, let alone anything else. I was in a catch-22 situation, stuck in a job paying the minimum wage, with never enough money left at the end of the month to save. Mum and Dad took a huge chunk of what I earned to contribute to running the household. If my dad got himself a proper job instead of poncing off his daughters, he'd be able to pay the bills without pleading poverty all the time. They had me over a barrel, and they knew it.

But that didn't mean I had to make things easy for them. Where was the fun in that? They couldn't really blame me, could they? If you forced somebody into something and they went along with it willingly, they were a complete doormat. That wasn't the way I was wired. The more they pushed, the more I pushed back. I wanted to choose my own path and not have *their* dream rammed down *my* throat. I was far from shy, but I didn't court the limelight like Lily did. She came to life when she was on stage; performing was her reason for living and breathing. It just so happened it bored me rigid. Admittedly, she had a better voice than me. She had a wider range and trained morning, noon and night to hone her craft. There was a lot of truth in the saying 'practice makes perfect'.

I didn't have a competitive edge or share the same incentive to achieve as my twin. Always being second best in our household had driven any desire out of me before it had even begun. Nothing I did was ever good enough. I was bored of coming last in the two horse race, so why bother trying?

I was consumed with feelings of jealousy. They had been eating away at me for years and were festering inside me, growing by the day, which made it impossible for me to have a relationship with Lily. If Dad's attitude towards us had been different, I might have been more enthusiastic. But he never gave me the opportunity to take the lead, even just for one song, to try and spark my interest. It was always my job to back Lily up, making sure her voice shone out above mine whenever we were harmonising. It was tedious and made me resent Lily even more if that was possible. I despised performing and felt like I was being forced into this to make my dad and sister happy, so I liked to make life as difficult for them as possible. Dad kept pointing out that a lot of our appeal came from the fact that we were twins. There wouldn't be an act if I wasn't part of it, but he still didn't appreciate the sacrifice I was making.

12

DES

'My God, we're going to get soaked,' I said, peering through the mist steaming the glass.

The heavens suddenly opened, and now the visibility was terrible even though I'd flicked the windscreen wipers onto the highest setting. The rain continued to pelt on the roof as pedestrians ran for cover.

'I'm not sure about the restrictions around here, so I'll drop you off at Eden's, and I'll leave the car at the station.'

I'd been hoping the rain might have eased by the time I pulled up outside the club, but it was still chucking it down.

'There should be an umbrella in the footwell behind my seat,' I said, looking at Daisy in the rearview mirror.

She was in one of her stroppy moods, so she didn't bother to answer me, but I must have been right because I saw her lean forward and reappear a moment later. I was tempted to have words with her over her rudeness, but she was looking for any excuse to get into an argument with me so that she could storm off in a huff and pull out of the audition. For once, I managed to hold my tongue and not play into her hands.

'I'm so nervous,' Lily said when I turned to look at her.

I could see her wringing her hands in her lap, and my heart went out to her. She'd be devastated if this didn't go well.

'You'll be fine; you've got this.'

Lily smiled, acknowledging my words of encouragement. Then she blew out a long breath, closed her eyes, and took a deep lungful of air in through her nostrils to try and calm herself down. I reached over and squeezed her hand. The unexpected contact made her jump out of her skin.

'Sorry, love, I didn't mean to startle you.'

'It's OK. I just feel a bit edgy.' Lily looked terrified.

'That's understandable, but you'd better go in. You don't want to be late. I'll just go and park, and then I'll follow you in. I won't be long.'

I turned to look over my shoulder and was about to offer Daisy a motivational boost, too, but she was already outside the car, standing on the pavement, sheltering under the umbrella.

The traffic was heavy; people always took to their cars at the first sign of rain, so while I waited for an opportunity to pull out, I kept one eye on the girls. The wind was whipping around them as they battled to stop the umbrella from blowing inside out. They'd been battered by the elements as they'd walked towards the front entrance, but they'd finally disappeared inside the foyer.

Watching them made me feel nostalgic all of a sudden. It took me back to their school days. I could have driven off before now, but if I was totally honest about it, I'd wanted to make sure Daisy didn't do a runner the minute she thought my back was turned. I wouldn't put anything past her.

13

LILY

Eden's was built between two brick viaduct arches beneath Denmark Hill Station. Its exterior was dark and industrial, but we didn't waste time taking in too many details as the weather was so horrendous.

'I'm Lily Kennedy, and this is my sister Daisy. We're here to see MacKenzie Cartwright,' I said to the man who opened the door for us.

He was tall and lean, dressed in a dark suit and tie, and his hair was plaited in cornrows.

'Nice to meet you, ladies. I'm Jermaine. Are you here for an audition?'

'Yes, it's at 2 p.m.; we're a bit early.'

That was the story of my life. I had no tolerance for people being late. Daisy was the worst. When left to her own devices, she couldn't be on time to save her life. Mum and Dad also had a casual attitude to punctuality. But I'd put my foot down today and made sure we'd left way before we needed to.

'No worries, I'll let Mac know you're here. Take a seat. He'll be with you shortly.'

Jermaine gestured to a pair of plush black velvet chairs to the side of where we were standing.

'Thanks,' I replied.

But I didn't want to sit down; I wanted to look at all the memorabilia hanging on the exposed brick walls under the heading 'Hall of Fame'. I was amazed at how many photos of famous people were lined up next to each other.

'Daisy, come and look at this,' I said as soon as Jermaine was out of earshot.

'No thanks. I'm good,' Daisy replied.

She was sitting in the chair with one leg crossed over the other, scrolling through her phone, showing absolutely no interest in our surroundings. I couldn't imagine anybody had posted anything so amazing on Instagram that it warranted her full attention.

I turned away from her. I wasn't going to let her wind me up. But I had a sinking feeling. This audition wasn't just about our voices; a lot more things came into it than that. No matter how well we sang or how flawless our performance was, I'd be very surprised if we were given the slot if one of us had a bad attitude. I mean, why would they bother? Not when hundreds of other hopefuls were nipping at our heels, grateful for the chance to sing at Eden's. The club had a fantastic reputation for discovering and nurturing newbies, turning them into successful artists. Opportunities like this came along once in a lifetime.

As my eyes swept across the photos again, I was surprised to hear the sound of a train above me. I looked up towards where the rumble was coming from and noticed three large-diameter spiral silver tubes bolted to the ceiling. If I had to hazard a guess, I'd say they probably housed the club's wiring. A place like this must have acres of cabling. But they looked like giant metallic centipedes crawling across the underside of the roof, which gave me the creeps, and I felt an involuntary shudder pass through me.

Time was dragging. I could feel its invisible presence. Wasn't it strange how it could speed up or slow down, depending on the circumstances? It flew by when you were having fun and inched along when you were dreading something. Weird how its passage could skew our perception. I supposed that was down to the amount of attention we paid it. You didn't notice the clock ticking when you were busy. But when you constantly looked at the dial, it never seemed to move. I just wanted to get this over and done with. Waiting for the audition to begin was torture.

'Are you nervous?'

Daisy looked up from her phone and fixed her blue eyes on me. If she was feeling anxious, she was hiding it well.

Daisy shook her head from side to side. 'You're shitting yourself enough for both of us,' she replied with a smile on her face.

She was right, I was a bundle of nerves, but Mum and Dad wanted us to get the slot at Eden's more than anything, so there was a lot riding on this for me. I didn't want to think about what the consequences would be if the audition didn't go well. My parents were in a lot of debt and we were in danger of losing our home. Dad had remortgaged the house when we were kids, chasing his dream of stardom. He couldn't keep up the repayments with the amount he was earning so he borrowed some money from Warren Jenkins, a local villain, to pay off the bank. But now we were in a far worse position. The debt was spiralling out of control.

Fast forward fifteen years and Dad still didn't have a regular wage coming in. Even when Mum worked overtime at Asda, she brought home barely enough to keep them afloat. Daisy and I contributed but neither of us had well-paid jobs, so we were on the breadline. All the stress seemed to go over Daisy's head. She couldn't care less; she was just going through the motions to keep them off her back. I sometimes wished we could trade places. The pressure on me to succeed was immense.

14

MACKENZIE

'Yo, Mac. There's a foxy set of twins waiting to see you in the foyer,' Jermaine said, sticking his head around the office door. 'I don't mind telling you, they're fit!'

I was mulling over my conversation with Castro's guy, looking for something positive to offer before I broke the news to Samson, so it had slipped my mind that I was auditioning acts this afternoon. I could do without this right now. I had enough on my plate to deal with. But then again, maybe Jermaine had just thrown me a lifeline. I'd go and listen to the acts and phone Samson afterwards. Hopefully, the situation would have improved by then.

'Thanks, mate, I'd completely forgotten!'

I pushed my chair away from the desk and got to my feet.

'You won't look so miserable when you catch sight of the stunners waiting for you,' Jermaine grinned.

'They're that hot, are they?'

'Yeah, man. They're on fire. Identical twins are every man's fantasy. I wouldn't say no to either of them,' Jermaine said over his shoulder as he swaggered down the hallway.

I was intrigued to see if they were as good-looking as he was saying. But something told me a couple of trolls were waiting for me. Jermaine was a proper clown so it was more than likely he was bigging the girls up as a joke. I'd have to reserve judgement until I saw them with my own eyes.

I hadn't intentionally kept them waiting, but no doubt they were currently being mesmerised by the foyer's hall of fame. Performers dreaming of stardom always were. They'd gaze at Samson's collection of memorabilia with wide eyes, hoping that one day their names would be on the platinum CDs and press reports and that their photos would hang next to the other successful artists lucky enough to have been given a start by Eden's.

Before the pandemic, Eden's was the place to be seen. There was no other venue like it for miles around. It was packed to the rafters every night of the week. You'd never know the country was in the grip of a recession and a cost-of-living crisis when you saw the amount of money that changed hands on a nightly basis. But that wasn't the case any more. Covid had wiped out more than just people. It had wiped out businesses, too. Eden's was no longer a success in its own right. Its future was bleak if things didn't turn around soon. Truth be told, we needed a successful act more than they needed us.

15

DAISY

'Sorry to keep you waiting.'

I looked up from my phone at the sound of MacKenzie Cartwright's voice and watched him as he sauntered into the foyer wearing ripped jeans and a black T-shirt. I wasn't sure what I'd been expecting, but I wasn't disappointed. He was younger and better looking than I'd imagined he'd be, so he'd ticked two boxes already. He reached Lily first and greeted her with a friendly handshake.

'Nice to meet you; I'm MacKenzie.'

I watched their exchange, letting my eyes roam over him without fear of being caught.

'Nice to meet you, too. I'm Lily.'

I could see my sister's hand trembling as she moved it towards his open palm. I scrambled to my feet before he reached my chair.

'So you must be Daisy,' MacKenzie grinned.

'That's right.'

'It's a pleasure, Daisy.'

When our eyes met and he shook my hand, my heart skipped a beat. It felt like an electric current had passed through my body, and my pulse speeded up. We'd only just met, but I was instantly attracted to him. My hormones had gone into overdrive. I wanted to ask if he'd mind if I ripped his clothes off. But I wasn't sure how he'd take that, so I decided to stick with the safe option.

'Likewise,' I replied.

Beads of sweat broke out on my upper lip, and the palms of my hands became clammy. I patted my face with my index finger before running my fingers down the front of my jeans to get rid of the perspiration. Although this was a sure sign of nerves, it wasn't the upcoming audition that was causing them. It was a reaction to the company we were in. I felt like a schoolgirl with a crush on her teacher. For God's sake Daisy, get a grip, I told myself. Don't make it so obvious. You need to play it cool, or you're going to make a complete tit of yourself.

Dad had drummed into us the importance of securing the slot. Warren Jenkins was circling. The shark was hungry and he wouldn't wait much longer to be fed. To save his own skin, my dad had forced us into this. If Lily and I messed up this opportunity, life at home was going to be even more miserable than before. Dad would be furious and he'd take his anger out on me. Having to perform merely to bail my useless dad out of a tricky spot sucked. I was resentful and bitter about it and had resisted with all my might, digging my heels in and being awkward just for the sake of it. Thank God Dad was as stubborn as I was. If he'd let me pull out, I'd have missed more than just the chance to further my singing career. I'd never have met MacKenzie.

'If you're ready, we'll get started with the tour,' MacKenzie said.

He looked at both of us in turn before he led the way along the carpeted hallway.

'There's a bar and a separate stage area for the live performances on this level and a dressing room and storage in the basement,' MacKenzie said over his shoulder.

'There's a dressing room?' Lily questioned.

'Yep,' MacKenzie replied before stopping outside the first set of classic oak doors we came to.

'Wow!' Lily mouthed to me. Her blue eyes were like saucers.

The double doors had a central stained glass panel and original feature door handles. Once we'd caught up with him, MacKenzie bent down and pulled up one of the bolts that secured the door at the bottom. Then he pushed it open, and we followed him inside.

'This is the bar. It's my domain,' he said, sweeping his arm around the empty space.

The room was large and echoey, with reclaimed timber floors, exposed brick walls and a sparse amount of stainless steel lighting dotted around, creating a cosy, industrial environment. Clusters of round wooden tables and chairs were scattered over the floor space. A large bar made from polished dark wood dominated the whole back wall, behind which an extensive range of premium spirits sat on glass shelving. Above that, a huge station clock stuck out from the wall on a wrought iron bracket. The Roman numeral dial gave the interior an old-world charm. This was the only part of the pub that was brightly lit. Your eyes were drawn to the bottles. Clever marketing, I thought.

'This is where the punters hang out while they're waiting for the live music to start,' MacKenzie said.

My stomach did a flip as his words registered. If Lily and I got the job, people drinking in here would have come to see us. It felt so surreal.

'Right, let's move on.' MacKenzie said, leading the way back out to the corridor. He pushed open the next door on the left. 'This is my office.'

He poked his head in the door, then stepped back so that Lily and I could have a look.

'As you can see, there's not much in there, so I won't bore you by taking you inside.'

Three filing cabinets ran along one wall, but judging by the piles of papers sitting on the edge of the wooden desk at the back of the room, they were either full or didn't get used much. A single ceiling lamp lit the small space, although the low-wattage bulb wasn't doing a very good job of it. The only other pieces of furniture I could see from the doorway were a wheelie chair pushed back from the desk and a tall metal cabinet lying against the other wall. MacKenzie was right. It was quite underwhelming.

'I'm sure you're both eager to see where you'd be singing if you get the job. I'll take you through to the stage area so you can familiarise yourself with the layout,' MacKenzie said.

He flashed us a warm smile, then walked down the corridor and stopped outside an identical set of doors as the bar. After pulling up the bolt at the bottom of one of the double doors, he pushed it open and stepped into the room.

I'd been expecting Eden's to have a modern, sleek interior, but there was more of a spit and sawdust vibe going on, which conjured up thoughts of beer-fuelled nights, not fancy neon-coloured cocktails in my mind. My grandad would have approved and would have called it a proper pub. It didn't have any airs and graces. What you saw was what you got.

'This place is a bit of a dump, but it's been going strong for the last twenty years. People don't come here for the decor. They come to hear the music,' MacKenzie said as though he'd just read my mind. 'As you can see, it's not massive, but it holds five hundred people,' he said, looking over his shoulder and smiling at us. 'It's pretty hard to imagine it now as the place is empty, but when it's full to capacity, it really rocks.'

'I bet it does,' Lily said.

I believed him, too. I could actually picture the crowd going wild and almost hear them singing along and their thunderous applause. My eyes scanned the room. There wasn't a stick of furniture in the entire space, but huge freestanding speakers were dotted around the stage. Smaller versions were suspended from the ceiling and attached to the walls with brackets.

'I know it looks a bit bare, but that's intentional. It's standing room only. Trust me, that's a good thing because people don't resist the urge to dance if they're already on their feet. If you get the slot, you'll see the energy in here's different to seated venues. The crowd engages more than when they're parked at a table nursing a warm pint,' MacKenzie said.

That made a lot of sense. A ball of nerves started rolling around in my stomach. I suddenly felt compelled to give the audition my all. This could be the break I'd been waiting for. Even though Dad would keep a big chunk of our earnings for himself, seventy percent to be precise, I might be able to scrape together a deposit for a flat. Then I'd be able to put some distance between myself and the overbearing control freak.

'After you,' MacKenzie said, gesturing to a small flight of stairs that led to the stage.

Lily's heels echoed as she walked over the reclaimed timber floors. I followed two steps behind, my Converse barely making a sound. I was suddenly regretting not making more of an effort. Lily looked incredible. It was obvious she'd spent time doing her hair and make-up and choosing her outfit. She preferred to wear natural tones, which suited her wholesome, girl-next-door image. Whereas I usually went for a bolder approach. The red-lipped siren look suited my personality better. I'd never choose a neutral pallet over a colourful one. Where the fun in that? But I couldn't be bothered to put any slap on today. I'd just thrown on a hoodie and some jeans and scraped my hair into a ponytail. I'd consciously dressed down for the occasion. It would serve me right if MacKenzie made a play for my sister.

Before MacKenzie joined us on the stage, he flipped the switches on a control panel at the back of the room, bringing the lighting to life. Multicoloured spotlights mounted on an overhead structure shone down on us, creating rainbow puddles on the floor and making the dust motes dance, changing the atmosphere instantly.

'The speakers and overhead lights are all controlled from the panel down there, and all of these can be synced with music,' MacKenzie said, sweeping his arm around the stage to point out the freestanding units peppering the perimeter and beyond. 'You'll be glad to know the acoustics are great in here, and because it's a small venue, it allows the crowd to be up close and personal to the artists.'

The idea of that sent a mild tremor running down the length of my spine. I stood at the front of the stage, looking out to where the audience would be. It was easy to imagine the room in years gone by, shrouded in cigarette smoke so thick you could barely see the act. Eden's might be a small venue compared to some, but it seemed huge to me.

'If you're ready, we'll get started,' MacKenzie said, as the door creaked open.

'Looks like I've arrived just in time. I'm Samson Fox, the owner of this establishment,' the man standing in the doorway said.

He looked just as I'd expected. Well-groomed and smartly dressed in a pale grey suit and a black shirt. But something didn't seem quite right about him. Something was off. His pleasantness felt false. Forced. Was it a mask? Sudden palpitations made my heart rate accelerate.

16

LILY

Samson Fox would be instrumental in us getting on in this business, so his presence had just ramped up the pressure. My head was about to explode. I hadn't expected MacKenzie to spring that on us so quickly. Dad hadn't arrived yet. He must have been having trouble parking the car. I wish we'd got an Uber now and saved ourselves all this unnecessary stress. An unpleasant thought started to form; if Dad didn't turn up soon, we might miss the chance to audition. I pushed that idea to the back of my head before I had a meltdown. I had to stay calm; working myself into a frenzy wasn't going to do any good.

'We're just waiting for our sound system to arrive. Dad must be finding it hard to get a parking. Would it be OK to wait a few more minutes?' I smiled at MacKenzie, hoping to appeal to his better nature.

I'd hated having to ask, but needs must. MacKenzie seemed like a decent guy, so I was hoping he'd understand. Bad timekeeping was a no-no as far as I was concerned. It was the height of disrespect. This shouldn't have been happening; I'd made sure we were here in plenty of time, for once.

As I looked towards the door for any sign of my dad, I saw Daisy flash me a look of contempt out of the corner of my eye. What the hell was wrong with her now? Whatever it was, it would have to wait. I couldn't deal with her throwing a strop at this moment. I had more important things to worry about.

'I have a question for you, Miss Kennedy.'

The unexpected sound of Samson's voice made my temples start to throb.

'Fire away,' I replied, resisting the urge to wring my hands together.

'Why do two grown women need to bring their dad along to an audition?' Samson asked with a smile on his face.

I felt like a complete idiot. There was no valid reason why Dad needed to be here, but I didn't think it was appropriate to say he was an aggressive control freak who was obsessed with taking charge of every aspect of our lives. Telling Dad we could manage without him wasn't an option.

'He's our manager and he likes to be hands-on, so he always insists on accompanying us,' I replied, inwardly cringing knowing how ridiculous that sounded.

Samson didn't look impressed, so he didn't bother to reply. He turned towards MacKenzie and glanced at his watch, which prompted MacKenzie to speak.

'Umm, I would if I could, but it'll put out the schedule if we wait any longer. We've got some other acts booked after you...'

My chest tightened as I processed his words. We were only a step away from losing the opportunity of a lifetime, and we had nobody to blame but ourselves. I couldn't bear being late. It stressed me out. Now, the audition Dad had fought so hard to get us was hanging in the balance over something completely avoidable.

17

DES

'Hi, I'm Desmond Kennedy. My daughters have an audition at two o'clock,' I said as a tall young man approached me.

I glanced down at my watch. It was almost a quarter past.

'No worries, mate. Feel free to take a seat over there,' the young man said, gesturing towards some expensive-looking chairs before he turned on his heel.

'Excuse me,' I called after him.

He stopped in his tracks and turned to face me.

'I was expecting to go in with my girls. I've got their backing tracks.'

I held up my laptop case to prove my point.

'In that case, you'd better follow me.'

He paced down the hall, past two sets of doors. I was nearly jogging to keep up with his long stride.

'Yo, Mac,' he said when he pushed open a set of doors. 'Desmond Kennedy's here to see you.'

Then he turned towards me and ushered me inside. I smiled at my girls. They were standing in the middle of the room with the stage behind them, on either side of a scruffy-looking bloke I presumed was MacKenzie Cartwright, the manager. He didn't really look the part dressed in ripped jeans and a faded black T-shirt, but I wasn't in a position to judge. He was the man who made the decisions.

'Hi Desmond, I'm MacKenzie,' he said, walking towards me.

'Pleased to meet you,' I said, shaking his outstretched hand.

'Likewise,' MacKenzie said before turning back to Lily and Daisy. 'Thanks for coming.'

What the hell was going on? Lily was on the verge of tears.

MacKenzie spun around again. 'Jermaine, do us a favour, see these guys out, please,' he said.

'See us out?' I questioned, feeling a scowl settle on my face.

'Sorry, dude, you've missed your slot,' MacKenzie said, turning the palms of his hands out. 'Now, if you'll excuse me, I've got another appointment.'

I felt my blood boil as MacKenzie went to walk away. But I knew if I unleashed my temper on him, I'd blow the girls' chance for sure. I needed to be apologetic. Grovel and drop on my knees if necessary. I'd do whatever it took to make things right.

'I'm really sorry I got held up, but I couldn't get a parking space. The girls were here on time, though, so please don't hold it against them...'

'I know they were, but I've got other people waiting to see me.'

MacKenzie gave me a weak smile and pushed the door open. I didn't dare look at Lily. She'd want my head on a block, and who could blame her? Arriving late to an audition was one of the worst things you could do.

'Please cut the girls some slack. We'd be happy to wait until the other auditions have finished,' I said, hoping to win him over.

'Listen, mate, if you want to be taken seriously in this game, you need to behave like a professional. That means being punctual, in case you didn't realise.'

I bit down on my lip to stop myself from tearing a strip off this cocky young man. He stood in the doorway looking at my beautiful daughters. He held eye contact with Daisy for several seconds before he spoke again.

'I tell you what, I'll let Lily and Daisy do their set, but you'll have to wait until I've seen the last act.'

'Thank you so much,' Lily said before I could form a reply.

'Thanks, I appreciate it,' I called as the door closed behind him.

'You'll need to wait in the foyer,' Jermaine said.

'That's fine,' I smiled.

I would have agreed to anything to put things right.

Lily shook her head and threw me a look of contempt as she waltzed past me.

'I'm sorry,' I mouthed.

If she'd heard my apology, she'd chosen to ignore it. I glanced at Daisy as she trailed two paces behind her sister. She was wearing an expression of mild amusement, which reignited my anger. But I couldn't afford to lose it now. We weren't going to get another second chance.

18

LILY

We followed Jermaine along the corridor like a row of ducklings. Once we were back in the foyer, I walked over to the Hall of Fame and started studying the pictures again to avoid making eye contact with my dad. I couldn't stand the sight of him right now.

I flinched when I felt Dad's fingers touch the small of my back. Why couldn't he just read the signs and give me some space? I didn't think that was too much to ask under the circumstances. The thing that irritated me most was that he didn't seem to give a shit that he'd kept everyone waiting. He was surprised MacKenzie thought it was a big issue. Why wouldn't he? And who knew what Samson had made of him? If we'd been hoping to impress the big boss, we were off to a bad start.

'Are you OK?' Dad asked as his fingers ran up and down my spine.

'What do you think?' I could feel my nostrils flaring as I glared at him.

My frosty response opened up a silence between us. The only sound was the distant rumble of trains on the tracks above us. It was strange. Eerie. Atmospheric.

'I'm sorry, Lily, it wasn't my fault. I couldn't get a parking space. I went around and around God knows how many times before I managed to find one.'

'We should have just got an Uber,' I spat back. Fury constricting my voice.

'Hindsight's a wonderful thing, isn't it?' Dad smiled, trying to make light of the situation.

I was livid. My insides were like a coiled spring, so much for staying cool, calm and collected before our big moment. My heart was racing. I couldn't catch my breath. I was on edge. My nerves were jangling.

'Why didn't you just leave the car on a yellow line or something? So what if we'd got a ticket,' Daisy said.

'I honestly didn't think it would be a big deal. These things never usually run on time,' Dad replied.

'Maybe not in your day,' Daisy said, ready to lock horns with Dad.

I could feel the tension building between them. The last thing we needed was for them to get into one of their back-and-forth slanging matches.

'I've already got a splitting headache. Don't you two start.'

I threw Dad and Daisy a look. I felt like a parent coming between warring siblings.

'I'm as shocked as you are,' Dad said, turning away from Daisy to face me. 'I can't believe he pulled the plug on us. It wasn't as though none of us had shown up on time. You girls were inside well before you needed to be.'

I'd been surprised when MacKenzie showed us the door, too. It was a jaw-dropping moment, so I wasn't going to let Dad off the hook that easily. And I'd been mortified when Samson had questioned me about my dad's involvement in the audition. It had been a humiliating experience. But I couldn't tell him about it in case he blew his top which was adding to the pressure. I was close to breaking point and didn't care how he tried to worm his way out of it. Nothing he said was going to change the facts. Dad was to blame. He'd caused this situation.

'MacKenzie's given us a second chance, so it's not a big deal,' Dad said, glossing over the catastrophe.

'It is a big deal, and now, thanks to you, I'm stressed out of my mind.'

I glanced over at Daisy; she was sitting in the same chair as before, scrolling through her phone like she didn't have a care in the world. I envied her laid-back attitude to everything; being highly strung was the biggest pain in the arse. Daisy might think she'd drawn the short straw in our house, but I'd give anything to be like her. Chilled. Laid-back. Unaffected. I'd be old before my time. Prematurely grey and wrinkled.

'Look on the bright side, now you've got extra time to mentally prepare,' Dad grinned.

He just didn't get it. Waiting to perform was torture. Time was inching by, and the anticipation was making me feel nauseous. Disastrous scenarios and what-ifs were whirling around in my head. I was trying to put them out of my mind, but the longer we were delayed, the more I was building them up. I kept dwelling on what could go wrong.

'Take some deep breaths and calm yourself down,' Dad said.

He didn't need to be a mind reader to know what was happening inside my head. I didn't hide my feelings well. I was an open book. Transparent. No air of mystery surrounded me.

Dad placed the flat of his hand on my back and moved it up and down, trying to iron out my worries. I took a deep breath in through my nostrils, held it for ten seconds and then blew it out slowly. My pulse rate started to decrease almost instantly, so I concentrated on my breathing until I was more composed.

'Are you feeling any better?' Dad asked.

I nodded.

'That's good. I know you've had a stressful start, but trust me, this is probably a blessing in disguise,' Dad smiled.

'Really?'

Dad's logic defied me sometimes.

'Nobody wants to be the first act to audition. By the time the panel get to the end, they can't remember the people they saw at the beginning. Being last is a huge advantage; you'll thank me for this later. Every cloud...' Dad winked and let his sentence trail off.

He was grinning from ear to ear. Brimming over with confidence, totally unaffected by the whole thing. I needed to do myself a favour and take a leaf out of my dad's and my sister's books before I ended up with high blood pressure.

19

DAISY

This whole experience was surreal. When Dad had burst through the door with the all-important backing track, he was wearing the expression of an expectant father about to miss the birth of his first child. It made me smile until I realised he'd almost lost us our chance to perform, which was ironic. This audition meant the world to him. He'd had big dreams that had never panned out. He knew that pursuing a career in music was risky and uncertain, being a performer could be a fleeting lifestyle. But he was a selfish bastard with an ego the size of Canada and wouldn't ignore the pull of his passion even for his family's sake. It was like a drug to him and he needed a fix.

If you'd given Dad the choice twenty-three years ago, I'd put money on the fact that he'd rather be here with his band than watching Lily and I take our first breaths. He bleated on about being a family man to anyone who would listen, but our importance paled into insignificance when an opportunity to perform presented itself. Mum was left holding the babies while he carried on like a single man. I don't know how she put up with it. I'd have put his balls in a vice if he was my husband.

Dad glanced at his watch before he announced. 'I better go and feed the meter. The parking's about to expire.'

Judging by the look Lily threw him, he'd be the one expiring if he took one step towards the door.

'Don't you dare go anywhere! You've caused enough trouble for one day,' Lily said.

She was making a stand, but inside, she must have been in turmoil. I watched the colour drain from her face as she waited to see if Dad would do as she'd asked.

'Mum will skin me alive if I get a ticket.'

'That's tame compared to what I'll do to you,' Lily replied, throwing Dad another warning look.

That was an idle threat if ever I'd heard one. Lily had no backbone, so she'd never be brave enough to take Dad on. That was my department. I was his sparring partner. She preferred to hide in the shadows waiting for the moment to pass like a spineless coward.

'OK, you win,' Dad said, backing down.

Lily was on the verge of tears, so he'd decided not to push things, which was the first sensible thing he'd done all day. It was just as well Lily stopped him in his tracks. We'd been waiting for ages for the auditions to finish, but barely a moment after Dad had threatened to abandon us, MacKenzie appeared in the foyer.

'Thanks for coming. I'll be in touch,' he said to four tattooed long-haired guys dressed in black.

I'd been sizing up the competition since we'd been waiting, and all of the acts seemed different to each other. The last guys looked like they were a rock band, but there were also solo singers and various-sized groups. I hoped for our sakes, MacKenzie was a fan of eighties cover versions.

My attitude towards this opportunity had changed as soon as I'd clapped eyes on MacKenzie Cartwright. He had a way about him, and I was drawn to him instantly. I suddenly liked the idea of working at Eden's if it meant I got to see him every week.

'Sorry to keep you waiting,' MacKenzie smiled, turning towards us.

'That's not a problem. Thanks for agreeing to fit us in. We really appreciate it,' Dad replied.

I had to suppress a smile. Watching Dad grovel was bringing me so much pleasure. Especially because MacKenzie seemed indifferent to his efforts. He was probably well used to people trying to butter him up to get in his good books.

'Lily, Daisy. Daisy, Lily,' he said. MacKenzie looked backwards and forwards at us while skilfully avoiding eye contact with Dad, who was doing his best to get himself noticed. I had to stop myself from laughing out loud. It was great seeing him brought down to size for once. He was always so hard on me, but MacKenzie wasn't putting up with any of his shit. He was calling all the shots and Dad was having to fall into line. I'd never seen my dad act like this before. MacKenzie was having a profound effect on him. I was in awe of the way MacKenzie was dealing with Dad. He was impressing me more and more by the minute.

'I'm sorry if you think I'm being rude, but you look so similar, I have no idea how to tell the two of you apart,' MacKenzie admitted.

'It's a common problem,' Lily smiled. Her nerves seemed to have evaporated into thin air. 'We like different coloured make-up, which helps people who don't know us well to distinguish between us. Daisy usually wears red lipstick. And her necklace has a 'D' on it.'

MacKenzie glanced over at me, but the white gold jewellery she was talking about was hidden beneath my hoodie.

'It's exactly like this.'

Lily's fingers found the pendant with the initial 'L' hanging around her neck. She held it up for MacKenzie to see before she slid it backwards and forwards along the chain. Mum and Dad had bought them for us last Christmas.

'OK, cool,' MacKenzie replied, flashing me a smile.

My heart was beating too fast and pounding against my rib cage, trying to break free.

'Let's get you down to the stage,' MacKenzie said.

'Technology's a wonderful thing, isn't it? All you have to do these days is download your backing track onto a laptop, and away you go. No musical equipment's necessary. As long as there's a speaker and a jack lead at the venue, the singer's in business. It wasn't like that when I used to play guitar in a band,' Dad said as MacKenzie led the way along the corridor.

This was getting funnier by the minute, and I had to stifle another laugh. Dad was running behind MacKenzie, spewing out the details of his life story. I'd wondered how long it would take him to mention that he'd been a musician in his younger days. He couldn't help himself. Every person Dad came into contact with was treated to the same patter. The hilarious thing was, MacKenzie wasn't even trying to humour him. He seemed completely disinterested, which was the best thing he could have done. If he'd engaged in the conversation, it would have only encouraged Dad and prolonged MacKenzie's agony. I was sure MacKenzie had better things to do than listen to the tales of a washed-up wannabe rockstar.

'Right, Desmond, I'll leave you to work your magic, but do me a favour, mate, be quick; the clock's ticking,' MacKenzie said when we reached the stage area.

'No worries. It won't take me a minute to set up,' Dad replied, still on his best behaviour.

'Chop, chop, we haven't got all day,' Samson said, dismissing Dad with a wave of his hand.

My dad looked shocked to see the big boss standing at the back of the room, but his words put a rocket up Dad's arse and he jumped to attention.

'I just need access to a speaker and a jack, and we'll be good to go.' Dad was like a puppy trying his best to please his master.

Daisy and I took up position on the stage behind two free-standing microphones. As we stood side by side, waiting for the first song to begin, I could feel Lily's nerves coming off her in waves. The pressure to succeed was mainly on her. Rightly so. I only had a supporting role and wasn't under the same stress. I heard her take a deep lungful of air as the opening bars of 'Time After Time' echoed around the room.

Lily might have been shitting herself, but she nailed her performance. 'Livin' On A Prayer' was the next song in the set. Dad had chosen it because it was hard to sing, especially for a woman. It showcased Lily's vocal range and highlighted the fact that she wasn't a one-trick pony. But as the opening bars started, Samson put his hand up.

'OK, thanks. You can leave it at that. I've heard enough.'

Samson wasn't giving anything away. He stared at us stony-faced. Now I knew how a contestant on *The X Factor* felt when Simon Cowell pulled the plug on their performance. Disappointment began creeping up inside me.

'Well done, that was bloody fantastic!' Dad gushed. 'So, what do you think of my girls?' Dad asked, turning to face Samson and MacKenzie.

I felt myself cringe. Talk about putting them on the spot. I wasn't sure I wanted to hear what they had to say. I wasn't ready to cope with the rejection.

'They're great, aren't they? Truly unique. There's no other act like them.' Dad pressed on, not put off by their silence.

It was mortifying, but he had no shame. He'd had years of practice, so being a pushy parent came naturally to him. I felt like I was seven years old again, back in the church hall when they were casting the parts for the Nativity. Lily was going to play Mary while I got the coveted role of the donkey.

Samson and MacKenzie stood looking at each other. A wordless exchange passed between them before Samson left the room.

'Once you've packed up your stuff, I'll show you out,' MacKenzie said, not being drawn into the conversation.

He was impossible to read, which intrigued me and frustrated me in equal measure. But a bit of unpredictability kept life exciting, didn't it?

Dad disconnected his laptop while Lily and I walked off the stage. It seemed to take much longer to cover the distance on the way back now that adrenaline wasn't fizzing around inside me. I wanted to make the moment last in case we weren't offered the slot.

'Are you ready to roll?' MacKenzie asked, checking the time on his watch.

He seemed distracted, like he had somewhere else to be.

'Yes,' I replied, deliberately making eye contact with him.

He held my gaze for a moment until Dad zoomed past me so that he could get close to MacKenzie. I was tempted to stick my foot out and trip him up to stop him in his tracks. I knew what he was going to do. The humiliation was real without him making it any worse.

'When will you decide if the girls are in?' Dad asked.

I knew that question was coming, but I still couldn't stop myself from squirming.

'The girls would be a great addition to your line-up...' Dad prattled on without giving MacKenzie an opportunity to speak.

I shook my head and let out a sigh. Did the man have no shame?

MacKenzie laughed. 'Thanks for coming. I need to chat things over with Samson. I'll be in touch in a day or two,' he said as we reached the foyer.

MacKenzie turned on his heel and walked back down the corridor before Dad had a chance to question him further. Dad looked shell-shocked that he'd been put firmly in his place.

'I don't think I've ever heard the two of you sing better. You were word-perfect and hit every single note. I was expecting them to offer you the slot there and then,' Dad said as we walked back to the car. 'If that jumped-up little tosser hasn't called me by tomorrow, I'm going to phone him.'

20

MACKENZIE

Samson was sitting behind his desk with a tumbler of Scotch in his hand when I walked into his office.

'Get yourself a drink,' he said, gesturing to the well-stocked bar in the corner of the room.

'Thanks,' I replied, helping myself to a generous measure of Kraken.

'You did good, MacKenzie. Those twins are a couple of stunners,' Samson said, leaning back in his chair.

'I couldn't agree more. They're the kind of women who turn heads and give you an instant hard-on.'

'I wonder how badly they want the gig.' Samson leered.

I had shit for brains. Why the hell had I said that? I hoped I hadn't just put ideas in his head. I didn't like the tone of Samson's voice or the look on his face. He had a predatory way about him where women were concerned, so I immediately felt protective towards the twins.

'What do you think they'd be prepared to do to get the slot? Suck me off?' Samson let out a belly laugh.

Disgust rose up inside of me, but I had to keep my distaste

hidden. Samson was a nut job and lost his shit at the drop of a hat, so if I valued my life, I'd need to keep my opinions to myself.

'I might install a pole on the stage. You never know, spicing things up a bit might improve the cashflow.'

'They're singers, not strippers,' I said, feeling the need to fight their corner.

'But I hold the key to the twins getting on in this business, don't I?' Samson winked.

I shouldn't have been surprised that he was exercising his power. Everyone wanted to impress Samson; from the women he screwed, to the hopefuls auditioning for a chance to be on stage at Eden's. He was a charmer and liked to keep himself looking sharp. He had his hair trimmed every week and was partial to a regular facial and manicure, but he bored easily. Samson didn't restrict himself to one woman and he was in the right business for variety. The club was always full of scantily clad babes looking for guys to buy them drinks. And he never went anywhere without a pocket full of notes.

'Why are you so offended? You know what birds are like. A lot of them have the morals of an alley cat and are more than happy to drop their knickers for a couple of Bacardi and Cokes. Especially the desperado's looking for a record deal. They'd prostitute themselves out on the promise of an introduction to Travis Steele. Now there's an idea,' Samson sneered.

This conversation was ringing alarm bells for me. Samson clearly had plans for the girls. It was true his good friend, Travis, was a record mogul, but he also had an appetite for women – the younger the better – which his long suffering wife chose to ignore.

'If Daisy and Lily play their cards right, I might even let them in on the action. Pretty girls make great drug mules. Having a set of identical twins on the team is about as good as it gets. Carbon copies give the Old Bill a massive ball-ache,' Samson said with a thoughtful look on his face.

I couldn't believe he was considering getting the girls involved in his operation. Was there no end to the lengths he'd go to exploit people?

'Right, I'm a busy man, so let's wrap this up. Offer the twins the slot.'

Samson took a sip of his Scotch and stared off into the middle distance.

'Don't you want to discuss the other acts?'

I'd been dreading having this conversation. Samson and I never saw eye to eye where musical talent was concerned. Where anything was concerned really. I'd asked myself countless times why I was sticking around. Eden's was going down the pan; like a lot of clubs, it was in financial trouble. And Samson had made some bad decisions lately. But he wouldn't take kindly to me abandoning the sinking ship. Desertion wasn't compatible with a long life. Nobody in their right mind upset the boss, so I was stuck working for him for the foreseeable future.

'There's no need. None of them compete in the looks department. You know me, I like a bird who's all tits and teeth. Long legs help too but they're not essential. They don't exactly fit my usual criteria but I'd be prepared to let that slide on this occasion,' Samson grinned.

So he was going to hire the girls based simply on their appearance even though they sang well, too. I felt a sense of injustice for them. I barely knew Lily and Daisy, but I didn't like the way he was talking about them.

'Can I leave you to draw up the contract?' Samson asked.

'Are you sure you don't want to hear them sing a second time?'

'I'm not interested in their voices. The contract, MacKenzie?'

This should have been a dream come true for the girls, but I had a horrible feeling it was going to be the beginning of their worst nightmare.

'I'll get it drawn up straight away,' I replied.

I felt a pang of guilt, but my hands were tied. I wasn't forcing Lily and Daisy into accepting the offer, but it would be a suicidal move on my part to defy Samson.

'Now if you don't mind, I've got a call I need to make,' Samson said, wafting his hand in the direction of the door.

I knocked back the contents of my glass, put it down on his desk and walked out of his office. After checking nobody was around, I stuck my ear up to his door.

'How's it hanging, Travis?' Samson asked.

I felt the contents of my stomach shift.

'I wanted you to be the first to know, I've signed a new act for the Tuesday night slot. You'll have to come and check them out. You're going to love them. They're just your type: long legs, long blonde hair, big blue eyes. And if that's not selling it to you, they're identical twins! Two for the price of one!' Samson roared with laughter.

The thought of Samson and Travis making a move on the girls sickened me. Both of them were beautiful, but I was especially attracted to Daisy, which was strange as they looked exactly the same. She had an aloofness about her and hadn't fallen over herself to engage with me like Lily had. But when she looked into my eyes, there was a definite spark. Only time would tell if something came of it.

21

DAISY

The rain had stopped, but now it was like running the gauntlet as we dodged the spray from the passing traffic.

'I take it you didn't like MacKenzie then?' I asked with a smile on my face.

'That's an understatement. He was an arrogant little shit, too cocky for his own good. And as for Samson. He was rudeness personified. It's the same the world over. You give people a little bit of power, and it goes straight to their heads...'

The sound of Dad's phone ringing put an end to his verbal assault on Samson and my future boyfriend. Dad scrabbled to pull his phone out of his pocket before the call rang off.

'Hello.'

Lily and I glanced at each other before turning our attention back to Dad.

'Hi, MacKenzie,' Dad continued after a brief pause.

I felt my pulse speed up. If Samson and MacKenzie had reached a decision so quickly, we were either going to hear fantastic news or the worst news ever.

'Thank you for giving them the opportunity,' Dad said.

I wished I could hear the other side of the conversation. I wasn't sure whether MacKenzie was letting us down gently or not. It was hard to second-guess what was going on.

'That's amazing! They won't need time to think about it. I don't even need to ask them; I know the girls will be delighted to accept your offer. We'll see you next week.'

And so it continued. I'd pictured this moment differently. I'd hoped Dad might have had the common courtesy to run it past us before he said yes to MacKenzie. Pretend we had a choice in the matter. But he didn't bother. He just steamrolled ahead, making plans on our behalf without consulting us. Same old story. Nothing ever changed. It was interesting that he thought Samson was rude when he was cut from the same cloth. Dad had tears in his eyes as he hung up. Then he flung his arms around Lily and me.

'I'm so bloody proud of you girls. I knew you could do it. MacKenzie said he was blown away by your performance. None of the other acts came close to you.'

I couldn't say I was accustomed to praise like this. I was usually the scapegoat. The one that was always in trouble. But it was nice, for a change, to bathe in the glory usually reserved for Lily and one hundred times better than being on the receiving end of one of his nags.

I wasn't sure how I felt about securing the slot at Eden's. The reality of what it meant hadn't hit me yet. As a family, we needed the gig desperately, so signing the contract had to be a good thing. I'd finally be earning more money, even after Dad syphoned off the lion's share, taking me one step closer to my goal of moving out. But I still had reservations. There was something really creepy about Samson. I couldn't put my finger on what it was, I just had a bad feeling about him. And the thought of performing to a room full of people was terrifying. Although I was sure I could get over my fear if it brought me into close contact with MacKenzie every week.

22

MACKENZIE

I'd barely walked back into my office after the auditions when my encrypted mobile started to ring.

'MacKenzie?'

It was the man with the Spanish accent.

'Yes.'

'I have some good news and some bad news. Which would you like first?'

I sat down in my chair and let my shoulders slump. 'I'll have the bad news.'

It was always better to finish on a high, wasn't it?

'Some of the containers have broken free from their lashings and were lost at sea...'

For fuck's sake. That was all I needed.

'How did that happen? Why weren't they secured properly?'

'They were, but the ship is being battered left, right and centre by enormous waves. The conditions are extreme. It happens. Hundreds of millions of shipping containers are transported by sea each year; not all arrive at their final destination.'

We imported our cocaine by this method all the time, and this had never happened before.

'Was our shipment one of them?'

'I'm not sure at this stage. It's too early to properly assess the loss. We won't know until the ship makes it to land and the containers are offloaded. Then we can carry out a full inventory.'

I supposed that was better than an outright yes.

'I'll be in touch when I know more,' the Spanish guy said.

After he hung up, I was left wondering what the good news was. I couldn't put it off any longer. I'd have to break this to the boss. If I told him the bare minimum and left out most of the details, it might keep the bollocking he gave me to a minimum. The pressure on me was mounting and I was genuinely scared for my safety. Samson had a habit of lashing out when things didn't go his way and I was right in the firing line. I didn't fancy being face to face with him when I dropped the bombshell so I decided to phone him instead. It was safer for me in the long run to have some distance between us.

'Hi Samson. I've had a call from Miguel's guy. The storm was too heavy to ride out, so the captain's had to divert the ship.'

I held the phone away from my face so he didn't burst my ear drum.

'Fuck! Is that going to cause a delay?' Samson asked.

'I'm not sure. He didn't say anything about the schedule. I'll ring you when I get an update.'

As expected, he hadn't taken the news well, so I didn't bother telling him there was a distinct possibility that our cocaine was sitting at the bottom of the ocean. Why worry him with something like that when I didn't know for sure?

'Oh, by the way, the twins have accepted the offer. They'll be starting next week!' I added, taking my own advice and ending the call on a positive note.

23

DES

'How did it go?' Tara asked when we walked in the front door.

'Not great,' I replied with a dejected look on my face.

'Aww, that's a shame.' Tara's eyes swept over the girls. 'You look like you've taken it well.'

'That's because they've been offered the slot,' I grinned.

'For God's sake, Des, you're such an idiot. You really had me going there.'

'Sorry, love, I couldn't resist it. You know what I'm like.'

'Don't keep me in suspense. Tell me all about it.'

'I think our girls deserve a drink first. It's not every day you get offered a gig at a prestigious club like Eden's. This could be the start of something big for them.'

Tara rushed over and hugged Lily and Daisy in turn. She was one proud mumma, beaming from ear to ear. I stood in the doorway, leaning against the architrave, watching the three women in my life. I was a lucky man. They were all so beautiful. Tara was just as gorgeous as the day we met. She had raven locks and dark brown eyes. Her olive skin tone made her look more Mediterranean than of Irish descent. But she was fiercely proud of her heritage and didn't take kindly to people questioning her roots when they decided she was far too exotic looking to have parents that hailed from Killarney. Tara's answer was always the same and was accompanied with or without an eye roll, depending on her mood that day. People shouldn't automatically assume Mediterranean ancestry for everyone who doesn't have fair hair and freckles! Needless to say, my heritage never came into question, thanks to my red hair, blue eyes and pale Celtic skin tone.

Tara was a stunner. My very own Catherine Zeta-Jones. She didn't look her age. Nobody ever believed she was fifty-one. She looked years younger. She could easily pass for one of the girls' friends, not their mother. Tara had good genes, so my daughters were beauties. They'd inherited their mum's honey-coloured skin, doll-like features, large eyes, full lips, and tiny noses, but not her colouring. They had long blonde hair that was naturally streaked with pale golden strands and bright blue eyes – my only contribution. They were slightly taller than their mum at five-foot-seven but every bit as slim.

I'd never felt more proud as I watched my wife and daughters interacting. I'd always known this day would come. If you wanted something bad enough, you'd get there in the end. There was more to singing than just using your voice. Lily sang from the depths of her soul. And I'd seen a completely different side of Daisy today. She was every bit as good as her sister when she bothered to put the effort in.

Having identical twins had felt like a blessing. Every time Tara and I left the house, people stopped us in the street totally mesmerised by the two little angels in the pram. We'd spent most of our lives dreaming of being in the spotlight; this was the closest we'd get to feeling like celebrities. The unearned adoration my girls received blew my mind. It was hard to get my head around the fact that people they'd never met were fixated by them. I couldn't help feeling a pang of jealousy. What I wouldn't give to have strangers acting like groupies everywhere I went. And once the girls started to talk, people would hang on their every word. I wished I could bottle the attention they received.

Lily and Daisy were beautiful, and they were told that on a regular basis. That must be every little girl's dream, right? Being showered with compliments, morning, noon and night was a tough life. Tara worried that all the fuss would turn them into egotistical brats. She didn't want them growing up to be divas. According to my wife, there was only room for one bitch in our household. And that was her. She was the queen bee. She wouldn't compete with her daughters for the role she'd claimed for herself.

Tara wasn't a bitch. She was a strong, independent woman who knew her own mind and didn't suffer fools gladly. You had to be tough in our profession. If you didn't have a thick skin to start with, you had to develop one pretty quickly, or you wouldn't stand a chance. My wife transferred her skills to motherhood and took a no-nonsense approach to keep our girls grounded.

They were undeniably pretty and had praise heaped upon them because of how they looked, but if they hadn't been carbon copies of each other, I doubted either one of them would have turned heads the way they did.

'For God's sake, Des, where are the drinks? We're going to die of thirst in a minute,' Tara said, glancing over at me.

Tara's voice brought me back to the present. I was lost in memories of the past and had completely forgotten I was meant to be bringing alcohol so we could raise a toast to Lily and Daisy.

As I walked along the hall to the kitchen, my thoughts turned to Daisy. She'd spent all that time kicking up about the audition, making out she didn't want to be part of it, but when it came down to the nitty-gritty, it was obvious she wanted this opportunity just as much as Lily did. They might have inherited their looks from their mother, but Daisy got that stubborn streak from me. She was a Kennedy through and through. If she wasn't careful, her defiance would land her in a whole heap of trouble one day. There was a fine line between pig-headedness and stupidity.

24

MACKENZIE

I'd been out for the count when my mobile started ringing. Stretching one arm out of the duvet, I fumbled around on the bedside table with my sleep-laden limb, trying to put my hand on the device while I kept my eyes glued shut.

'Hello,' I said into the receiver before clearing my throat. My voice was low and croaky from all the weed I'd smoked last night.

'Hello, MacKenzie. I just wanted to let you know the ship has arrived at Rotterdam, and I've had confirmation that your container wasn't lost at sea,' Miguel's guy said.

As his words registered, my eyes slowly opened, and I raised my head.

'That's great.'

Finally, something was going right. We were only a couple of days behind schedule, so the diversion hadn't caused too much disruption.

'Unfortunately, there's another problem...'

My head flopped back into the pillows. I was losing the will to live.

'The storm has hit the mainland, and now the port's being battered by heavy winds.'

That sounded like a stalling tactic if ever I heard one.

'What difference does that make?'

'The port can't operate the cranes they use to unload the cargo. The conditions are too dangerous.'

'Let me guess, this is going to cause yet another delay.'

We sold the popular recreational drugs MDMA, LSD, speed, ketamine, ecstasy and cocaine. I had plenty of everything apart from the coke, and that was all anybody seemed to ask for at the moment. It was as though the clubbers knew it was in short supply.

'What are we talking about this time?' I asked when Miguel's guy failed to elaborate.

'It depends on how long the cranes are out of action and how congested the terminal gets in the meantime. The port authorities said it could be anything up to a month.'

'A month?'

'I know that's not what you wanted to hear, but that's the worst-case scenario.'

For fuck's sake. We might as well order another shipment from Ecuador at this rate. It would probably be with us sooner. Our cocaine might as well have gone overboard; we still couldn't get our hands on it.

I glanced at the time on my phone before I tossed it onto the bedside table. It wasn't even 7 a.m., so it was way too early to phone the boss unless I wanted my bollocks ripped off. It was still dark outside, so I rolled onto my side and tried to go back to sleep, but my mind was in overdrive. We couldn't afford to wait a month for the shipment to be released before it made the last leg of its journey to the UK.

If it came to it, I'd have to buy some cocaine at inflated prices and sell it on until our stock arrived. Samson wouldn't be happy, but I didn't have another alternative as far as I could see. I'd have to tread carefully and not upset the local dealers, but I needed to get the best price I could for the gear. Reinforcements were needed if I was going to be able to pull this off.

Leroy and Jermaine still lived with their mum on a council estate in Brixton, only a stone's throw from where I'd grown up in a similar high-rise hell hole. They were depressing places. Washing flapped on balconies, colourful graffiti tattooed walls and the lifts and stairwells always stank of stale piss. The only differences between the two were the postcodes.

Drug use was rife in the area, but I didn't want to trade on my old manor. It was too close to home. My mum and two younger brothers still lived there, so it would be better to find a source on another estate. There were plenty to choose from, but having a man with connections helping me would be the best way forward.

'Hi, Leroy, it's MacKenzie,' I said when he eventually picked up.

'Do you know what time it is?' Leroy's voice was thick with sleep.

'I know. I'm sorry to call you so early, but it's an emergency. I need to get hold of some coke urgently.'

'Fuck off, man. You'll have to score from some other mug who didn't finish work four hours ago.'

Leroy wasn't impressed.

'It's not for me. It's for Samson. His order's stuck in Rotterdam. It could be delayed for a month, and we'll have run out of gear by then. I haven't told him yet. I was hoping to have a plan in place before I dropped the bombshell.'

'I wouldn't want to be in your shoes when he finds out. How much do you need?'

'As much as you can get. But it needs to be cheap. And do me a favour, keep this to yourself.'

Even though none of this was my fault, Samson would hold me

personally responsible. My life wouldn't be worth living if I didn't get my hands on some coke before our stock ran out. The cost of running a club was huge and since we'd lost a lot of the clientele, Eden's had become dependent on the money we raised dealing drugs. No gear meant no dough. And that wouldn't be good for any of us.

25

DES

'I always knew our girls were destined for stardom,' Tara said.

'All the hard work has finally paid off,' I replied, smiling at my wife.

The girls were in their respective rooms, and Tara and I were sitting side by side on the sofa, talking about yesterday's audition while sharing a bottle of red wine.

'Right from the day they were born, there was something incredibly special about them,' Tara said with a wistful look on her face. 'Neither of us were lucky enough to get a break like this, but I'd always dreamed this day would come.'

'It's fantastic, isn't it? I can't believe it. I reckon I'm more excited than Lily and Daisy are.'

'I'm sure they're over the moon, but it probably hasn't sunk in yet.' Tara reached forward, picked her glass up from the coffee table and lifted it to her lips.

I didn't want to talk about what the consequences would have been if they hadn't got the slot because it would have ruined the moment. But the much-needed cash would keep Warren Jenkins and his threats on my life at bay for the time being. Who knew where this opportunity could lead? The sky was the limit. Pretty soon, the debt that had hung over us for so long would be a thing of the past. I could feel it in my bones.

'I don't think Lily and Daisy realise how lucky they've been. It's so hard to get anyone to listen to a demo. There's so much competition out there I don't usually get past first base.'

'Well, Desmond, you hit the jackpot this time. The stars must have been aligned just right when you contacted Eden's.'

Tara put her glass down on the table, then she reached towards me and planted a big kiss on my cheek, which brought a smile to my face. She hadn't called me Desmond for years. My full name was only used in formal situations and by my parents. Everyone else referred to me as Des. Desmond was her affectionate term for me. Hopefully, things were looking better for us.

Our marriage had been in and out of trouble because of the debt. Tara had been to hell and back over the years. She'd begged me to get a nine-to-five when the girls were born, but I wasn't prepared to walk away from the band. I felt like fame and fortune were just around the corner. I just needed a little more time and some financial backing. Unfortunately, that day never came.

Tara had hit the roof when I remortgaged the house. She'd called me a selfish bastard and threatened to leave me. She probably would have if we hadn't had kids. Things went from bad to worse when Warren Jenkins came into my life. I'd thought he was my saviour, handing over the money to enable me to clear the crippling mortgage repayments with no questions asked. But the interest he was charging was so steep it was impossible to reduce the amount we owed him. I had a bad credit rating and no friends or relatives I could turn to, so I didn't have any option other than to let the loan shark terrorise me. And he did at every opportunity, day and night.

'I wish my mum and dad were still around to see this. Our girls could be on the cusp of making it big,' Tara said, breaking into my thoughts. She was brimming over with pride.

If you wanted to reach the top, you had to put in the effort. Both Lily and Daisy had been born with the voices of angels. Lily used her gift, honing her craft for hours every day. Whereas Daisy couldn't be bothered. The difference in their ranges started to show a while ago, which was another reason I wanted Lily to take the lead. But there was more to it than just their ability. Daisy had a bad attitude when it came to band practice, so I wasn't going to reward her for not giving it her all. But something had changed today. I hoped it continued.

'You know, even Daisy stepped up to the mark when they went on stage,' I said.

'And you spent all that time worrying that she was going to ruin things just to spite Lily. I've told you before she does this to wind you up. You're your own worst enemy; you shouldn't let her get a rise out of you.' Tara gave me that knowing look.

I tore my eyes away from her and slumped back on the sofa.

'What's wrong, Des?' Tara turned towards me with a worried look on her face.

'I nearly cost the girls the audition.' I turned away when I saw the look of horror spread over her features.

'What do you mean?'

'I was late...'

Tara threw me one of her looks.

'Only by a couple of minutes.'

'Even so, I bet Lily nearly killed you. You know how she feels about timekeeping.'

'It wasn't my fault; I couldn't get a parking space, and when I arrived, the manager said he had other acts to see, and he showed us the door.'

'Jesus, Des. Why didn't you say something? I wondered why

you'd been gone so long, but I know these things have a habit of running over.'

'Exactly. I really didn't think it would be an issue. The girls were there early. To cut a long story short, I had to use the old Kennedy charm to talk him into giving us a second chance,' I grinned.

I could talk myself out of trouble most of the time and had a knack of twisting myself around little fingers. My mum used to say I had the gift of the gab.

'Thank God it worked. I'd say you're a bit out of practice these days,' Tara laughed.

'Listen, don't knock it. Do I need to remind you that my silver tongue won you over?' I winked.

Tara was way out of my league, but I'd still managed to pull her somehow. None of my mates could believe a bloke like me had ended up with such a beauty. I was no oil painting, but she fell for me, and the rest, as they say, is history.

26

MACKENZIE

'Who's this?' I asked when I picked up my personal mobile. I didn't normally answer the phone to withheld numbers, but I was distracted, so I'd done it without thinking.

'I'm phoning on behalf of Willem,' a guy with a Dutch accent said.

Who the fuck was Willem?

'Doesn't ring a bell, mate. Is this a sales call?'

'No. I'm calling from Rotterdam...' the voice trailed off just as I was about to hang up.

'What's this about?'

'I was part of the team unloading cargo this morning—'

'Hang on a minute, mate, I thought the port was closed because of the storm?' This didn't add up, so I cut him off mid-sentence.

'It was, but there's been a break in the weather, so we were able to start operating the cranes.'

That was music to my ears. I felt myself riding high on this glimmer of hope.

'That's great. Sorry, I interrupted you. What were you saying about the cargo?'

'Willem's one of the officials at the port. He asked me to let you know there's a problem with the shipment of coffee you were expecting from Colombia.'

I came crashing back down to earth, and now my head felt like it was about to explode.

'What sort of problem?' My tone was abrupt, but I couldn't help being rude. There was no time for pleasantries.

'I'm afraid I don't know. I'm just passing on the message...' the Dutchman replied before he hung up.

I couldn't really blame him for not wanting to stick around and get an ear bashing from me. I didn't even know the bloke.

I dropped the phone onto the desk. Why did crap always land on my doorstep? How the fuck had this Willem guy got hold of my number in the first place? No prizes for guessing. Samson must have given it to him. It would have been nice if he'd asked if I minded beforehand, though. But that was a perk of being the boss. I was an underling, one of his skivvies. He gave the orders, and I did what I was told, or else.

I glanced at my watch to check the time. It was just after one. Samson probably wasn't even up yet; he wasn't exactly an early bird. I'd have to tell him the bad news, but maybe I should wait a bit; he wouldn't be impressed if I woke him from his sleep. Who was I trying to kid? He'd shit a brick if I didn't pass on an important message like this as soon as it came through. I'd told him that the ship had arrived at Rotterdam, but I hadn't mentioned the problem the storm had created with the cranes because I valued my life too much. On top of everything else, a month's delay would have been too much for him to handle. It was better for all concerned that he didn't know, especially as Leroy was still trying to source some gear at a good price to tide us over. In the meantime, I'd been cutting our dwindling supply of cocaine with creatine to make it go further. There hadn't been any complaints so far.

'Samson, it's MacKenzie,' I said as soon as the call connected.

He cleared his throat before he spoke. 'Why are you phoning me so early? This better be important.' Samson's voice was thick with sleep.

The way he was talking, anyone would think it was the crack of dawn, not lunchtime.

'I'm sorry, boss, but I've just had a call from Rotterdam, and I thought you'd want to know.'

I could hear the rustling of bedclothes before Samson spoke again. 'What's going on?' he asked, sounding much more alert than he had a moment ago.

'I'm not sure. The guy I spoke to had a message from Willem.'

'Has the shipment left for Felixstowe yet?'

I could hear the impatience in Samson's voice. I knew I was in for a bollocking even though none of this was my fault.

'He didn't say. He just said there was a problem with the shipment.' I spat the words out as though they were burning the inside of my mouth.

'What sort of problem?'

I didn't need to see Samson to know that the part of his cheeks not covered by his designer stubble would be turning red, and his big brown eyes would be out on stalks.

'The guy didn't say.'

'Why didn't you ask him? You're a fucking half-wit, MacKenzie.'

There was no point trying to fight my corner. Samson wasn't listening. He was lost in the red mist. Thank God I wasn't within striking distance or he'd have had his hands around my throat.

'Are you at the club?' Samson asked through gritted teeth.

'Yes.' Where the hell did he think I was?

'Go home and pack a bag. We're getting the next available flight to Amsterdam,' Samson barked down the phone before he hung up.

I'd been really looking forward to seeing Daisy again, hoping to make a move on her before Samson or Travis beat me to it. Now, thanks to the boss, that wasn't going to happen for another week. My day was going from bad to worse. The pressure was mounting and there was nothing I could do about it. Going to Rotterdam wasn't going to change the situation, but being alone with Samson at a time like this could have deadly consequences for me. I wasn't being dramatic. The man was a raging lunatic who acted first and thought about what he'd done later. If at all. When Samson wasn't happy, somebody had to pay. And I had a horrible feeling in the pit of my stomach, that the somebody with his head on the block was me.

27

DAISY

'For God's sake, hurry up; we're going to be late!' Lily shouted up the stairs.

I was in the middle of topping up my bright red lipstick, so I didn't bother to reply. After checking my reflection in the full-length mirror one last time, I walked out of my bedroom and sauntered down to the hallway.

'You look nice. Very rock chick,' Mum said as her dark brown eyes scanned over me.

I was wearing skin-tight black faux leather trousers and a black corset-style top which laced up the back with ribbon. I'd even put on heels for the occasion, hoping I'd be able to impress MacKenzie with more than just my singing voice.

Lily had chosen something similar to me. She was dressed in dark blue skinny jeans and a black cold-shoulder top with needle-thin stiletto-heeled strappy sandals.

'Knock 'em dead,' Mum called after us as we left the house.

The icy December air whistled around us as we walked the short distance from the station car park. I pulled my fake fur coat around me in a bid to keep out the cold. It might have looked warm and cosy, but it was an illusion. The fabric had no heat-retaining properties, so it had little effect at repelling the sub-zero temperature. A sudden gust lifted my hair off my shoulders and made it dance around my head. The sooner we got inside the foyer, the better. I'd spent ages getting ready, and I was going to look like I'd been dragged through a hedge backwards at this rate.

Leroy greeted us at the entrance. It was the first time we'd met him, but it was easy to tell he was related to Jermaine. It wasn't just the cornrow hairstyle that was giving the game away. They had similar features and were both over six feet, although Leroy had a bigger frame.

'Mac's asked me to show you to your dressing room,' he said.

My heart fluttered at the mention of MacKenzie's name. I'd been hoping he'd have been here to meet us himself and had to make a concerted effort not to look too disappointed.

'If you'd like to follow me,' Leroy said, flashing us a smile which exposed a gold front tooth.

He walked along the carpeted hallway, pointing out the bar, MacKenzie's office and the stage area as we passed them. Lily was immediately behind him, I was next, and Dad was bringing up the rear.

'Nearly there,' Leroy said, pausing above a flight of stone stairs.

Our shoes echoed around the stairwell as we made our way down to the basement. Lily and I both held on tightly to the handrail. The steps seemed very steep in three-inch heels. We followed Leroy along the corridor. Bulkhead lighting and concrete flooring gave the space an industrial look, so I hadn't been expecting much. But I was in for a pleasant surprise.

'That leads out to an alleyway. You can bring your van down and unload your gear through here,' Leroy said, pointing over to the double-width door.

'Thanks, mate, that's good to know,' Dad replied, even though he was carrying the only equipment we needed with him.

'And now for the moment of truth. Here you go,' Leroy said.

When he opened the door, it almost banged against the arm of a two-seater sofa that had been wedged into the corner.

'After you,' Leroy said, gesturing for Lily, Dad and me to step inside.

I couldn't help feeling a little starstruck when my eyes scanned around the backstage room Lily and I were allowed to use before gigs. Two light-up mirrors, the type with bulbs sticking out from a rectangular frame, were stuck to the wall opposite the door. A piece of white countertop lay beneath them. It stretched almost the entire width of the small room so that we could spread out our make-up when we were getting ready.

The room wasn't exclusively for our use, so there was shelving under the counter with rows of plastic baskets to store our things in. Two swivel stools covered in black faux leather sat beneath that. A full-length mirror took up most of the wall space adjacent to the dressing tables. On the wall opposite that, there was a mini fridge. The kind you'd find in a hotel room, whose presence created a buzz of excitement in me, but in reality, there was only enough room for a couple of beers or maybe a bottle of wine and Lily's precious mineral water. Heaven forbid she should have to drink water from the tap like the rest of us did.

'The room's fitted with soundproofing so you can relax before your set. Nobody wants to be disturbed by the noise of other bands when they're preparing to go on stage, do they?' Leroy said.

We hadn't been expecting treatment like this, so Lily and I had already put our faces on, but I was definitely going to make use of the area before next week's show.

'You guys are on at nine. How long do you need to set up?' Leroy asked.

'Not long. Fifteen minutes should do it,' Dad replied.

'Cool. I'll give you a shout. In the meantime, feel free to make yourselves at home. Take whatever you want from the fridge. It's on the house,' Leroy smiled.

'Will Samson and MacKenzie be watching the girls' performance?' Dad asked.

The mention of Samson's name sent a wave of panic coursing through my veins.

'Usually, they would, but they've been called away on urgent business,' Leroy said.

I breathed a sigh of relief that Samson wouldn't be here, but I was bitterly disappointed that I wasn't going to see MacKenzie and had to stop myself from letting out a groan. I'd been looking forward to this moment since the audition. Now that I knew MacKenzie wasn't here, I wasn't sure I could be arsed to go on stage.

'What's wrong with you?' Dad asked as soon as Leroy closed the door behind him.

'Nothing,' I replied.

'Really? You could have fooled me. You were full of the joys of spring a minute ago, and now you've got a face like a slapped arse,' Dad pointed out.

'I'm nervous, so do me a favour and leave me alone. The last thing I need is you winding me up,' I snapped.

I wasn't about to own up to what was really bothering me.

'Fair enough, I've got the message loud and clear. You didn't need to bite my head off.'

Dad held his hands up in front of him as though he was shielding himself from the lash of my tongue.

28

MACKENZIE

Samson must have checked the time on his watch at least fifty times since the plane took off. We'd managed to get the last two seats on the British Airways flight to Rotterdam and made it to London City Airport by the skin of our teeth, thanks to Leroy's skill behind the wheel. He'd had to jump more than one red light and endured verbal abuse from other road users, but the man had nerves of steel and wasn't put off by countless middle fingers and long, drawn-out blasts of the horns – no wonder he'd been employed as a getaway driver on more than one occasion.

I craned my neck, peered out the window. A sea of lights were below us. My eyes fixed on them as they grew closer and closer. A moment later, the plane's wheels hit the tarmac. I loved flying at night. Cities always looked much more impressive against a night sky than in the daytime.

'Thank fuck for that. I thought we'd never get here,' Samson moaned.

It had taken just under an hour, but by the fuss he was making, anyone would think we'd just endured a long-haul flight.

'The amount of legroom they give people is inhumane. Talk about travelling cattle class,' Samson whinged.

I was going to say welcome to the world of economy, but I thought better of it. At least he had the aisle seat. I'd been stuck in the middle, sandwiched between him and a guy who must have weighed at least twenty stone, and I hadn't complained once.

Samson was accustomed to the finer things in life: airport lounges, VIP service, and free drinks as part of the package. That was the way he liked to travel. But they didn't have a first class option on this route, and when you booked a flight at a moment's notice, you were lucky to get a seat on the plane. He couldn't really expect to be treated like a king. He should be thanking his lucky stars we were with BA and not one of the budget airlines.

As we only had hand luggage, we emerged into the arrivals hall a short while later. A driver was waiting for us and whisked us away to the hotel in the city centre that Samson's PA had booked. Fifteen minutes later, we were standing at the front desk.

'I'm starving. Where's the restaurant?' Samson asked the receptionist after she'd booked us in.

'I'm sorry, sir, it closed at nine o'clock,' she replied.

Samson stared at the young woman, who was barely out of her teens, with a look of horror on his face.

'It's closed?' he questioned, as though she'd said something alien.

'Yes, I'm sorry, sir. It's almost ten o'clock now. I could arrange some room service for you instead,' the receptionist offered.

'I want a proper meal,' Samson replied with his hands on his hips.

I gave the receptionist a sympathetic smile. Samson was behaving like a total prick. It was embarrassing to see a grown man acting like this.

'We're in the middle of the city centre. There must be loads of restaurants around here that are still open,' I said, trying to take the heat off the young woman.

'I can recommend Delphine's. It's just across the road from here, a two-minute walk,' the receptionist pointed dead ahead. 'It holds a Michelin star and has a very good reputation. Would you like me to phone them and make a reservation for you?'

'Don't worry; that won't be necessary,' I replied as Samson was already heading towards the door. 'Thanks for your help,' I called over my shoulder.

I paced across the shiny marble floor to catch up with him. My boss could be a prize pig at times. Being rich didn't give you a hall pass to be rude. But he got away with it time and again. I felt sorry for the receptionist, but to be fair to her, she handled the situation well. I'd say she was used to people speaking to her like that. It shouldn't be the case, but when you worked in an expensive hotel where money was no object for the clientele, they expected you to stand on your head to please them.

Samson was in a foul mood, so we spent our time in the restaurant in virtual silence. We were almost at the end of our meal when he finally spoke.

'I don't think much of her recommendation. I hate foreign muck like this,' Samson said as he pushed his food around the plate.

You'd swear the man was starving to death with the fuss he was making. He had a well-covered, five-feet-ten-inch frame, although he always told people he was six foot. You only needed to see him standing next to our bouncers to know that wasn't true. I didn't know why he felt the need to lie about it; being tall wasn't the be-all and end-all, but I supposed when you had a personality like his, height would be the only thing he had going for him. His arrogance never stopped women from falling at his feet, though. There was no better fanny magnet than a wallet full of fifty-pound notes.

'I have to say, I enjoyed mine,' I replied, scraping the last mouthful of black Angus beef bourguignon onto my fork.

A fancy French restaurant wouldn't have been my first choice either, but it was the best bourguignon I'd ever had, and he'd ordered the same as me, so I couldn't work out what he was complaining about. But the way Samson was behaving this evening, in one of his moods, he'd have found fault with whatever dish had been served up.

'I can't believe you enjoyed that.' Samson prodded a piece of beef with his knife.

The way he was gawping at it, you'd swear he'd just discovered somebody had placed a huge turd in the sauce. My boss was an arsehole, and I hated working for him, but once you got into this game, there was no getting out, even when you wanted to. I would love to have a safe, mundane job, but a man like me had very limited options. If you made the mistake of walking down the wrong path, it was virtually impossible to go straight. I'd been a petty criminal since my early teens. That wasn't something I was proud of, but shoplifting and selling hooky gear had become a necessity after my scumbag of a dad fucked off with some tart he met down the pub, leaving my mum skint and alone to bring up three kids. If I didn't steal, we didn't eat. It was as simple as that.

I tilted my empty plate towards him. 'I thought it was delicious.'

My only issue was I could have eaten it twice over. The portions in expensive restaurants like this were always tiny, but I kept that to myself. I didn't want to give him any ammunition.

Samson rolled his eyes at me.

'I've said it before, and I'll say it again, you'd eat any old shit, wouldn't you? Proper dustbin you are, MacKenzie.'

He threw me a look of disgust before he clicked his fingers at the waiter to get his attention. Then, he settled the bill without leaving a tip. It always amazed me how the wealthiest people were also the tightest.

'I'll meet you down in the lobby at seven forty-five,' Samson said as the lift doors opened on the fifth floor, and we both got out.

The hotel had given us adjoining rooms, but Samson wasn't about to invite me in to share the contents of his mini bar, which was a blessing as far as I was concerned. The more distance I could put between us, the better my evening would turn out to be.

29

DAISY

Our opening gig had gone well. Better than well. It was an amazing experience. The crowd danced and sang along to our playlist. They'd poured booze down their necks while the music blared out and behaved exactly as we dreamed they would. Seeing them enjoying our set, enjoying life, was a pinch-me moment.

At the end of the evening, when a cheer went up and the audience called for an encore, it brought tears to Lily's eyes. No surprise there. I could always count on my twin to be predictable in that department. My sister was highly strung. Dramatic. She could turn on the waterworks at a moment's notice; whatever the occasion, happy tears, sad tears, worried tears. You name it. She could find a reason to blub. And then she always excused her wailing by saying she couldn't help it, she was an emotional person. My arse. She was an attention seeker. Nothing more. Nothing less.

'Thank you all for coming. You were the best crowd ever,' Lily said, lapping up the applause when we finished the last song.

'It's been a blast,' I said into the microphone before I walked off the stage.

Even though our first show had gone better than any of us

could have expected, I was down in the dumps. My mood was low. Disappointment hung over me like a dark cloud on a summer's day. I'd been looking forward to this evening, but I'd pictured it ending very differently. I'd hoped MacKenzie would have been here to watch us perform. Then we'd celebrate the success of the night with a few drinks. Share our first kiss. Maybe more. Who knew what would happen? If you were open to things like I was, possibilities were endless. Risk and intrigue walked hand in hand as far as I was concerned.

'What's up with you? You've got a face like a slapped arse,' Dad said when he walked into the dressing room.

I couldn't help feeling blue. I didn't just fancy MacKenzie, there was more to it than that. He could be my escape route out of home. My dad made my life hell, tormenting me at every opportunity, but he literally shrank in his shoes in MacKenzie's presence. If we became an item, Dad wouldn't dare try to control me or lay his hands on me ever again. MacKenzie seemed like a lovely guy and I could picture a new life with him, a more exciting existence where I wasn't in conflict with my dad all the time. It couldn't happen soon enough for my liking.

'You should be grinning from ear to ear. The two of you were bloody brilliant. Considering that was a live set, it was virtually faultless.'

I tilted my head to one side before I flashed him my best fake smile.

'Is that better?'

Dad rolled his eyes and shook his head, but he didn't reply. The last thing I wanted to do was get into a back-and-forth power struggle with him. I wanted to get out of Eden's and back to the house where I could hide in the sanctity of my bedroom and be alone with my thoughts. I spent a lot of time in my room to avoid being in my dad's company. It was the only way not to end up in an argument with him. Things sometimes got so heated between us that he'd unleash his violent temper on me. I could do without that tonight. MacKenzie was on my mind and I needed space to think.

I'd had big expectations for tonight, so the roar of the crowd and the loud applause didn't make up for MacKenzie's absence. I might have been mistaken, but I'd thought there'd been a spark between us. Maybe I'd imagined it. But one thing was certain, the Tuesday night slot at Eden's was soon going to lose its appeal if he was away on business every time we were due to sing. Fingers crossed, it was a one-off. My heart wasn't in performing the way Lily's was.

* * *

'You seem to be under the impression that your time is more important than ours,' Dad said, shaking his head in irritation when I dragged myself into the garage for band practice.

'I'm five minutes late. Big deal. Get over it,' I replied.

'You should take a leaf out of your sister's book and be five minutes early next time,' Dad fired back, never missing the opportunity to compare us to each other.

It was no wonder we'd always had a strained relationship. Lily was the first-born golden child. She'd had a fifteen-minute head start on me, but it had given her a massive advantage. Lily was treated differently by our family and everyone we knew. I remember my grandad warning my parents about it. He told them no good would come of having favourites and that they'd drive a wedge between us. Did they listen? Hell no. So now they only had themselves to blame for the situation they'd created.

'I can't believe you've got the cheek to tell me off about my time-keeping after you nearly cost us the audition.' I shook my head from side to side.

'I should have known you were going to throw that back in my face. You can't help yourself, can you?' Dad snorted. He glared at me with his fists clenched down by his sides, not bothering to conceal his anger.

'For God's sake, give it a rest, or we'll get nothing done,' Lily said, trying to stop us from tearing strips off each other.

'Why don't you shut the fuck up? Nobody asked for your opinion.'

Lily's face was a picture. She hadn't been expecting me to turn on her, but it pissed me off when she waded into one of mine and Dad's arguments like a United Nations peacekeeper trying to negotiate a ceasefire.

'Don't you dare speak to your sister like that!' Dad roared. He grabbed a fistful of my hair and spun me around to face him. 'Apologise right now.' He was literally foaming at the mouth.

All I had to do was say sorry, but my stubbornness wouldn't let the words out of my mouth, even when Dad tightened his grip.

'I'm warning you, Daisy,' Dad said, his blue eyes bulging.

I glared at him with a defiant look on my face and that's when his patience wore out. He let go of my hair and swung his arm back. The sound of the slap connecting with my skin echoed around the garage before pain shot through my cheek. It was throbbing. Burning. But I wouldn't give him the satisfaction of crying out.

'Dad, stop! You've really hurt her. Look at her face! I can see your handprint on her cheek,' Lily screamed, before she burst into tears.

'I barely touched her. I'll tell you something, kids today are too bloody sensitive for their own good. A good clatter never did us any harm,' I heard Dad reply as I walked away.

How ironic that he was accusing me of being sensitive when my sister was the one crying her eyes out.

30

MACKENZIE

Samson had a really annoying habit of agreeing a time and then arriving early. He'd done it to me on countless occasions, so I made sure I was down in reception at 7.30 a.m. so that he couldn't be pissed off that I'd kept him waiting. When he stepped out of the lift, he seemed more than a bit surprised to see me sitting in the leather bucket chair opposite. He was dressed in one of his trademark grey suits and black shirt combos. His tanned hands peeked out from the bottom of his shirt, gold cufflinks glinting in the bright overhead lighting that flooded the foyer.

I didn't do flash at the best of times, and we were only heading to the port, so it hardly warranted wheeling out his Savile Row finest. But that was Samson all over. It was all about outward appearance. He liked to look the part. You'd be hard pushed to find a more shallow, self-centred person if you tried. I couldn't be bothered with that crap; jeans and a hoodie suited me just fine.

'Morning, boss,' I said, leaping out of the chair.

Samson turned over his wrist and checked the time on his Breitling watch.

'You're early,' he remarked before he walked towards the glass doors.

We were all in for a treat; his mood hadn't improved one bit from last night. If anything, he was even saltier than before.

Willem was waiting for us at the entrance of the Customs Office. He was about the same height as me, had short brown hair parted on the left and swept over his shiny forehead. He had a round moon face, which mirrored the shape of his glasses, an ultra-straight nose and small beady eyes.

'Mr Fox,' he said as Samson approached him.

'Pleased to meet you,' Samson replied, holding out his hand and giving Willem a warm smile, doing his best to be charming and polite. 'MacKenzie tells me there's a problem with my shipment of coffee.'

'Yes, I'm afraid so.'

Rotterdam was Europe's largest port. It was a hive of activity. Everywhere I looked, giant cranes were unloading containers from cargo ships before stacking them side by side along the quay. They stretched as far as the eye could see.

'Come inside where we can talk in private, and I'll explain,' Willem said, looking over his shoulder to a group of armed customs officers standing by one of the port's perimeter fences.

He led us up the steps of the boxy structure, which looked like a site office used by the construction industry.

'Take a seat. Would you like some tea or coffee?' Willem asked.

'No thanks,' we replied as we sat next to each other on the opposite side of the desk.

It was stifling in the room. You wouldn't think three small oil-filled radiators would kick out so much heat. The temperature was unbearable. I felt like I'd fallen headfirst into a volcano, so I burrowed my way out of my hoodie the moment I sat down.

'Let's just get down to business, shall we,' Samson said; his Mr

Nice Guy front was starting to slip already. 'What exactly is the problem?'

'The container is due to be scanned this afternoon, and there's a possibility it will be searched,' Willem said as beads of sweat appeared on his forehead.

'What the fuck!' Samson shouted, leaping out of his chair. He held onto the side of the table and leant across it so that his face was inches away from Willem's.

Willem was wearing the expression of a man whose balls had just been grabbed by a silverback gorilla.

'I'm not sure I heard you right. Did you say the container is going to be searched?' Samson practically had steam coming out of his ears.

Willem nodded his head as his Adam's apple bobbed up and down. He looked like he was on the verge of tears.

'How the fuck has this happened?'

When Samson slammed his fist down on the desk, Willem jumped out of his skin. Then he swallowed hard, and his eyes began darting around the room as though he was looking for an escape route. Lucky bastard. I wish I could go with him. But if I tried to run from Samson, he'd track me down and end my days. I knew too many of his secrets to be able to walk away.

'The port is taking major steps to stop drugs entering Europe. We've been told to step up customs checks and scan all containers arriving from Latin America.'

'Why am I only just hearing about this change in procedure?'

Willem squirmed in his seat.

'We've been digging our heels in and bitterly resisting the changes. It's time-consuming checking everything that arrives, so we've told the powers that be that we need to find a good balance between the speed of unloading the cargo and checking for contraband,' Willem replied.

'How come they're sniffing around our shipment? It doesn't make any sense,' Samson questioned.

He had a valid point. Our cargo was in a terminal with one hundred thousand other containers, so why had it been singled out?

'We use risk analysis to determine whether inspections are needed,' Willem said.

'What's so risky about a shipment of coffee then?' Samson was on the verge of losing it.

'Thousands of shipping containers depart from Guayaquil each month. It's one of South America's busiest ports. The authorities in Ecuador only search a small percentage of them. They don't have any scanners, so the task falls to the port officials and drug-sniffing Belgian shepherds. They have to painstakingly inspect the containers by hand. Rumour has it, the dogs can only reliably search three containers a day, so we've been told to be extra vigilant.'

Samson looked less than impressed by Willem's long-winded explanation.

'Colombia and Peru are two of the biggest producers of cocaine. Ecuador is sandwiched between them. Because of its geography and lax security, the authorities know it's a transit hub for cocaine,' Willem continued.

'That still doesn't answer my question. Why do they think a shipment of coffee is so high risk it warrants being scanned?' Samson was chewing the inside of his lip, trying to keep a lid on his explosive temper.

'Coffee, pineapples, bananas, it makes no difference. Anything coming from Ecuador raises a red flag. About forty-five per cent of the cocaine produced in Colombia now passes through Ecuador.'

'For fuck's sake.' Samson's nostrils were flaring. 'So what's going to happen?'

'We'll scan the container if we're told to, but it will only be opened as a last resort,' Willem replied before pushing his glasses back up his nose with his index finger.

'There's no way we can let this happen. Why aren't you doing something about it? You need to stop the search from going ahead, you fuckwit!' Samson's large eyes bulged as a curly vein appeared on his temple and started to throb.

'I can't. It would raise too much suspicion if I intervened.' Willem threw the palms of his hands up.

Samson's head rocked back, and he let out an elongated sigh. Then he dropped down onto the spindly office chair, which appeared to let out a groan of displeasure in response to his weight. This was disastrous news for all of us. Eden's was at the point of going under. Even though we'd just signed the twins, I was worried it was too little, too late. While Samson was using the club as a front for his drug-dealing empire, there was some hope for its survival, but now that we were having difficulty obtaining coke, the reality was we might have to shut up shop. If I wasn't very careful, I could end up losing everything.

'Please don't distress yourself. I have a plan in place,' Willem smiled and held his hands out towards Samson. 'I've arranged for one of my close associates to carry out the scan. I'll be on hand to help him, so don't get too stressed out about this. We'll make sure nothing shows up so then we can clear the shipment for its onward journey.'

'Clear it through customs as quickly as possible.'

The charming, well-dressed man who had shaken Willem's hand barely twenty minutes ago was unrecognisable.

'I will, of course, but it will cause a slight delay to the schedule; there's no way around that.'

Willem was a brave man for admitting that. I wouldn't want to be in his shoes.

'I'm not leaving Rotterdam until my gear is on its way, so you'd better sort this out pretty damn quickly, or your head's on the block,' Samson said, pushing back his chair with such force that it flipped over. 'The scan had better not show anything hidden in that cargo of coffee.' Samson was leaning across the desk so he could get up in Willem's face.

'I can assure you I'll do everything in my power to make sure nothing shows up,' Willem replied.

'Not good enough,' Samson said over his shoulder as he flung open the flimsy office door and powered down the steps.

Now, it was going to be my turn to get an ear bashing.

'I'm not buying that crap he was trying to spin us. Somebody must have tipped the port off,' Samson said in a low voice as we walked over to the car.

I'd been thinking the same thing. There was a grass in the ranks.

'What happened to the useless fuckers that were meant to move the cocaine to a different container so there was less chance of the authorities checking it? Every man and his dog knows shipments coming from South America are more likely to be scanned.'

Willem hadn't told Samson anything he didn't already know.

'They had one job to do, and they fucked it up. How hard is it to get the drugs out of the container and away from the docks? I pay those fuckers thousands of euros to get the batches through. They're not getting a penny off me for this fiasco.'

Samson's rant was finally over. I'd stayed quiet while he'd offloaded. There was no point in trying to talk to him while he was in a mood like this. I knew that from experience.

31

MACKENZIE

Samson was the one who set up the deal between his suppliers and his distributors. Then he stepped back. Everything else was dealt with by the people who worked for him. I was his second in command and knew what was expected of me. I was bricking it. If I didn't follow orders, my days were numbered. Drug dealing was a dangerous business. Death at the hands of your boss or the competition was a real possibility.

I'd been keeping my head down since we got back from the port, trying to stay out of the firing line. Samson had gone to the hotel gym to let off some steam, so I took the opportunity to phone Leroy while he was out of earshot.

'How's it going, mate?' He answered my call on the second ring.

'I've been better, I can tell you.'

'Any news on the shipment?' Leroy asked, sounding upbeat.

'It's stuck in customs. The container's being scanned this afternoon,' I replied.

'No way. First the storm and now this.' By the sound of his voice, I could tell Leroy's mood had taken a downward turn.

'Samson's doing his nut. We're going to be in a right fucking mess if anything shows up. Have you had any luck finding us another source?'

Jermaine and Leroy lived on a dodgy estate. There was bound to be somebody selling coke. It was the kind of place you could buy anything, so a bit of cocaine should be really easy to come by.

'Are you sure about this? Samson won't be happy if you start buying from a dealer at an inflated rate,' Leroy replied.

'I know, but I might not have another option. I'm running low on stock. Surely it would be better to make a smaller profit than lose our customer base while we wait for our supply chain to sort itself out.'

'I hear what you're saying, bro, but I still don't think the boss will go for it.'

'Do me a favour, keep looking into it for me. Don't buy any gear yet, but check it out, please.'

I'd do it myself, but I didn't live on an estate any more, so I didn't have contacts like he did. It would be better coming from him. If I started trying to buy a large volume, the dealers would think I was an undercover cop attempting to bust them. I just sold the gear. I didn't usually get involved in sourcing it. We had enough marijuana, MDMA, LSD, speed, ketamine and ecstasy stashed at Eden's to supply half of south-east England. I'd been hoping to flog it in place of the coke. But I hadn't had any takers. Our clubbers weren't interested in it. I supposed I got where they were coming from. If you fancied a steak, chicken was a poor substitute.

* * *

Willem had just called to say the shipment had cleared customs, but it could be weeks before it left Rotterdam as the storm had caused a huge backlog at the docks. Samson wasn't going to be happy. He must be back from the gym by now; it was time to go and ruin his day.

'I've been talking to Miguel Castro about this shit show, and he's almost certain Vincenzo Lombardi's behind it. He reckons the Italians tipped off the port authorities as payback,' Samson said, after I'd filled him in on the latest development.

'He could be right.'

Vincenzo had told Samson that he'd end up regretting taking his business elsewhere. And this was the first shipment he'd ordered from his new Mexican supplier. It seemed like there was more than bad luck behind the official interest in it.

'The more I think about it, the more I'm convinced Miguel's hit the nail on the head. Tens of millions of pounds worth of drugs are imported into the UK from Europe and South America every year. We'd never had any issues while we'd been buying our gear from Lombardi's stock. But the minute I cut him adrift, my shipment gets scanned. We came this close to getting the lot seized.'

Samson held his thumb and forefinger an inch apart.

'It does seem like a very convenient coincidence that our cargo was inspected.'

'Vincenzo's not going to get away with trying to stitch me up. Mark my words. He'll be sorry he started this.'

Samson was a man of his word. If he said something, he did it. He always followed through, so Vincenzo should be worried. I was worried for him. Samson wasn't going to give him a wrap on the knuckles for meddling in his business. There would be far darker consequences for Lombardi and his crew. I was sure of it.

32

LILY

The common assumption people had was that parents loved their children equally. Even if they did have a favourite, I was sure they made a conscious effort to treat their children the same. That didn't happen in our house.

Daisy thought I got the better end of the deal, but being the golden child was harder than you think. It wasn't the enviable position she thought it was. I paid dearly for my spot on the pedestal. Everything I achieved was used as an example for Daisy to follow. We were constantly compared. The pressure on me to succeed was immense. I never felt brave enough to voice my opinions or go against the rules of the home. My dad's violent outbursts put paid to that. There was no doubt in my mind the way Mum and Dad raised us caused the problems I had with Daisy. It was their fault our relationship had become so bad. So toxic.

As children, we'd both craved their attention and did what we could to get it. My dad was incredibly strict. He was a tyrant and lashed out without much reason, which made me retreat into my shell. I learned pretty quickly it was safer to avoid confrontation and go along with his plans than challenge them. My main purpose in life was satisfying my parents' needs. I became a people pleaser from an early age. On the other hand, Daisy was a hellraiser and pushed the boundaries at every opportunity. I sometimes felt she kicked back against conformity whether or not she objected to what was being asked of her. My dad would say she was awkward for the sake of it and I agreed with him.

After we'd landed the spot at Eden's, Daisy had been on cloud nine. We'd all noticed the change in her. She seemed to be taking our singing career seriously for once. Thank God. I constantly set unrealistic goals in my search for perfection and got frustrated if everything wasn't just so. I could be very hard on myself, but that stemmed from a fear of failure. Performing alongside my sister sometimes felt like dragging an unwilling donkey up a hill. I thought we'd turned a corner, but she'd been in a foul mood since our opening night, and her attitude was worse than ever. I couldn't work out what was going on with her.

'For God's sake, Daisy, how many times do we have to go over this before you hit the right note.' Dad's face had turned purple.

'I did hit the right note. Maybe you need to get your hearing tested,' Daisy fired back.

The two of them were at each other's throats again. It was a constant battle of wills. They were both as bad as each other. Stubborn. Strong-willed. They wouldn't entertain the possibility that the other person could be right, they preferred to argue their point of view until they were blue in the face. Neither of them would back down, and it was draining. Sometimes I tried to intervene, but they were impossible to reason with, so I often found myself tuning them out instead until the battle was over. Now that we'd secured the gig at Eden's, it was more important than ever that we tried to get along. But Dad and Daisy seemed determined not to put their differences aside. I didn't understand why they couldn't just call a truce? Why couldn't they just let the animosity go? Was that so much to ask? Not from where I was standing. I was losing patience with both of them.

'Give it a rest, will you? You're stressing me out, and now I've got a headache.'

'He started it.' Daisy's bottom lip was turned out in a pout.

'You need to learn to handle criticism better,' Dad replied.

'You never do anything but criticise me.' Daisy put her hands on her hips and glared at Dad.

'Why don't we try a different song? We're not getting anywhere with this one,' I said, hoping to stop their back and forth.

'I think we should keep going until we nail it; quitting is a loser's attitude,' Dad replied, throwing Daisy a look.

His comment didn't go down well. The result was like pouring petrol onto a naked flame.

'That suits me just fine. I'd be delighted to quit. I'm fed up with this crap. I've got better things to do than spend my nights going over the same old shit in a freezing cold garage.'

Here we go again. Dad always pushed it too far, and Daisy always responded by refusing to sing.

'You can't just walk out! You're part of the duo who've just signed a contract with Eden's,' Dad fumed.

Dad and Daisy were locked in a death stare contest.

'Stuff the contract.' Daisy's blue eyes flashed with anger.

'No can do. It's legally binding.'

The smug look on Dad's face was like a red rag to a bull.

'So sue me,' Daisy said through gritted teeth.

'They will,' Dad replied.

'Well, in that case, I've got a brilliant idea. Why don't you take my place? You're always telling us what a fantastic musician you are, and you can hold a tune, so I'm sure you'd do a far better job harmonising with Lily than I do.'

Now, it was Daisy's turn to be smug. Dad looked like he'd just stepped in a pile of warm dog poop with bare feet. He was so stunned by the way Daisy had just spoken to him. He couldn't think of a response. Dad was rooted to the spot, staring at my sister with his mouth open.

'I was going to leave you to it, but I think I'll hang around to critique your performance.' Daisy's lips parted and stretched into a smile.

My dad and sister were so hostile to each other that it was impossible not to be affected by it. When they started fighting, they stressed me out.

'Get out of my sight,' Dad shouted, pointing towards the door.

'Gladly. The way you're carrying on, you'd think your band of talentless hopefuls had got the slot at Eden's. Your only part in our performance is plugging in your laptop and starting the backing track. I'm pretty sure either one of us could manage to do that without you,' Daisy announced as her parting gesture.

My head felt like it was about to explode. I wished she hadn't brought me into her battle. I hated confrontation. Dad turned towards me with a wounded look on his face, but he wasn't going to get any sympathy from me.

'Oh, for God's sake. The two of you do my bloody head in. That's another practice session wasted. We might as well call it a night,' I said, shaking my head in frustration.

Even though I wanted to perfect the vocals, I'd only have to listen to Dad moaning about Daisy if I stayed behind and I wasn't in the mood. He loved a good whinge and could win a gold medal in complaining. He was a true professional when it came to griping, but he'd have to find somebody else to listen to him droning on tonight. I was about to take myself out of the equation.

'I'm sorry, Lily. But you know what Daisy's like. She's impossible.'

They were both impossible if you asked me.

'Are you sure you don't want to go over a few more songs from the set?' Dad asked.

'No.'

'Don't be mad at me.' Dad tilted his head to one side and smiled at me.

'What am I going to do if Daisy won't sing this week?'

Disastrous thoughts were spinning around in my head. I was going out of my mind with worry. This was my dream. Everything I wanted in life and it felt like it was slipping through my fingers. Daisy never tried to hide her resentment of me. It had been long-simmering since our childhood and had eaten away at our relationship over the years. But her attitude towards performing was making me resent her too. She was behaving like a spoiled brat. Storming off when things didn't go her way. I was the meek one. The weak one. The doormat everyone walked all over. But I was determined to dig deep. Too much was riding on this for me, so I wasn't going to let my sister ruin the opportunity.

I knew where her jealousy stemmed from, so I'd tried to turn a blind eye to the way she treated me. But the tension between us kept building. It felt like things were going to come to a head sometime soon. Maybe it would be a good thing if they did. Then we could confront the problem. My parents might have caused the rift, but ultimately, we were responsible for fixing the broken dynamic between the two of us. Our future at Eden's depended on it.

'Don't worry about that. Daisy quits at the end of every practice session, and she still turns up to the next one,' Dad said, glossing over the situation he'd created.

I was furious with him and Daisy and needed some space. I knew from experience that when people started to make me feel tense and overwhelmed, the best thing I could do was take a break from them. Dad was a serial offender. I couldn't always be at his disposal when he wanted to offload his thoughts and frustrations.

My mental capacity had reached its limit. Once I felt the onset, I had to walk away until I could regain my composure. Privacy. Solitude. Isolation. They were calling to me.

'I'm pretty tired actually. I think I'll have a bath and get an early night instead.'

That was the best excuse I could come up with in the timeframe.

'Fair enough,' Dad said.

I stretched out my neck and then forced out a yawn before heading over to the door.

I found all the arguing incredibly stressful. Life was too short to waste time squabbling over stuff that wasn't important. There were so many other things that deserved our attention. I had a mental to-do list as long as my arm. And if something was worth doing, it was worth doing well. I put my heart and soul into everything. Daisy and I couldn't have been more different if we'd tried in that department. It frustrated me beyond words that she went through life being content with achieving a mediocre result. She never applied herself to anything. Our act could be truly amazing if she gave it her all.

33

DAISY

Dad's criticism was never constructive, always destructive. I'd worked out a long time ago there were two ways to deal with it. I could either listen carefully. Or I could ignore it completely. Guess which one I chose? I'd trained myself to only half listen, which wasn't difficult. Pressing the mute button and switching off was the only way to preserve my sanity. I'd heard his lectures so many times before. I could repeat them word for word.

Even by Dad's standards, he'd hit an all-time high this evening. He'd found fault in every note I'd sung. I couldn't do anything right in his eyes. He'd turned pointing out my mistakes into an art form and seemed to really take pleasure in it. I didn't care what he thought about me anyway, so he was wasting his time and energy. But I wasn't the type to roll over and take the beating when somebody kicked me in the gut. I stood my ground and fought back. It was no wonder we always ended up arguing.

I'd definitely got one over on Dad in our latest fight. I was used to him wearing a look of disappointment, which seemed to be a permanent fixture when he was in my company, but when I slammed the door shut behind me, I was glad to see his freckled face had turned bright red with anger. My scathing comments must have got to him. He was very good at dishing it out but useless at taking it, incapable of dealing with the role reversal. He hadn't appreciated me pointing out some home truths. My parents had been desperate for us to hit the big time so that their dream would live on through us. Dad, in particular, viewed our success as his own.

Dad didn't play the guitar much any more. He maintained he'd given up his days in a band to focus on mine and Lily's career. I used to wish he'd carry on jamming with his guys, but if he hadn't been so persistent, I would never have crossed paths with MacKenzie. Obviously, I'd never tell him I'd be eternally grateful. It wouldn't do him any good if I stroked his enormous ego.

I lay on my bed staring up at the ceiling, daydreaming about MacKenzie and what the future might hold for us. I couldn't stop thinking about him. I loved the way his brown hair flopped over his eyes. As for those eyes, they were large and almond-shaped and totally mesmerising. I'd had an instant magnetic attraction to him. I wondered if he felt the same about me.

I sat bolt upright as a worrying thought pierced my brain like a spear. Lily and I looked identical, so if he fancied one of us, he'd also be attracted to the other. We were very different characters, but it was too early for him to have formed an opinion about our personalities. We'd only just met, so he hadn't got to know us yet. Once he did, he'd realise we were wired differently. I hoped for my sake he liked a girl with a spirited side to her.

My heart suddenly sank. I hadn't been looking my best at the audition because I couldn't be arsed to make the effort. Lily had looked incredible though. And she was always everyone's favourite, so my chance with MacKenzie could be over before it had begun. A feeling of resentment started gnawing away at me again. It didn't take a lot to arouse my jealousy. It was a complex emotion and struck me when I least expected it to.

I didn't usually have a defeatist attitude, so I was surprised at myself for thinking like this. It was time to snap out of this mindset and get back on track. I was confident in myself and my own capabilities, open to whatever life threw at me. I didn't fret over the future or spend time worrying about what-ifs. I was a positive, determined person, and I'd set my sights on MacKenzie. I wasn't going to let anyone or anything stand in my way. Especially my perfect sister. Tuesday couldn't come around soon enough for my liking.

34

MACKENZIE

'We might as well head back to London. There's no point staying here for weeks on end waiting for the shipment to set sail,' Samson said.

'Sounds good to me. Willem's just sent me a text asking if we can go and see him at the port as soon as possible.'

'Did he say why?' Samson's features hardened.

'Nope.'

'There better not be another problem with the fucking shipment,' Samson replied, looking thoroughly pissed off.

'The sooner we go, the sooner we'll find out.'

The December air had a sting to it, I thought, when Samson and I stepped out of the taxi. I pulled up my hood and shoved my hands into the front pockets of my jeans. The sky was grey and thick with clouds, threatening rain. Willem appeared a short while later and ushered us towards his office. I knew before I even stepped over the threshold that it was going to be boiling in there again. Rivers of condensation were running down the misted-up windows.

'Thanks for coming,' he said once we were inside the stifling office with the door closed firmly behind us. 'I'm not sure whether you are aware or not, but ten young men in their early twenties had to be rescued by the emergency services from the port last night.'

Willem's beady eyes flicked between Samson and me. They were dark and shiny like a hamster's, and although small, they were incredibly intense.

'What's that got to do with us?' Samson asked.

'Nothing, but there's going to be a police investigation—'

'Let me guess; that's going to cause another delay,' Samson said, interrupting Willem before he'd finished his sentence.

I couldn't help feeling that Samson was missing the point. He hadn't even asked what had triggered the call to the emergency services.

'So you haven't heard about it?'

I shook my head. Willem adjusted his glasses and cleared his throat before he began to speak.

'I'm surprised. All the news channels are covering it.'

'We're here on business. Not to keep up with local current affairs,' Samson replied.

Willem looked uncomfortable, so he turned his attention away from Samson and focused on me instead.

'What happened to the men?' I was curious, even if Samson wasn't.

Willem let out a sigh. 'This has been an ongoing problem here for some time. We've been trying to crack down on it, but drug gangs operating locally still manage to drive containers concealing their workers into the port undetected.'

'What for?' That seemed like an odd thing to do.

'The workers get paid to get drugs out of other containers and away from the docks,' Willem replied.

'How do they do that?' I was intrigued.

'The drivers leave the containers concealing their workers close to where a known drug shipment has been unloaded. They stay hidden until there's an opportunity for them to get at the drugs. We call them the cocaine collectors. They make around two thousand euros for every kilo they carry out. They're a vital link in Europe's cocaine chain,' Willem said.

'Jesus. Who knew that went on?'

I was genuinely shocked, but when I glanced at Samson to gauge his reaction, I wasn't sure he was even listening. He was plucking imaginary fluff from his suit jacket and seemed disinterested in the conversation. He had a habit of constantly brushing himself down, but I would have thought what Willem was telling us warranted his full attention.

'So let me get this straight. They just walk out of the port carrying the gear?'

That seemed way too easy. We'd seen armed police patrolling the perimeter fences.

Willem nodded. 'Unless they're caught red-handed, they only risk a fine for trespass, which is less than one hundred euros, so it's not really a deterrent compared to the money they earn if they make it out of the port.'

'Surely, it would just be easier to drive it out.'

'You'd think so, wouldn't you, but the port is huge. It's forty-two kilometres long, so it's difficult to police, and corruption is commonplace,' Willem said.

'Well, you should know all about that,' Samson said.

Willem's cheeks flushed, and then he began to speak.

'The collectors' success rate is high, and the money is so good, young men are queuing up to do the job. Those chosen operate with military precision. The Italian gangs who control the local drug distribution around the port prefer this carry-out method to any other.'

'Why's that?' It didn't make any sense to me.

'The drugs in the consignment are divided up between the collectors, which spreads the risk of the whole shipment being seized. Even if some of the men are caught, it's unlikely they'll all be detained,' Willem explained.

That wasn't how our shipments were handled. But I supposed it made sense if the cocaine was being sold to the local market. It wouldn't work for us as our consignment had another sea journey before it reached its final destination. Port workers transferred our coke to another container, which was then loaded onto a ship bound for Felixstowe.

'Even though the money's good, the work can be extremely dangerous. The collectors have to bide their time in the containers, waiting for the coast to be clear. They can be holed up for days on end,' Willem said.

'That sounds grim,' I replied.

Willem nodded. 'We regularly find abandoned units equipped with food, sleeping bags and buckets that provide makeshift toilet facilities. No doubt the men last night have done this job before, probably lots of times, but something catastrophic went wrong, and the workers got locked in.'

'I wonder how that could have happened,' Samson grinned.

I looked over at my boss. He looked so smug. I suddenly suspected he knew more than he was letting on about the unfortunate accident.

'They're lucky they didn't die,' I said.

'Six of them did.'

'No way.' I felt my eyes grow wide.

He might not be admitting to anything, but I'd heard Samson make threats towards Vincenzo. He'd said Lombardi would be sorry he tried to stitch him up and now this has happened. But this was more than a threat. People were dead. I couldn't help feeling the Italian crew weren't the only ones in danger. Willem and I needed to watch our step too or we'd end up six feet under.

'If they hadn't called for help when they did, there would have been more fatalities. We don't know how long the men were trapped, but they were enclosed with a cargo of bananas. Biological matter uses oxygen, so the air was getting thinner...' Willem's sentence trailed off.

I could see Samson examining his suit jacket, looking for invisible particles. He wasn't making any effort to hide the fact that he was bored with the conversation.

'Jesus. Death by banana! You couldn't make it up,' I said, shaking my head from side to side.

'According to the survivors, when the temperature started to rise, they knew they had no other option but to phone the emergency services. The men were in a bad way when they got them out. The ones still alive were suffering from serious breathing difficulties,' Willem replied.

I couldn't imagine taking such a risk. I dealt drugs inside the club to boost my income, but that was safe by comparison.

'The rescue team had trouble finding them. The collectors didn't know where they were, and time was running out. It took hours to pinpoint where they were hiding. A hundred thousand containers lie within the port compound, and the whole premises had to be searched. It was a huge job,' Willem said.

'I wouldn't have wanted to be in their position, slowly suffocating to death while they waited for help to arrive. It must have been pure torture,' I said before looking out of the steamy windows at the sea of near-identical metal containers lined up along the quay.

'The rescue party said it was like looking for a needle in a haystack. But they pulled out all the stops. A police helicopter with a thermal imaging camera was scrambled to assist from above while customs officers, the fire brigade and ambulance services searched the area on foot. It's a miracle any of the men survived.' Willem shook his head.

'What a waste of resources. It's a pity the bananas didn't suck every last breath out of the scum,' Samson said, checking the time on his watch.

Willem seemed horrified by his remarks.

'Why are you looking at me like that?' Samson asked.

The tone of his voice was threatening, and Willem squirmed in his seat in response.

'If that's all you wanted to see us about, we'd better hit the road. We've got a plane to catch. Come on, MacKenzie, the taxi's waiting,' Samson said, getting to his feet.

I dragged in a huge lungful of air once we were outside. The heat was so oppressive in Willem's office it was easy to imagine what the men trapped in the container had gone through.

'What a terrible way to die,' I said, shaking my head.

'You do the job, you take the risk.' Samson shrugged.

'Did you, by any chance, have anything to do with that unfortunate accident?' I asked when the driver pulled away from the port.

'Now that would be telling,' Samson replied, tapping the side of his nose, pretty much confirming his involvement.

I'd always known it would be dangerous to cross Samson, but now that I was almost certain he was a murderer, it pretty much cut off any escape routes I might have been tempted to try. If I wanted to stay alive, I'd have to keep my mouth closed and do what was asked of me.

35

MACKENZIE

'Welcome back,' Igor said when I walked into Eden's. 'Could I have a quick word?'

'Yeah, sure, just give me a couple of minutes.'

I'd barely put my arse cheeks on the chair when there was a knock on my office door.

'Sorry to bother you, but I really need to talk to you.' I looked over and saw Igor's huge frame filling the doorway.

'You'd better come in.'

'I thought it was going to all kick off while you and Samson were away,' Igor looked like he had the weight of the world on his broad shoulders.

'Why? What happened?'

'This car pulled up at the entrance, and the front passenger window went down. The guy sat there staring at me for the longest time,' Igor said.

It had to be the Albanians trying to take advantage while the boss was away. That was the last thing I needed. As if I didn't have enough to worry about.

'Let me guess; was it a matte black BMW?'

'Yes. They showed up just before opening. I was trying to control the queue with Caleb while Leroy and Jermaine carried out searches and checked IDs. The crowd were being a bit rowdy, so we already had our hands full.'

Igor seemed concerned as well, so it was best to take this seriously. Igor was on his feet all the time he was on duty. While he patrolled the queue, he'd also have been on the lookout for underage people trying to get into Eden's, checking if people were drunk, using drugs or hiding weapons. Being a bouncer was like being a babysitter. But instead of little kids, they were dealing with people whose behaviour could be unpredictable.

'Did you have words?'

Igor was Polish and spoke fluent English, but he never said a lot. He was naturally reserved and respectful of everyone he encountered, but he laid down the law if the moment called for it. Assertiveness was a character trait he had by the bucket load.

'No. Nothing actually happened, but they were making their presence felt, so I thought it was worth mentioning. Something felt off. I could sense trouble was on the horizon.'

Igor had a good nose for spotting potential dangers. He was good at thinking on his feet and knew how to act in any situation, springing into action in the blink of an eye when necessary.

'Sounds like you handled things perfectly.'

'Thank you, Mac. I've briefed the team to be on the lookout for anything suspicious,' Igor said before leaving me alone with my thoughts.

It was good to be back in the UK, even though trouble was brewing. I felt safer now that I had my guys around me and wasn't on my own with the boss.

* * *

Igor towered over the three Albanians as he showed them to Samson's office several hours later. They formed a line side by side, facing our boss as Igor took up position next to the man who paid his wages.

'I'm Arben Hasani. Nice to meet you, Mr Fox.'

Samson shook Arben's outstretched hand, but he said nothing.

The Albanian frontman was younger than I'd expected him to be. I'd say he was about the same age as me, in his early thirties. He had dark hair and dark eyes and was dressed in smart black trousers and an expensive-looking pale blue shirt. He must be good at his job to be holding a position of authority already.

'A little birdie tells me you're running low on stock,' Arben said.

Samson bristled at his remark.

'You shouldn't always believe what you hear.'

'In that case, it looks like I've had a wasted journey. I was going to offer to help you out of your predicament. I'd be happy to loan you some stock until your order arrives.'

'That's very noble of you, but I don't need you coming to my assistance,' Samson replied.

'I was just trying to be neighbourly,' Arben smiled.

'And I appreciate the offer, but I don't need your help. Now, if you don't mind...'

Samson threw Igor a look, and the two men shared a silent exchange. A moment later, Igor walked over to where Arben and his two men were standing.

'I'm sure you can appreciate that Mr Fox is a very busy man. Let me show you out,' Igor swept his arm in front of them, gesturing towards the door.

'Being neighbourly, my arse,' Samson said after Igor and the Albanians were out of earshot. 'That smarmy bastard just wants to muscle in on my territory. If he thinks he can start throwing his weight around, he's got another think coming. Only a mug would let themselves become indebted to a bloke like that.'

Samson's chest was puffed out. He was doing his favourite 'I have a big swinging dick routine', which definitely meant he felt intimidated by Arben.

'How the fuck did he get wind of our trouble?' Samson's eyes were blazing.

'Maybe he's behind it. Willem's contact said the port received an anonymous tip-off, and Arben's only started sniffing around recently,' I replied.

'I suppose it's possible, but I still reckon the Italians were responsible,' Samson said.

If you asked me, there was no point wasting brain power on this; it didn't matter who had grassed us up. The bottom line was we couldn't get our hands on the coke. Full stop.

'I'd say right about now Vincenzo's wishing he hadn't threatened me. Let's see how smoothly his distribution runs with a shipment of cocaine lost, six of his men dead and another four hospitalised,' Samson said.

I didn't know how he'd managed to pull it off, and there was no point in asking him. He never divulged his secrets, but Samson must have arranged for somebody to stitch up Lombardi's crew. He'd never stand back and let a person get one over on him without retaliating. I hoped for our sake he hadn't started an all-out war. Trouble didn't stand still. I wasn't ready to lose my life over this.

'Arses need kicking at the port. They were all meant to be fatalities. There weren't meant to be any casualties. Everyone knows I hate a sloppy job.'

A muscle in Samson's jaw was twitching. I wouldn't want to be the person who failed to carry out the mission correctly. Their punishment was coming as sure as summer followed spring.

'Tell the guys to pay extra attention on the door tonight,' Samson said as he dismissed me with a wave of his hand.

'Have you got a minute?' I said to Igor as I walked into the foyer.

He nodded and followed me along the corridor and into my office.

'Samson had a bit of beef with the Italians while we were in Rotterdam. And Arben didn't look happy when he was shown the door after the frosty reception he received. I'm sure I don't need to tell you this, but make sure you're extra vigilant for the time being,' I said.

'Don't worry. We'll be on the lookout. We'll keep our eyes peeled for any aggro heading our way,' Igor replied.

He was a professional who could clock a problem a mile away. Working on the door was his life. Igor had a great team. The smallest guy was six feet tall, and all of them could handle themselves. Door staff had a reputation of being muscle men in suits. I was inclined to agree with that.

'I know you've got it covered, but Samson asked me to mention it,' I smiled, trying to stay positive.

'Everything will be fine.'

Eden's was the only late-night venue in the area, which meant everybody gravitated here after the pubs kicked out. There used to be other places nearby, but they'd all closed down following a council clampdown. Clubs that didn't introduce strict drug control measures found themselves targeted by the police. Samson tried to resist the new rules, but there was no way around it if he wanted to remain open. We were only one step away from being regulated into oblivion ourselves.

'Your guys have enough to deal with without the Albanians complicating things.' I could feel a frown settle on my face.

I usually had complete faith in my guys. In this line of work, it was essential to be ready in case it suddenly all kicked off. And they were great, but the Albanian outfit was massive and if they decided to come on strong, Igor and the lads would be no match for them. They'd be completely outnumbered.

'Sometimes being on the door reminds me of my army days. It's like being in combat, back on the front line. I've had a gun pulled on me, stitches in my head.' Igor ran his fingers over the top of his bald head. 'And I came this close to being jabbed in the face with a glass.' Igor put his thumb and forefinger about an inch apart. 'Don't worry, Mac. The Albanians don't faze me.'

I wished I could say the same.

36

DES

'I still can't get over the way that little bitch spoke to me the other night,' I said.

'Just let it go, Des. Dwelling on it isn't going to change anything,' Tara replied.

'That's easy for you to say, but she said some really horrible things.'

Daisy had really hit a nerve when she'd implied my band were rubbish. That was rich coming from her. She'd never have got the break if it hadn't been for her sister's amazing voice. But good as Lily was, getting noticed wasn't all about talent; luck played a huge part in a performer's success. Being in the right place at the right time definitely counted for something.

'I can see she's upset you, but you'll have to try and put all of this behind you. Think of Lily. She's worried sick that Daisy's not going to sing on Tuesday. She hasn't been to rehearsals since you two had the falling out,' Tara said.

My wife was always the voice of reason. Umpiring the war raging between my daughter and me wasn't an enviable position.

'The last thing I want to do is stress Lily out.'

'Well then, you know what you'll have to do,' Tara replied.

I looked at her with a blank expression on my face.

'You need to *apologise to Daisy*.' Tara stretched out every syllable of the last three words to drive her point home.

'No way. She's the one who should be saying sorry to me.'

'For God's sake, why are you so stubborn?' Tara's dark eyes looked daggers at me.

It was true I wasn't easily swayed when my mind was made up, but my wife always gave me a run for my money in the digging your heels in department. But dogged determination was a good quality to have, in my opinion. Stubborn people knew what they wanted, so they tended to be more decisive and had greater focus.

'I know you don't want to be the one who backs down, but for once, you're going to have to swallow your pride and make peace.'

Tara threw me another one of her looks.

'I mean it, Des. If you don't, you can kiss all of this goodbye. Eden's didn't sign a contract with a solo artist.'

Much as I hated to admit it, Tara had a point. But what she was asking me to do didn't sit easily with me, to put it mildly.

'You can be such a selfish bastard sometimes. Don't you dare ruin this for Lily because of a stupid argument with Daisy!'

'All right, you win,' I said, holding my palms out in front of me.

Tara was on the warpath, and it would take a braver man than me to upset her any further. I'd been on the receiving end of her quick temper many times before. One lash of her tongue could cut you in two, so I knew when to call it quits however much I hated to admit it.

37

DAISY

Mum didn't come to hear Lily and I sing last week because she didn't want to jinx our first gig, but she was going to be watching us tonight. I had the sneaking suspicion there was more to it than that. My bet would be that Mum wanted to be on hand in case the cease-fire Dad and I were having collapsed.

You could have knocked me down with a feather when Dad asked if we could call a truce. If I'd been expecting a grovelling apology, I'd have been bitterly disappointed. But I had no intention of saying sorry to him either, so drawing a line under it suited me fine. I couldn't be arsed to waste precious energy on it. Arguing with my dad was draining, and I had other things occupying my mind. MacKenzie Cartwright, for one.

'How's it going?' MacKenzie said as he paced towards us with his hand outstretched and a smile filling his face.

'Good, thanks,' Lily and I both replied.

Mum and Dad were in the bar having a few drinks while we were chilling out in the dressing room. Lily had flashed me a disapproving look when I'd poured myself a large glass of white wine, but it was none of her business how I prepared to go on stage. I didn't have an issue with her sipping on a bottle of Evian. Each to their own.

'Sorry I wasn't here last week. I got called away on some urgent business, but I've heard the feedback from the gig, and it was really positive, so I'm looking forward to seeing what everyone's raving about myself tonight,' MacKenzie said.

'Aww, that's fantastic! We never get tired of hearing that people have enjoyed our performance,' Lily replied.

'You were a big hit.'

I watched their exchange and knew I should join in, but it was as though somebody had glued my mouth shut. My heart started pounding so loudly I was worried he'd be able to hear it. It took all my strength not to pounce on him and shove him up against the wall. Now that was an idea! I wondered how he would react. If Lily wasn't sitting next to me, I'd have been tempted to find out.

'So tell me a bit about yourselves. Are you single?' MacKenzie asked with a cheeky glint in his eye.

'Yes,' Lily said, flashing him a smile.

I felt indignation tighten my chest as a wave of jealousy swept over me, I had an overwhelming desire to lash out at my perfect sister. I hadn't told her how I felt, but even so, what the hell was she playing at? Lily and I never found the same guys attractive. She was into clean-cut, pretty boys. I preferred a proper man who was a bit rough around the edges. I seriously had the hots for him, so I'd been hoping the feeling was mutual. I should have known he'd go for Lily. Everyone always did. This was the story of my life. She was the first choice. Numero uno. Fucking fantastic.

'That's good to know,' MacKenzie replied.

Then he flashed her a smile. And she smiled back. They were flirting with each other right in front of me. Bastards. We were twenty minutes away from going on stage, and the only thing I wanted to focus on was getting out of the room. I couldn't stand watching Lily stealing the man I'd set my sights on out from under my nose.

I swallowed a few times to compose myself. I was boiling mad but also on the verge of tears. It was a weird combination I knew so well. I would have given anything not to be in this situation. The worst thing I could do was make a fool of myself. Lily would love that, so I was determined to retain my dignity. They were welcome to each other. My sister was probably only interested in him because she knew he'd be my type. Good old Lily never missed an opportunity to get one over on me.

'We're going on stage in a few minutes. Where are you going?' Lily asked when I suddenly stood up.

'I'm going for a smoke,' I replied, pulling my bag out from under the chair.

The lazy smile she'd been wearing while she'd flirted with MacKenzie slid from her face. She was trying her best to hide it, but I could see her breathing had become erratic. Lily knew she couldn't control me, and that stressed her out. I found a small amount of compensation, knowing her anxiety levels were soaring right now.

'I don't think that's a good idea. Can't you wait until after our set?' Lily fixed me with a pleading look.

'No.'

She only deserved a one-word answer. I opened the dressing room door and stepped out into the corridor. As I paced towards the double-loading doors, I heard the rush of the train above me. It startled me. Snapped me out of my mood momentarily. But then it settled over me again.

A gust of cold air hit me in the face when I pushed open the door, and I wished I'd had the sense to pick up my jacket before I'd stormed off in a huff. But I hadn't been thinking straight. I was blinded by the red mist. I flattened myself against the wall so that I could escape most of the draught before I pulled a Marlboro out of the pack and lit it. I was still drawing the smoke into my lungs when I heard the door behind me open. Why the hell had Lily followed me? She couldn't possibly let me have a couple of minutes to myself, could she?

'Mind if I join you?'

My neck snapped around in surprise at the sound of MacKenzie's voice. He was standing in the alleyway with a cigarette clamped between his lips. I gave him a shrug and tried to look indifferent, but a goofy smile threatened to paste itself onto my face, and I had to battle to suppress it.

'It's a free country.'

I tore my eyes away from his, which wasn't easy to do. It was as though he had an invisible magnet drawing me towards him. The attraction was so strong it was like a physical force. I could feel his eyes on me even after I'd looked away, which made my heart start hammering in my chest.

There was an atmosphere between us now, and I was the one who'd created it. It was tense. Awkward. Uncomfortable. A true tumbleweed moment. Beads of sweat formed on my upper lip. I hoped he wouldn't notice as the alleyway was dimly lit. My mind was racing as I tried to think of something to say to fill the empty void that was hovering around us. Don't panic. Deep breaths. Stay calm, I told myself. But the silence stretched on. I cleared my throat as I searched for a suitable topic of conversation. The weather. Small talk. Anything. Being alone with him had shattered my confidence. My nerves were paralysing me. I could see my hands trembling as I put the cigarette up to my lips.

'Daisy. You'd better come in. We're going on in a minute,' Lily said from the doorway.

Her interruption would have normally pissed me off, but she'd actually saved me from the situation by giving me a reason to leave.

I'd been looking forward to this moment, but now that it was here, I was a ball of anxiety and felt out of control.

'On my way,' I replied before I dropped my cigarette onto the floor and ground it out with my shoe.

I was too embarrassed to speak to MacKenzie, so I smiled at him instead. He smiled back.

'Hey, Daisy. Do you fancy having a drink with me after your set?' MacKenzie asked as I reached the door.

'Yeah, why not?'

I tried to keep my voice reserved, but my stomach was doing cartwheels. Maybe I hadn't blown things with him after all. As I walked back to the dressing room, I was grinning from ear to ear, but the smile slid from my face when a horrible thought came into my head. Had MacKenzie asked Lily the same question? I didn't want my imagination to run away with itself, but that idea sent a fresh surge of jealousy flowing through my veins.

38

MACKENZIE

'What can I get you, mate?' I leaned across the bar so that I could hear over the racket.

'A pint of Stella and a bag of your finest,' the guy replied, handing me a fifty-pound note.

After I poured his drink, I ran the booze through the till and then put the pint glass on the counter. I passed him a one-gram bag of cocaine as I gave him his change.

Daisy was perched on a barstool right next to where the guy was standing. I wasn't sure whether she'd seen the exchange or not, but if the two of us were going to become an item, she'd find out sooner or later that I made most of my income from dealing. Don't get me wrong, being the manager of Eden's paid well enough, and I wasn't a greedy man, but it was a drop in the ocean compared to what I could make shifting gear. My side hustle gave me a stream of additional cash that I'd come to rely on.

If Daisy and Lily played their cards right, I might let them in on the action. From a criminal's perspective, having a set of identical twins on the team was about as good as it got. Even though advances in DNA could now find tiny differences in their genetic makeup, the procedure was expensive, so it wasn't widely used. Carbon copies still gave the Old Bill a massive ball-ache if one of them committed a crime and blamed it on the other.

I'd worked in bars before, where I'd had to be far more discreet about peddling drugs, but as my supplier was also the owner of the club, dealing had been written into my job description. Samson controlled most of the pubs in the area. A couple of small independent watering holes, The Bell and The Railway Tavern, hadn't fallen into his clutches, but they only attracted old men and local anoraks, neither of which required our services, so they didn't interest the boss. Eden's had the biggest customer base out of all of Samson's pubs.

'Aren't you worried you'll get caught?' Daisy asked after the bar had closed.

So she had seen me dealing. I had to give it to her. She'd been very discreet.

'Nah. If I was the nervous type, I'd be in the wrong business,' I laughed.

'Be careful. I wouldn't like to see you lose your job.' Daisy flashed me her killer smile, and then she crossed one long slender leg over the other.

My eyes were drawn along the length of her pins. I wouldn't object to her wrapping those around me tonight.

'Don't worry. I won't.'

'You seem very confident about that. What if one of the bar staff tells Samson you're selling drugs on his premises? You'd be out for sure,' Daisy warned.

If only she knew that Samson was a nightclub owner on the surface but led a double life as a drug kingpin. Eden's was a smoke-screen. I'd let her in on that little secret in time, but I'd have to get to know her better first to make sure she was completely trustworthy. On the plus side, she looked very concerned for a woman who wasn't interested in me. Something told me she'd just been playing hard to get when she'd given me the cold shoulder earlier.

'If I lose my job, my old boss, Roscoe, would welcome me back with open arms. He was gutted that I didn't go with him when he took over The Castle, but Dover's a long way from here,' I replied to keep the charade going.

'Has Eden's ever been raided?' Daisy asked.

She was a lot more talkative now that she'd had a few drinks.

I shook my head. 'We sometimes get undercover cops in here, but I can usually spot them a mile off, so when they ask to buy drugs, I call the door staff and have them ejected, telling them we operate a zero tolerance to illegal substances and not to bother coming back. Their type of custom isn't welcome in our establishment,' I said with a wink.

'That's hilarious,' Daisy laughed.

When her mouth stretched open, I got a glimpse of her straight white teeth. She was beautiful. A real hottie. I was definitely punching, but that wasn't going to stop me. Behind every gorgeous woman was an ordinary bloke like me.

'Wait, you're not undercover filth pretending to be a singer, are you?'

'As if,' Daisy replied.

'It's good to see you've loosened up a bit,' I said, leaning towards her. 'You were proper frosty with me earlier.'

'No, I wasn't.'

Daisy denied it, but her cheeks flushed just enough to give away her embarrassment.

'Erm, the term ice maiden springs to mind,' I smiled. She definitely seemed to be thawing to my charms.

39

DAISY

'I see what your dad means. He is a cocky little shit, isn't he?' Mum said.

I was sitting opposite her, mindlessly spooning Crunchy Nut Cornflakes into my mouth, trying to mop up yesterday's alcohol. I didn't usually overindulge on a Tuesday, but the opportunity had presented itself, and I wasn't going to turn it down. I wasn't hungover, but my temples were throbbing a little bit, reminding me that more than one bottle of wine had passed my lips. I usually downed a pint of water before I went to bed when I was on the piss, but it had slipped my mind. My thoughts had been preoccupied.

'Who's a cocky little shit?'

I knew exactly who Mum was talking about, but I wanted her to do the work.

'MacKenzie,' she replied.

'I can't say I've noticed,' I shrugged.

My mum and dad had taken an instant dislike to MacKenzie. I didn't share their opinion. And the fact that my parents didn't approve of him would only drive me further into his arms.

After last night, I was smitten. He wasn't the classic tall, dark and handsome by any means. I'd say he was five feet eight inches if he was lucky, barely taller than me. I'd have to put my heels away for now. Otherwise, I'd tower over him. He was very slim. Wiry but not in an athletic way. MacKenzie had the kind of physique that screamed heroin chic. His body fat percentage was so low that veins were visible on his forearms. He had brown hair which flopped over his eyes, and he always seemed to look unkempt. So far, I'd only seen him wear T-shirts that had seen better days and a pair of ripped jeans. I was probably painting a bad picture, but he oozed sex appeal and was confident and friendly. MacKenzie had a nice face and gorgeous eyes, but he wasn't classically good-looking.

I was all for a modern man taking his turn with the household chores, but I drew the line at sharing my eye cream and hair products with my other half. I couldn't think of anything worse than being in a relationship with somebody who spent longer getting ready than I did in the morning. I wouldn't have to worry about any of that with MacKenzie. He was more of a roll out of bed and throw on the first set of clothes that came to hand sort of guy.

'You're probably too young to remember Pete Doherty, but that's who he reminds me of,' Mum said.

'Of course, I know who Pete Doherty is. I work in the music industry, don't I? He looks nothing like him if you ask me, but everyone's entitled to their own opinion,' I replied before scooping a spoonful of my breakfast into my mouth.

'Why are you so cranky? Have you got a sore head?' Mum's voice had a bitchy tone to it.

'No, but I'd just like to eat in peace,' I replied, hoping to put an end to the conversation.

'Suit yourself,' Mum said before she walked out of the kitchen.

Not a moment too soon if you asked me. Now, I could go back to daydreaming about MacKenzie. Did I mention he had the most amazing greeny-hazel eyes, which seemed to change colour depending on the lighting? They were large and almond-shaped, framed by ultra-long lashes and seemed almost too big for his face. I found them mesmerising. When he fixed me with them, it made me go weak at the knees. I got the impression he was a talker, not a fighter. My granny would have said he had the gift of the gab, not unlike my dad.

I'd always been drawn to bad boys and people who didn't conform, but I'd never been involved with anyone on his level before. When I saw MacKenzie dealing last night, logic told me I should run a mile and not get involved with him, but where was the fun in that?

40

MACKENZIE

I'd had to resort to cutting my dwindling supply of cocaine. So far, there hadn't been any complaints, but this was a short-term measure. Our customers had an insatiable appetite, and if I ran out of gear, my regulars would take their business elsewhere.

'Yo, Leroy, what's happening, man?' I said when I saw him walk past my office.

Surprise, surprise, he didn't look best pleased to see me.

'How's it going, Mac,' he replied, sticking his head around my door.

'Come in a second, will you? Any luck getting your hands on the coke?'

'I can get you some, but not at the price you want to pay. The guys I've tried are street dealers, not wholesalers,' Leroy replied.

Albanians at the top of the criminal ladder had established themselves as key distributors. By sidelining the middlemen, and buying in bulk, it helped them to secure low prices. They could buy cocaine in Colombia for around one thousand dollars and sell it for thirty thousand euros once it reached European ports. That was some profit margin.

The amount Samson sourced was tiny in comparison to the volume Arben imported. My boss was used to being a big fish in a small pond, but the opposite was true in this case. At this stage, I was seriously tempted to start importing the white stuff myself. What was to stop me from travelling to Rotterdam on an overnight trip and returning with kilos of cocaine hidden in secret compartments built into the floor of a van? How hard could it be? People did it every day of the week. A stunt like that would need careful planning though. And time was the one thing I didn't have.

'Samson won't like it, but we might have to take the Albanians up on their offer,' I said.

'He'll never agree to that,' Leroy replied.

'He might not have a choice.'

The Albanians seemed to be the only big player not having supply issues. After Samson fell out with Vincenzo Lombardi, we started buying our stock from the Mexicans. We were yet to receive the first shipment, so that had turned out to be a disastrous move. But there was no going back, not since the trouble Samson had caused at Rotterdam. Our relationship with the Italians was dead and buried, along with six of their men.

Willem had called this morning to say there were too many police sniffing around to move anything. Everyone was on edge, and even though he was helped by a dense network of corrupt officials placed in key positions inside the port, which usually allowed them to easily bypass security checks, they couldn't risk releasing the shipment for its onward journey until the investigation was complete. Samson would do his nut, but he only had himself to blame for the current mess.

Samson got most of his drugs from Rotterdam. But he might have to consider sending the shipment through Antwerp next time if things were going to be like this. Willem had told us the Dutch authorities were cracking down on imports from South America, so we were always going to have issues unless they stopped the extra checks.

41

DAISY

Lily had a goal-oriented mindset. She set her expectations a lot higher than the average person. Way higher than mine. Everything had to be perfect. But we both had different definitions of the word. Lily didn't just put pressure on herself. She pressured everyone around her as well. She was uptight. Tense. Highly strung. I had to put up a mental wall to keep her stress levels away. She was taxing, and I didn't want to waste vital energy on her when I could be thinking about MacKenzie.

I wasn't a prude by any means, but I was shocked when I saw MacKenzie dealing openly at the bar. I didn't have a problem with people doing drugs. Everyone seemed to take cocaine these days. I wasn't really in a position to judge; I smoked weed, but I'd never felt the need to try anything stronger. Dabbling with illegal substances was a slippery slope, wasn't it? One minute, you were smoking a joint, and the next, a syringe of heroin was sticking out of the crook of your arm.

Being a user and being a supplier were poles apart. MacKenzie had tried to brush my concerns under the carpet when I'd questioned him about what he was doing. Even though he didn't seem bothered by the risk he was taking, losing his job would be the least of his concerns if he got caught. He'd definitely do time if he was convicted. Sitting opposite him on a plastic chair during a prison visit didn't appeal to me in the slightest. Irresistible as I found him at the moment, I was pretty sure I'd go off him rapidly if he got sent down. I was a twenty-three-year-old woman, so I wouldn't want to waste the best years of my life waiting for my partner to become a free man. No relationship would be worth that sacrifice.

Why was I overthinking this situation? That was very out of character for me. Lily was the one who excelled in stressing herself out over what-ifs. That wasn't my bag at all. I was a go-with-the-flow kind of girl, so I pushed my concerns to the back of my mind.

'For God's sake, Daisy. What's taking you so long?' The sound of Lily's voice thundered up the staircase.

I was late. That was the story of my life. I needed to work on my relationship with time. I could see Lily pacing backwards and forwards along the hallway when I came out of my bedroom and looked over the bannister. She glanced up at me. Her blue eyes were filled with concern.

'Chill your beans,' I said as I sauntered down the stairs, which sent her stress levels into overdrive.

'You do this every week. No wonder I get wound up about it,' Lily said.

She threw me a look of contempt before she turned on her heel and paced towards the front door. Dad scurried after her, clicking the car's remote control so it would unlock before she got to it. Heaven forbid he should keep her waiting. His head would roll for sure.

* * *

'I'm going for a smoke,' I said when we reached the dressing room.

It was the first time I'd spoken to Lily since we'd left the house. There was no way I wanted to be stuck in a room with her, so I didn't even bother taking my coat off. I got my lighter and Marlboros out of my bag and headed out into the corridor.

When I pushed open the door and stepped out into the alley, my teeth chattered as a blast of icy wind hit me full force. I pulled my fake fur calf-length coat around me and huddled against the wall to keep out the chill. Underneath, I was only wearing a black leather mini skirt and strappy top. It was a great combination for performing in a warm venue, not such a good choice on a December evening.

I took a cigarette out of the pack and attempted to light it, but the sudden gusts kept blowing out the flame, so I put it away again. I was just about to go inside when I heard the door creak open.

'I thought I might find you out here,' MacKenzie said.

I turned my head towards the sound of his voice. He was smiling as he walked towards me, which sent my pulse soaring. Even at this distance, I could feel his energy pulling me closer. I had an inexplicable connection to him. Stupid really. I barely knew the man.

'Lily's in one of her moods again, so I'm staying out of the way.'

'Sounds like a smart move,' MacKenzie said. 'I thought you'd be having a smoke.'

'I had planned to, but it's like a wind tunnel in here. I gave up trying to light it on the fourth attempt,' I replied as another arctic blast howled past us.

'What's up with Lily?' MacKenzie asked.

'She's in a strop because I kept her waiting, and we left the house ten minutes later than planned. Big deal.' I rolled my eyes.

MacKenzie shook his head and wagged his forefinger at me. 'You naughty girl.'

I let out a belly laugh.

'Anyone would think I'd committed a crime the way she's carrying on. She can be so anal at times.'

'You're not a bit alike, are you? Well, apart from the fact that you look identical. That came out wrong, but I'm sure you know what I mean.' MacKenzie hit his forehead with the palm of his hand.

'Lily's the golden child in our family. I'm the scapegoat.'

'Sounds intriguing. Don't stop there.' MacKenzie's stare was intense. Flecks of gold danced in his eyes.

'Lily and I have spent our whole lives being pitched against each other. Whether it's intentional or not, people can't help but compare the two of us. It's jarring.'

'I bet.'

'As a kid, I was always in trouble.'

'Me too,' MacKenzie smiled.

I wasn't a bit surprised we had that in common. It felt good to open up to MacKenzie. Slagging Lily off was a favourite pastime of mine and he seemed to be enjoying listening to me spout.

'Mum and Dad were strict with me, hoping it would decrease my rebelliousness. If anything, it intensified my defiant behaviour. I like giving the orders. I don't like being told what to do.'

'There's nothing wrong with being assertive. You sound like my ideal woman.'

MacKenzie's reply sent my pulse racing. I felt my cheeks flush, and my heart started hammering in my chest.

'Aren't you cold?' I asked, glancing at his bare forearms so that I could tear my eyes away from his.

'If you're offering to warm me up, I won't say no,' MacKenzie grinned.

My coat was an open-fronted design. I'd wrapped it over my chest and was clutching the edges of the fabric to hold it together, but I let my fingers uncurl, releasing my grip so that the coat fell open. MacKenzie wasted no time snaking his arms around my waist.

As he pulled me towards him, I threw my arms around his shoulders, and our lips met. Heads tilted. Eyes closed. Tongues explored. A siren wailed in the distance and then died away, but the rumble of traffic from the busy street was constant. Inner city. Bustling. Urban. This wasn't the most romantic of settings, snogging up against a cold brick wall, under the arches. But this wasn't a fairytale. It was real life. A real situation. If I had to rate it, I'd say it was the best first kiss I'd ever had. It was incredible.

'I'd better go before Lily sends out a search party,' I said when we pulled apart.

'If you weren't about to go on stage, you'd be in serious trouble. Nice outfit, by the way. The long coat, short skirt and strappy heels are spot on. You look like sex on legs.'

MacKenzie's eyes ran up the length of my body.

'Thanks,' I replied.

As I went to walk away, MacKenzie grabbed hold of me and pulled me back into his arms, locking lips with me again. While we kissed, his hands started roaming over my body, so I wriggled out of his grasp before we got too carried away. Having sex in an alleyway wasn't on my bucket list.

* * *

'Is something going on between you and MacKenzie?' Lily asked, tucking a strand of her shiny hair behind her ear.

Was it that obvious? I thought we'd been really discreet.

'No. What makes you say that?'

I tried to paste a puzzled expression on my face. Judging by Lily's response, I wasn't sure I succeeded.

'I've seen the way the two of you look at each other. You can't keep your eyes off each other. There's definitely a spark...' Lily let her sentence trail off.

I wanted to whoop with joy. This was a first for me. My previous boyfriends never got the opportunity to choose between us. I'd met them when I wasn't with Lily. She had loads of friends, and her name was always on the guest list. More often than not, I was allowed to tag along so the host didn't appear rude by not inviting me. I knew my presence was surplus to requirement. And that hurt. She was a better version of me in every conceivable way. Although MacKenzie didn't think so. I was over the moon, but I had to keep up the pretence.

'So nothing's going on then?' Lily crossed her arms over her chest and studied my face. She seemed a bit put out if you asked me, which felt good, but I couldn't afford to let my pleasure show through.

'Give it a rest, Lily. What are you going to accuse me of next?'

I threw the palms of my hands up, doing my best to act indignant.

'You might want to fix your lipstick before we go on stage,' Lily replied.

I sat down on the stool just as MacKenzie walked into the dressing room. Our eyes met in the mirror, and I nearly burst out laughing, but I managed to hold it in. He looked like The Joker in the *Batman* films. I tore my eyes away from him and fixed them on my own face. There was a bright red smudge circling my mouth, and my lipstick hadn't looked like that when I'd gone out for a cigarette. No wonder Lily was suspicious.

Lily's eyes flicked from MacKenzie to me several times before she spoke.

'So are you still going to try and convince me that it's a figment of my imagination that something's going on between the two of you?'

Lily tilted her head to one side and glared at me.

I could see she was waiting for an answer, but I couldn't think of anything to say. My jaw locked. Silence filled the air around us. MacKenzie and I exchanged a glance, but both of us refused to comment. Unspoken words hung between us.

Lily looked at us in turn. I could see her frustration growing by the minute. A smile was threatening to spread my lips widely. I couldn't let it. I stared at my sister. Stony-faced. Defiant. Challenging.

'Give me some credit. I'm not that stupid, Daisy.'

There was anger in her voice. It was stamped into every word. I thought she'd tone it down as MacKenzie was in the room. It wouldn't do to let her halo slip while there were witnesses around. But it had all got too much for her. Lily always buckled under pressure. I watched her expression change with a wry smile on my face. Her nostrils flared as she tried to control her breathing. When I saw her chest rise and fall; I knew she'd lost the battle. A moment later, she made a break for the door, no doubt hoping I hadn't noticed the tears welling up in her eyes. Stupid bitch. She did my head in.

My heart swelled with pride as Lily rushed out of the room. I felt victorious. Triumphant. Some people were lucky enough to have a great relationship with their siblings. I wasn't one of them so I loved getting one over on my sister. Hurting her gave me a lot of pleasure. It was payback for all the crap I had to put up with on a daily basis because of her.

42

LILY

When I felt the sting of infuriating tears stab my eyes, I knew I had to get out of the room. I needed to put some space between myself, Daisy and MacKenzie. The way the two of them were looking at each other, trying not to smile, was making my blood boil. I was absolutely fuming. I'd dug my heels firmly into the ground and was determined not to back down until Daisy admitted what was going on. But I should have known I'd never be able to last. Daisy was the most stubborn person in the world. She made Dad look like a lightweight, and that was saying something.

I didn't want the two of them to have the satisfaction of seeing me break down, so I'd taken off like a scalded cat instead. Great idea. Not. I couldn't help myself. Daisy was winding me up, and my frustration got the better of me.

I burst out of the door but wasn't sure where to go. I wanted to let my feelings out somewhere private – some chance of that. Dad was in the bar, so I couldn't go up there. We'd agreed, for everyone's sake, it was better if he kept his distance before we went on stage. I didn't fancy freezing my bits off in the alleyway. The ladies' toilet wasn't appealing either, so I was running out of places to go. I paced along the corridor and plonked myself down on the bottom step. I could hear the sound of glasses clinking and customers laughing above me. People were having fun. That was how it should be.

I swiped at the tears running down my face with the back of my hand. I was annoyed with myself for letting my sister reduce me to tears, albeit angry ones. She'd be gloating that she'd won. Daisy could be such an arsehole sometimes; she loved getting one over on people. Being emotional didn't mean I was weak. Out of control. A drama queen.

I wasn't jealous of Daisy and MacKenzie being an item. He wasn't my type by any means. I was angry that she'd lied to me and treated me like a fool. Why the big secret? She was a grown woman. She could snog whoever she liked. I didn't give a shit as long as it didn't affect me. But this did. So, I was worried about the outcome. I had to hope for all our sakes that things worked out between them. If they got bored of each other, and knowing Daisy's track record with men, she'd be fed up with him in a week or two. Where would that leave us?

We performed in the club MacKenzie managed, which would make things awkward if their relationship soured. I was sure he could even find a reason to terminate our contract if he was the jilted party, which he was likely to be. Who could blame him? He was in the position of power, not us. I'd never forgive her if she messed up this opportunity. Dad will go ballistic when he finds out. I wouldn't snitch, but it was only a matter of time until he got wind of it. Gossip travelled like a fire.

I couldn't believe Daisy had hooked up with MacKenzie. What a stupid thing to do. True to form, my sister was only thinking about herself. Her wants. Her needs. Jump in feet first. Fuck the rest of you. That was her motto. She could be so bloody selfish at times and didn't give a shit about the consequences.

People assumed we had an unbreakable bond because we'd

shared a womb. They put way too much emphasis on the fact that we'd materialised from a single fertilised egg that had split in two. But I hated being a twin as much as Daisy did. We might have started our lives together, but we'd never been inseparable and clingy like some twins. We developed our own identities from an early age.

I sat on the cold stone steps as the minutes rolled by. Time was running out, but my head was scrambled. Daisy really knew how to pick her moments. I'd give her that. I didn't know how I was going to get through this gig. I had to pull myself together. The show had to go on. I was a professional, even if she wasn't.

43

DAISY

'You might want to clean yourself up.'

I swivelled around on the stool to face MacKenzie as soon as Lily left the room and held out a facial wipe. He looked at me with a puzzled expression, so I got to my feet and started wiping the bright red lipstick off of his face.

'I think our secret's out in the open,' I smiled.

'I didn't realise we were keeping one,' MacKenzie replied.

'Lily asked me if something was going on between us, and I denied it.'

MacKenzie looked wounded. 'Cheers.'

'Don't be offended.'

'I'm not.' MacKenzie gave an indifferent shrug, but his face told another story.

'It's just my dad will think it's unprofessional if he gets wind of it.'

'And I thought you said you were a rebel. The non-conformist daughter who does as she pleases.'

I could see MacKenzie was doubting what I'd told him.

'I am. But I also enjoy a quiet life, and my dad could win a gold medal in nagging. I was always in trouble when I was a kid. I couldn't do anything right. My mum and dad despaired of me, but to be perfectly honest with you, it was the only way I got any attention. So I learnt from an early age, if I acted up, somebody would notice.'

'Listen, you don't have to justify anything to me. It's none of my business. I don't really know your dad, but from what I've seen, he seems a bit intense,' MacKenzie replied.

'He is. We fight like cat and dog. Whereas my perfect sister is the apple of his eye.'

'That bothers you, doesn't it?'

When MacKenzie fixed his gaze on me, I felt the need to confess.

'My mum idolises her too. They treat me very differently. I try not to be jealous of Lily, but it's hard not to be when you're blinded by the halo of light that surrounds her.'

MacKenzie wrapped his arms around me.

'You've got no reason to be jealous. You're incredible. If you ask me, she's jealous of you.'

'No way,' I laughed and shook my head.

'Trust me. She is; I've seen the way she looks at you.'

That was a revelation to me. I'd never considered that to be the case.

MacKenzie was kissing the side of my neck when I heard the dressing room door open. I glanced up and saw Lily standing in the doorway.

'Oh, for God's sake. Get a room, will you?' Lily said, throwing us an evil glare.

Then she stormed past us and plonked herself down on the sofa.

'I'll see you after your set,' MacKenzie said, planting a kiss on my cheek.

Once he'd left the room, I glanced over at Lily. She was staring straight ahead, biting the side of her lip. Her legs were shaking. That always happened when she was stressed about something and in a state of fight or flight. Was I bothered that it was my fault she was feeling like this? Nope. Lily was a constant thorn in my side, so I was glad I'd managed to piss her off.

44

MACKENZIE

The following week, I had to take matters into my own hands. Samson was a Jekyll and Hyde character. His mood changed depending on which way the wind blew. He'd agree to something one minute and then go back on it the next. I couldn't risk running my plan past him, so I arranged to meet Arben Hasani behind his back.

Samson had set me up with a customised Android phone featuring self-destructing messages that were deleted from the recipient's device after a certain amount of time. It also had a panic wipe facility. All data could be removed from the device by entering a four-digit code. I used it to arrange drug deals and my clandestine meeting with the Albanian frontman.

I left my car a short distance away from the barber's shop in Barking town centre, paying for parking with my mobile. I had no idea how long I was going to be and wanted the option to top up the meter if need be. If this borough was anything like where I lived, you couldn't leave your motor for ten seconds without getting a ticket. The traffic wardens were like vultures swooping down to catch anyone brave enough to take a chance.

I was probably taking a bit of a risk coming here alone. I'd seriously considered asking Igor to tag along, but I didn't want to put him in an awkward position by testing his loyalty to me or the man who paid his wages.

Two dark-haired bearded guys were standing behind the barbers' chairs when I opened the door and walked inside. They both looked at me in the mirror while cutting their clients' hair.

'You here to see Arben?' one of them asked.

'Yep,' I said.

'He's in the back room,' the guy replied, flicking his head sideways to indicate where I needed to go.

'Thanks, mate.'

I felt all the pairs of eyes in the room on me as I made my way across the patterned grey and white tiled floor. When I approached the doorway, a large hand swept the beaded curtain to one side.

'Come in, MacKenzie,' I heard Arben say.

The room was bigger than I'd been expecting. A large, dark red traditional-looking rug with white tassel ends covered most of the floor. Only a slim border of wood ran around the outside of it. Brass lanterns with white porcelain shades hung from the centre of the room, below which a small square table sat. Four individual armchairs were arranged around it. They were covered in white lace throws. I felt like I'd just stepped into Arben's mother's living room. It was a far cry from East London, more like rural Albania.

'I'm so glad Mr Fox has come around to my way of thinking,' Arben said.

When his lips stretched into a smile, I suddenly felt nervous and wanted to run from the room before I did something I suspected I might end up regretting, but I was already in way over my head, so there was no point in trying to back out now.

'In our culture, it's incredibly rude to refuse an offer of help. Our people have a generous nature and don't expect anything in return. We are famous for our hospitality. Please sit down,' Arben continued.

He gestured with a nod of the head to one of the two guys standing behind him wearing an Adidas puffer jacket, tight dark jeans and white trainers. Moments later, the young man placed a bottle and two glasses on the table.

'Have you tried raki before?' Arben asked.

'No. I can't say that I have.' I stopped short of adding 'or want to'.

I'd been to Greece before and remembered the taste of the ouzo only too well. The two countries were neighbours, and the clear liquid looked suspiciously like the stuff I'd nearly poisoned myself on years earlier.

When he uncorked the bottle and poured two measures, it took me back in time to a lads' holiday when I was in my late teens. I'd spent most of the week with my head down the toilet, spewing up the alcohol I'd spent my hard-earned cash on. My stomach was so raw by the end of the trip that it nearly put me off booze for good.

The guy that had been standing next to him followed closely behind with a platter full of meat and sausages.

'This is Tave Mishi. Please help yourself,' Arben smiled.

It looked good. Charcoal marks equalled flavour. Even I knew that, but I hadn't come here for a teddy bear's picnic and didn't have much of an appetite. My nerves had got the better of me, but I knew I couldn't risk offending Arben by snubbing the food and drink he was offering me. If it all kicked off, I was severely outnumbered. Four Albanians were in the room with me, and another two were in the barber's shop. I inhaled deeply, trying to stop the rising panic filling my chest.

I reached forward and took the smallest piece of meat on the plate. I bit into it and started chewing. It was lamb. I hated lamb. But I munched through it at record speed and then washed it down with the raki. The neat alcohol burnt as it slid down my throat. My mouth was on fire, but at least the strong flavour took the taste of Baa Baa Black Sheep away.

'It's good, huh?' Arben asked.

'Delicious,' I lied.

'You must try the chicken, pork, beef and the sausages. All of them are good, too,' Arben beamed.

Then he picked up the bottle of raki and went to refill my glass. I reached over and covered the top of it with my hand before he had a chance to.

'I'd love to, but I'm driving. I better not risk being over the limit. I can't afford to lose my licence,' I said.

That was a great excuse. It was just as well that Arben didn't know I regularly drank and drove. It didn't prick my conscience to have ten pints and get behind the wheel.

'Samson will be disappointed that he missed out on all of this.' I swept my hand over the platter of food on the table.

'Maybe he'll see fit to join us next time,' Arben replied.

Implying that this arrangement was going to become a regular occurrence.

'Maybe,' I smiled.

Samson would have my balls on the block if he knew what I was doing. And Arben wouldn't want to trade with me if he thought he wasn't getting one over on the main man himself, so in order to keep everyone sweet, it was safer to leave both of them in the dark. That way, everyone would be happy. Well, that wasn't technically true. Samson had taken umbrage to Arben offering to help him out. Sniffing around another outfit's front was a big no-no and seen as a direct threat. I'd have to do more than pass around the peace pipe if he ever found out.

'Rotterdam port is still in chaos. You're lucky your stock hasn't got stuck in the backlog,' I said, trying to steer the conversation towards the purpose of my visit.

'Luck has nothing to do with it. Our global network is extensive and very well-established. That's why we're the largest supplier of cocaine in the UK's market,' Arben said. 'Corrupt Dutch police officers working at the port make sure our shipments get through no matter what's going on.'

'I'm impressed by how smoothly your operation runs.'

A little bit of flattery usually worked like a charm, and by the look on Arben's face, my words were having the desired effect.

'Thank you. That's kind of you to say,' Arben replied. His face was brimming with pride.

'Do you always source your cocaine from Colombia?'

It wouldn't hurt to do some homework.

'Not always, sometimes the supply chain begins in Peru, but we always send the shipments via Ecuador. The long Pacific coastline is a smuggler's paradise. Our drivers usually transport cocaine to the Guayaquil port two or three times a month,' Arben said.

'Is that all? I thought you'd have a lot more shipments in circulation than that.'

Maybe the Albanian outfit wasn't as big a player as they were making out they were. The Mexicans moved their drugs on a constant conveyor belt because it took such a long time for them to get from A to B. They had shipments moving on a near-daily basis.

'Our couriers carry larger quantities than some of the other wholesalers. We move two thousand kg at a time,' Arben said.

'Two thousand kilos. Isn't that a bit risky?'

'Ecuador is a small country with institutional weaknesses at its core, so it's ripe for exploitation,' Arben said.

'Even so, that's a lot of coke,' I said.

Ecuador was on the verge of becoming a narco-state. The kingpins had used their vast financial resources to buy themselves into power. Everything had a price, so criminal organisations took advantage of that.

'When we ship in bulk, we get away with making fewer journeys. Each trip takes around twelve hours, and our couriers have to bribe police and officials along the way. It's the same price, however much we're moving. So shifting a large amount in one go saves us a lot of money and increases our profits,' Arben explained.

If they were exporting two thousand kilos at a time, their profit margins must be enormous.

'There's a good markup. In Colombia, a kilo of cocaine costs around one thousand dollars. By the time it arrives in Ecuador, the price has increased to three thousand dollars. By the time it reaches Europe, it's worth thirty thousand euros. And as you know only too well, that price doubles once it reaches UK shores,' Arben said.

Ten years ago, a kilo of cocaine sold for around one hundred thousand pounds. But the Albanian organisations have forced the price down. We've all had to follow suit or risk losing our place in the market. They could afford to take the knock if they were shifting as much gear as that. Samson's operation was small fry in comparison.

'How much cocaine were you hoping to buy?' Arben asked.

'Just enough to tide me over until our shipment arrives,' I replied.

'I can't sell you less than a kilo.'

When Arben fixed his eyes on me, I felt beads of sweat prickling my forehead. I wouldn't live to see another day if this deal went wrong.

45

DAISY

Christmas Eve

It was only mid-afternoon, but dusk was already falling when Lily and I left the house. We'd been invited to a party Samson was hosting at Eden's. Dad's nose had been pushed out of joint when his name hadn't been mentioned, but I was glad he wasn't going. I wouldn't be able to let my hair down with him breathing down my neck. He'd offered to give us a lift, no doubt hoping the hospitality would be extended to him if he was right outside the door, but Lily said she'd drive. She didn't drink anyway, so it made perfect sense to me.

'Welcome, ladies. You're both looking lovely,' Caleb said when Lily and I walked into the foyer.

'Thank you,' we both replied.

'Mac's in his office waiting to escort the two of you to the party. He's a lucky man!'

Caleb flashed us his gap-toothed smile. He was such a sweetheart. I had a real soft spot for him.

'Well, we'd better not keep him waiting,' I said, smiling back at him.

'You look incredible,' MacKenzie said when I walked into his office.

'Thanks,' I smiled.

I was wearing a silver sequined mini dress with matching shoes and bag. I'd decided to treat myself with the extra money I was earning singing at the club, and by the look on MacKenzie's face, it was worth the investment. I'd thought twice about buying the shoes, knowing they'd make me taller than MacKenzie, but he seemed to love me wearing high heels, so he clearly didn't have a problem with the height difference. No law stated that men had to be taller, and I liked being different. Not everyone aspired to be Ken and Barbie. Speaking of which, Lily was doing a great job of imitating her this evening.

She was dressed in a shocking pink, floor-length one-shoulder satin dress. It was eye-catching, and she did look stunning in it if you liked that kind of thing, but it didn't appeal to me. There was no way you'd miss her in the sea of little black dresses, which was precisely why she was wearing it. Lily liked to stand out from the crowd. My dress wasn't understated either, but you could spot Lily's a mile off.

'You scrub up really well.' The gold flecks danced in MacKenzie's greeny-hazel eyes.

'You seem surprised!' I laughed.

Lily let out a loud sigh, bored with our flirting. If we were irritating her already, she had a long night ahead of her.

'You look nice too,' MacKenzie said.

Lily pursed her lips and begrudgingly said, 'Thank you.'

She had a real attitude with MacKenzie, which surprised me as he was always very pleasant to her.

'Let's get this party started,' MacKenzie said, pushing his chair back from the desk and getting to his feet.

'Oh wow! You scrub up well, too. You've gone to so much effort. You really shouldn't have, not on my account,' I smiled.

MacKenzie was wearing a navy T-shirt and dark-washed jeans with a pair of battered Nike trainers. But I wasn't complaining. He looked good to me. I couldn't picture him in a shirt and tie.

'How cruel. The outrage,' he grinned.

His lips grazed my cheek on the way past, but he stopped short of kissing me. No doubt that was for Lily's benefit. It was bad enough being the third wheel, but when the couple were all over each other in front of you, it made things ten times worse. He was more generous than I was where her feelings were concerned. I'd have been happy if he'd snogged my face off right now. Who gave a shit if it made her feel uncomfortable? I didn't. Once Lily had turned her back, he ran his hand over my buttocks before giving the left cheek a squeeze.

'I don't think you've been to Samson's office yet, have you?' MacKenzie asked when Lily glanced over her shoulder at us.

'No,' Lily replied.

Good recovery, I thought.

'Well, in that case, let me lead the way.'

MacKenzie walked towards the stairs that led down to the basement and our dressing room. He stopped outside a door at the end of the corridor, behind the stairwell, that I'd never really paid any attention to before and entered a code into the wall panel. A moment later, I heard the door click open. MacKenzie pulled it towards us and then gestured for us to go inside.

I wouldn't really call it an office. It was more like a suite of rooms. We walked along a short passageway, past the ladies, then the gents, and then a door with a gold plaque bearing the name Samson Fox in black letters.

'Keep going,' MacKenzie said.

He was bringing up the rear. Lily did as instructed, following the sound of the music coming from a room ahead of us. The space was cavernous. I felt like we'd just stepped inside a magical winter wonderland. Huge white Christmas trees were dotted around the room. They were decorated with white lights and silver decorations. Sparkling stick trees with the same lights were clustered around them, creating an indoor forest. The place looked amazing. Tables and chairs lined two of the walls. Each one had a vase of long-stemmed white flowers making up the centrepiece, while white church candles sat in groups around them. Who knew this incredible space was hiding behind a very ordinary-looking door? I must have walked past it countless times and never given it a second thought.

'So what do you think of Samson's entertaining space?' MacKenzie asked.

'It's awesome,' I replied.

It was decked out like a boutique nightclub with a black sparkly floor, rotating overhead lights and a massive bar along the entire back wall. There was a buffet table on the opposite wall to the bar with freestanding snowflake ice sculptures at either end. Two men wearing chef's jackets stood behind it. Samson had put a lot of effort into the party. He'd really pushed the boat out and spared no expense.

Somebody I'd never seen before stopped MacKenzie as soon as we'd walked in, but that was fine by me. It had given me a chance to drink in the surroundings. What I'd seen had gone to my head.

While MacKenzie was busy chatting, a tall young man carrying a tray approached Lily and me. He was dressed in black trousers and a white shirt.

'Would you ladies like some champagne or a cosmopolitan?' he asked.

'Not for me, thanks,' Lily replied.

'If you'd prefer something else, there's a fully stocked bar.' He gestured towards the back of the room with a flick of his head. 'It's free, by the way,' the man grinned.

'I can't. I'm driving,' Lily smiled.

Why did she always say that when people offered her alcohol? She didn't drink, so why not just admit it? But that was typical of Lily. She always had to be the martyr even though she wasn't depriving herself of anything.

'Oh, that's a shame.'

The young man's eyes doubled in size. He looked mildly horrified to think there was a guest at a party with a free bar who couldn't take advantage of the host's hospitality. Little did he know. When he gave her a sympathetic smile, I rolled my eyes.

'I'll go and get you a soft drink. What would you like?'

The man fixed his eyes on my sister. He was falling over himself to be helpful.

'A mineral water with ice and a slice, please,' Lily replied.

I had to resist the urge to let out a loud groan. She was more than capable of getting a drink herself. She didn't need him to wait on her hand and foot.

'What's in a cosmopolitan?' I asked before Lily demanded anything else.

'Vodka, Cointreau, cranberry juice, and freshly squeezed lime juice,' he replied.

'That sounds nice. I'll try one of those.' I picked up the martini-shaped glass containing the pinky-red liquid. 'It's delicious,' I said as the chilled alcohol flowed down my throat.

'I'm just going to get myself a whisky,' MacKenzie said, coming up behind me.

'No worries.'

Samson Fox was dressed in a charcoal grey suit and a black

shirt. He'd spotted us from the doorway and was now making his way towards us.

'I've been hearing some really good things about your act.'

Samson stood between us and smiled. As he did, the skin at the side of his soft brown eyes crinkled. His brown hair was greying at the temples, but he was still an attractive man even though he must have been well into his forties. His chiselled jaw was covered in designer stubble, but he was reeking of aftershave.

'It's great to finally meet you face to face. I thought you looked stunning on the stage, but you're even more beautiful close up.'

Lily beamed with pride, won over by his silver tongue. I would have been flattered, too, if he hadn't been groping my arse while smiling sweetly at her. It was so unexpected that I almost choked on my drink. Mr Fox owned the club, but that didn't give him free rein to touch me up whenever he wanted to. He had another think coming if he thought he could put his hands on me uninvited. Samson was getting away with it now because he'd caught me off guard, and I didn't want to make a scene, but this was the first and last time he'd cop a feel at my expense.

I'd been really looking forward to the party, but the man was a creep. I froze as his fingers moved over the fabric of my dress. My muscles tensed involuntarily. I was so relieved when he lifted his hand away that my nerves got the better of me. I swallowed my cosmo down in one so I wasn't tempted to fling it into his face.

'Somebody's thirsty,' he laughed, then he clicked his fingers and summoned the waiter.

I felt my pulse speed up when Samson locked eyes with me. He had to prise the glass out of my hand. I hadn't realised I was gripping the long stem so hard until I was forced to let go.

'I don't like seeing my guests with an empty glass,' Samson said as he handed me another cosmopolitan.

His gaze was intense, and it lingered a little too long for my liking.

'What's that you're drinking?' he asked, turning to face Lily.

I felt myself breathe a sigh of relief as his focus switched from me to my sister. I discreetly looked over my shoulder to see what was taking MacKenzie so long.

'Mineral water,' Lily replied.

'Are you serious? Didn't anyone tell you it's a free bar? My parties are legendary,' Samson boasted.

'I don't doubt that, but I'm driving,' Lily replied.

Here we go again.

'But it's a Christmas party. You have to have a drink. I insist. I'll pay for your cab home,' Samson said.

How was she going to get around that?

Lily was beaming from ear to ear. She wouldn't have been smiling if she'd been in my shoes. My blood was boiling. Trust Lily to catch the attention of the head honcho. Samson was fawning over her while treating me like a piece of meat. Where was the justice in that?

'That's a very generous offer, but I'll be driving first thing in the morning, so I'd better play it safe.'

'On Christmas Day?' Samson questioned.

Lily nodded. 'Straight after breakfast, we always go and lay flowers on my grandparents' graves. It's a family tradition.'

'That's a nice thing to do,' Samson replied.

Sensing that their conversation was over, I excused myself so that he couldn't turn his attention back to me.

'I'll be back in a minute. I just need to use the ladies,' I said, putting my glass down on the nearest table.

As I walked across the dance floor and down the corridor, I asked myself the million-dollar question only a man would know the answer to. Why were the women's toilets always the furthest away from the bar?

Lily hadn't seemed bothered that I'd left her alone with the big boss. In fact, she seemed delighted to have his undivided attention. More fool her. She was welcome to him. He made my flesh crawl.

I locked myself inside the cubicle and then leaned against the door. I couldn't concentrate, distracted by the sound of the blood rushing around my head. My first proper encounter with Samson had been about as pleasant as a throbbing pimple on my arse cheek. He was being so brazen it made me question whether he'd done this before and got away with it.

I put the lid down on the toilet and sat on it. I couldn't face going back too soon, but I knew if I stayed away too long, people would wonder if I'd had a dodgy curry last night. I glanced at my watch; ten minutes had passed. I'd better not overdo it. Lily would usually be breathing down my neck by now. Where was she? She must have been distracted by something. Someone. It could only be Samson Fox. I let out a sigh. Reluctant as I was to go back to the party, I couldn't hide in here all evening. That would send him the wrong message.

The thought of what he'd done lit a fire in my belly, and I felt a sudden urgency to get myself back into the room. But I stood up too quickly, and the motion made me feel lightheaded. The fact that I'd been swallowing cosmopolitans like they were going out of fashion probably hadn't helped either, but it was Christmas Eve, and I had every intention of getting drunk.

I was just about to unlock the cubicle when I heard the exterior door open. I stopped in my tracks and held my breath, trying not to make a sound. My heart was in my mouth. Panic was clawing its way up from the pit of my stomach. I was scared to death that Samson had come looking for me.

'Daisy, are you in here?' Lily asked.

Her words sliced through the silence. I'd never been so relieved to hear the sound of my sister's voice before, so I flung open the door without hesitation.

'Are you OK?' Lily looked concerned.

'I'm fine. I should have known you wouldn't be able to resist checking up on me,' I snapped, trying to conceal my true feelings.

'There's no need to bite my head off. We were getting worried; you've been gone for ages. MacKenzie asked me to come and see if you were all right. You've been knocking back those cocktails, and they're lethal.'

Lily was right, but how would she know the alcohol content of anything?

'Spare me the lecture. I've heard it all before. What I drink is none of your business.'

I stared into Lily's eyes, and a thousand unspoken words stared back at me.

'What?'

Lily didn't reply.

'I didn't realise I'd been gone that long. I got chatting to a couple of people on my way here,' I lied, realising I had to come up with an excuse to explain the time I'd been away.

Lily waited while I washed and dried my hands. She seemed reluctant to let me out of her sight. I wondered if Samson had been touchy-feely with her, too, but I didn't ask. I wanted to forget about my employer's pervy behaviour.

My eyes darted around the room as I walked two paces behind my sister. There was no sign of the grey-suited bottom pincher anywhere, so I breathed a sigh of relief and then helped myself to another cosmopolitan from a passing tray.

'Go easy on those. Like I said, they're lethal,' Lily warned before throwing me a disapproving look.

Would I listen to her advice? Of course not.

46

MACKENZIE

'Mac, have you got a minute,' Jermaine said.

There was an undertone of panic in his voice, which was very out of character for him. He was the youngest member of the team and the joker of the pack. A proper wind-up merchant.

'What's up, bro? It's Christmas Eve. Why are you stressing? Are you worried you're not on Santa's good list,' I smiled.

'It's all kicking off on the door.'

I felt the smile slide from my face.

'Oh, for fuck sake,' I replied.

It was the same every year; punters, full of booze, with only one thing on their minds. Alcohol made people think they could take on the world. They felt invincible. Their self-confidence went through the roof, and their common sense went out of the window. They'd pick a punch-up with their own shadows.

I was on my fourth double of Samson's finest top-shelf whisky. Up until a moment ago, I'd been surrounded by a warm fuzzy glow only an eighteen-year-old single malt like Highland Park could give. Now, I suddenly felt stone-cold sober. It was as though every drop of alcohol had left my system instantly.

'I'll be back in a minute,' I said to Daisy.

'Please don't leave me on my own.'

She looked like a deer caught in the headlights.

'You're not on your own. Lily's standing right next to you.'

The way she looked at me, anyone would have thought I was a total stranger, and had just gone up to her in the street and said, 'Excuse me, love. Would you mind giving me a quick blow job?' She'd almost recoiled in horror.

It was crystal clear she didn't want to stay with Lily, and I felt bad deserting her, but I had no choice. Jermaine wouldn't have called me if it wasn't an emergency. I could see she wasn't about to leave it at that, so I made a break for it. I didn't have time to get caught up in a conversation with her.

'You'll be fine; get yourself another cocktail. I'll be back before you know it,' I said over my shoulder.

Jermaine's back was disappearing out of the door by the time I caught up with him.

'What's going on?'

'Four of Arben's guys are in the foyer. They're refusing to leave until they've seen you.'

I felt the colour drain from my face. But I pushed my shoulders back and pasted on a smile as the Adidas Army came into view. Igor and Leroy were standing guard over them, which meant Caleb must be trying to control the queue single-handedly. That was likely to spell trouble. I needed to send this lot packing as soon as possible so my guys could go back to what they did best.

'Good evening, fellas. What can I do for you?'

'I have a message from Arben. You need to pay for the cocaine by Boxing Day,' one of the men said.

'Boxing Day?' I questioned. I wasn't sure I'd heard him right over the commotion coming from the street.

Igor threw me a look and then rushed off towards the entrance.

'That's right,' the man sneered.

'I'll do my best, but that's such short notice.'

I wasn't working this evening, and the club was closed tomorrow.

'You better make sure you pay up on time, or he's going to remove one of your fingers for every day you're late. If you run out of digits, he's going to take your beautiful girlfriend and sell her to the highest bidder,' the man grinned.

There was no evidence of any Christmas cheer in the air tonight. Having delivered the message, the Adidas Army filed out of Eden's, one after the other. I followed closely behind.

'Get your fucking hands off me,' I heard a man shout.

I went to get a closer look as the action unfolded. Two drunks were trying to have a sparring match. Igor moved quickly and decisively. He went in for a bear hug, wrapping his biceps around the nearest guy's elbows to stop him from flailing his arms around as he tried to retaliate. Caleb went up behind the other bloke and got him into an arm bar, twisting his limb up behind his back, he lifted the bloke onto his toes until he squealed like a pig. The rowdy bloke had been trying to land a punch on the geezer next to him in the queue. Jermaine grabbed his other arm, and they dragged him out of the line.

'This is the second time I've warned you. Now fuck off home. You're not coming in,' Caleb shouted in the bloke's face.

As Caleb and Jermaine released their grip on him, Caleb pushed him in the centre of his back to help him on his way. The man stumbled. I thought he was going down, but he managed to stay upright, just about. I watched him sway off into the distance with his tail between his legs.

'Settle down, you piece of shit,' Igor said.

'Who do you think you're calling a piece of shit. Fuck off back to your own country,' the man shouted. A mist of spit sprayed out of his mouth as he ranted.

He was going to be sorry he said that.

'Caleb,' Igor called before he kicked the man in the back of the knee, making his leg fold.

Igor had decided the best course of action was to take the man down. His patience had worn out, so he was going to turn the aggression on. It was time to teach the cheeky git a lesson he wouldn't forget in a hurry. Don't take the piss out of the bouncer unless you want to suffer. Igor was an army veteran. The guy didn't stand a chance.

Once the guy was down on the ground, Caleb and Igor tried to restrain him, but he wasn't going to give up easily. He was thrashing about calling them every name under the sun. The man was a typical angry drunk. He had the strength of ten men. But I knew my staff, and they would be prepared to hold him there until he wore himself out. He was riled up, but adrenaline was exhausting. He had to tire soon. Igor was twenty-three stone of bulging muscles, and Caleb wasn't far behind him, tipping the scales at nineteen stone. The guy had forty stone pinning him on the pavement. I was amazed he had any fight left in him.

'I can't breathe,' the man protested.

'You can get up once you settle down,' Caleb said, crushing the man's cheek into the paving slab.

Realising his struggle was in vain, the man finally gave up the fight and went limp. For one moment, I thought my guys might have gone too far, but they got to their feet and then dragged the drunk up by the scruff of his jacket. He staggered around the pavement for a bit, trying to find his feet before stumbling towards the tube. I watched him weaving his way there.

'Well done, guys,' I said as I turned my attention away from the troublemaker.

But my team were already back at work. Security staff faced violence and danger on a nightly basis, so they took it all in their stride. Getting blood on their hands was part of the job description. Some people couldn't handle their drink. That was a fact. They lost all control and went wild when they were on a night out.

I was proud of my crew. They all had a good work ethic, which was essential to the smooth running of the team. My guys needed to be able to rely on each other. And they could. They were close-knit. Brothers in arms. They were a good mix of characters and had more than proved their capabilities tonight. If it all kicked off with Arben, I was going to need their help to save my skin, which made me appreciate them more than ever.

47

DAISY

'Where's your beautiful sister?'

Samson had come up behind me and whispered in my ear. I could feel his breath on my neck. I went to answer, but the words lodged in my throat. My mouth was dry, and my heart was pounding. I didn't want him to know I was on my own. He made me feel uncomfortable. Tense. Edgy. But I didn't want him to realise that, so I summoned every bit of courage I possessed, swung around, and looked him right in the eyes.

'She's gone home,' I replied as though being alone didn't bother me.

I'd been relieved when she'd called it a night. She'd been watching my every move like a hawk, constantly nagging me about my drinking, smoking and unhealthy diet. The more she lectured me, the more I indulged. My eyes followed her as she walked out of the door. I thought I'd be able to relax now. How wrong could I have been?

I'd been under this strange illusion that Samson would have more important people to mingle with than little old me. But he was staying as close as prolapsed haemorrhoids. Where was a tube of Anusol when you needed it?

Lily had never been a party animal like me. I supposed a boozy do like this wouldn't have the same appeal for somebody who was teetotal. She'd stuck it out for a good few hours, but there was only so much mineral water with lime a person could drink before they reached their limit, and as there weren't any networking opportunities on the horizon, she'd decided to cut and run. I was beginning to wish I'd gone with her.

I'd imagined the place would be full of Samson's success stories. None of the people who appeared in the pictures in the hall of fame decorating Eden's foyer had shown up. Why was that? Maybe they hadn't been invited. Who knew? I'd been hoping this was going to be a star-studded event. I'd been looking forward to rubbing shoulders with the rich and famous. But only the current line-up was here.

I'd been delighted when Lily had cleared off as I'd hoped MacKenzie and I could be alone together, but he still hadn't come back. Something bad must have been kicking off to keep him away for such a long time. And now I was stuck with Samson again. I thought I'd got rid of him. It was going to be a long night. I was seriously tempted to bail, too. If MacKenzie didn't appear very soon, I'd make an excuse and get out of here.

'Oh, that's a pity. I was hoping to introduce her to my good friend Travis Steele. He's a record producer,' Samson said.

My ears pricked up. Travis Steele's name was legendary in the music business. He'd launched thousands of careers. Things looked like they were on the up. Maybe I should stick around for a bit longer. Lily would be livid when she realised she'd missed out on this opportunity.

This had to be the guy Samson was talking about, I thought, when I spotted a man with bleached blond hair and a bright pink complexion who looked to be in his mid-fifties making his way towards us. He was wearing an open-necked blue and white flowery shirt and pale blue designer jeans with patent lace-up shoes.

'It's a pleasure to meet you, darling.'

'Nice to meet you too,' I said, but I didn't mean it. There was something unsettling about him.

As he stopped in front of me, the smell of his aftershave sent me reeling. Just like Samson, he was reeking of it. While they stood side by side, the aroma of woody outdoorsy vibes were battling for supremacy with citrusy top notes. They smelt like they'd bathed in the stuff rather than sprayed a quick spritz. The fumes were suffocating.

Travis took hold of my right hand and lifted it up to his mouth. Then he planted a kiss on the back of it while gazing into my eyes, which made a shiver run down my spine. What a weird thing to do. We weren't living in the 1800s. I shifted uncomfortably. Fidgety. Nervous. Keen for all of this to be over.

'What's your name, beautiful?' Travis asked as though he was chatting me up in a bar.

'Daisy,' I replied.

Samson clicked his fingers, and a moment later, a waiter appeared. He was carrying a tray with a cosmopolitan and two crystal tumblers of dark spirit. Samson picked up the cosmo and handed it to me. I was already holding another one, which was more than half full.

'Not for me, thanks; I've already got one.'

I tried to glance down at my watch discreetly, but my vision was a bit blurry, so I couldn't read the numbers on the dial. The party was drawing to a close, and the room was emptying out at an alarming rate. I'd been sinking cocktails to pass the time while waiting for MacKenzie to return. I'd had a lot to drink and suddenly felt vulnerable.

'It's late. I should get going,' I said.

'Let's have one for the road. I insist,' Samson said.

This was only the second time I'd met Samson, but I knew he was a man who was used to getting his own way, so I didn't put up any resistance. I just took the glass out of his hand and said nothing. I didn't want him to realise how uneasy I was feeling.

'Bottoms up,' Travis grinned.

'One of my favourite positions,' Samson replied.

The men started to laugh.

What the hell was taking MacKenzie so long? I cast my eyes around the room. The place was deserted, apart from a solitary bartender, myself and the gruesome twosome standing in front of me.

'It's a shame your sister had to rush off. I wanted to have a chat with the two of you about your future,' Travis said. 'I'm sorry, I can't remember her name. Samson did tell me, but I'm not as young as I used to be, so once I've had one or two sherbets, everything goes out of my head.'

Travis touched the thick gold chain around his neck with his liver-spotted hand, and I caught sight of his wedding ring. How could a simple gold band give a person so much reassurance?

'She's called Lily.'

I knew what he meant about the alcohol fog, and I was considerably younger than he was, but I wasn't convinced age played any part in the equation. When you'd had as many cocktails as I'd had this evening, it affected your brain power. Simple as that.

'The two of you have a bright future, and I should know, I've launched plenty of careers in my time. I know what it takes to make it big. You have it by the bucket load, so seeing that mirrored when you're standing next to your twin will multiply your appeal tenfold.

Believe me, the public won't be able to get enough of you when I propel you into the spotlight.'

I felt like I was having an out of body experience. I could see Travis's lips moving as his words buzzed around in my head like a swarm of angry bees. That last drink had sent me over the edge. I'd had one too many, and now I felt out of it.

'Are you OK, darling?' Travis asked.

The room had started spinning like the twister at the funfair. My stomach was churning. I knew I was going to be sick. How embarrassing. Even though I was drunk, I knew I'd be mortified tomorrow.

'Excuse me a minute.'

I forced out a half smile for his benefit, then tried to breathe through the wave of nausea threatening to wash me away. I staggered across the empty dance floor, praying I'd make it to the ladies in time. I hadn't even got halfway when I felt an arm snake around my waist. I turned my head, expecting to see MacKenzie.

'I've got you,' Samson said.

He flung my left arm over his shoulder, holding it in place at the wrist as he guided me into the toilets. I could feel the imprint of his fingers on my skin. Holding me too tightly. Digits digging into my flesh. I'd barely made it to the sink before the contents of my stomach hit the porcelain. Samson let go of me and held my hair back as I clung to the rim. I retched into the basin as the smell of vomit filled the air around us.

Once the sickness had stopped, I ran the tap to wash out the sink. Then, I cupped my hands and let the cold water fill the space before lifting them to my mouth. I swilled it around several times trying to get rid of the disgusting taste. I looked in the mirror and saw Samson's eyes roaming over my body in the reflection. He stared at me with undisguised interest. His gaze was scrutinising. Blush inducing. Disconcerting. Unnerved by the sudden feeling of his hands on my waist, I opened my mouth to protest. The words died on my tongue before I had a chance to spit them out. But then Samson moved his hands up and cupped my breasts, and I knew I had to find my voice.

'What the hell do you think you're doing?'

I couldn't look at him. My mouth was trembling. Tears weren't far away, threatening to spill.

'Don't be such a prick-tease.'

Samson lowered one hand and began pulling up the hem of my dress while grinding his groin into me from behind. He shoved his hand into my knickers, forcing two fingers inside me.

'Stop. Please don't do this,' I begged, looking at him in the mirror.

He didn't meet my gaze. He was too focused on what he was doing. Was he going to rape me? My heart started pounding. I had to get away. Samson grabbed hold of my arm and turned me around to face him. He looked at me strangely as though he'd just heard my thoughts. It was unnerving to think somebody had seen the inner workings of my mind.

'Get off me.'

I put my hand on his chest and pushed him backwards.

'You think you're something special, but women like you are ten a penny,' Samson said before he dusted off the front of his grey suit and then pulled the sleeves of his jacket over his shirt cuffs.

I breathed a sigh of relief when Samson walked out of the toilet and then looked in the mirror. My face was wet with tears. This industry was dominated by men at the top who had access to young, impressionable females desperate to further their careers. But I wasn't going to sleep with him to get a record deal. If that's what he thought was going to happen, he was mistaken. Now that my fear was subsiding, I was furious with him. Talk about abusing his position. I was riled up. Ready to give him a piece of my mind, but when I walked back into the room, there was no sign of Samson or Travis, so I sat down at the table to wait for MacKenzie.

My body started trembling as a mixture of fear and adrenaline raced through my veins. I wished I'd trusted my gut and not left myself wide open to Samson by getting drunk. From the moment I'd met him, I'd felt there was something creepy about him even though I couldn't put my finger on what it was. I should have been on my guard around him. Wary. Not allowed myself to be vulnerable. Defenceless. He'd taken advantage of me in the worst way possible.

48

MACKENZIE

Daisy was slumped in a chair with her head resting on the table nearest the door when I finally made it back to the party.

'Hey, babe, I'm sorry I was so long,' I said, sitting down beside her.

Daisy didn't stir. She was completely out of it.

'Are you OK?'

I rubbed Daisy's arm, but she was out for the count.

'Oi, MacKenzie,' Samson called.

He was sitting at the bar, sharing a drink and a joke with Travis. The two of them were thick as thieves. They'd been friends for years.

'Where did you disappear to?' Samson asked as I got closer to him.

'It was all kicking off on the door, so I went to lend a hand.'

'Did somebody need a toothpick then?'

Samson laughed. Travis joined in, braying like a donkey as if that was the funniest thing he'd ever heard.

'You're hilarious,' I replied, rolling my eyes.

'I like to think so. Aren't you going to tell me what happened?'

'Two meatheads got into some argy-bargy in the queue. But Igor and the guys sorted it and sent them both packing.'

Igor had trained my guys not to get caught up in the nonsense. People tried to draw them into the drama all the time. Drunks loved a verbal altercation, but he didn't have the patience for it. He was a busy man with no tolerance for listening to bullshit. I couldn't say I blamed him. Igor maintained his actions spoke louder than any words he could say, so he rarely found the need to enter into a disagreement with a customer he was about to eject. It just wasted everyone's time and didn't change the outcome, so why bother?

'Is that all? Why did they get you involved?'

I had no intention of saying anything about my visit from Arben's guys or that he'd sent me a Christmas present in the form of a verbal threat.

'Igor could see trouble was brewing, so he wanted to separate the two of them before it kicked off. I kept watch on the door while our guys did what they do best; a bit of good old-fashioned bouncing.'

When my guys were forced to intervene in a situation, they tried to work in pairs. Two bouncers were better than one whenever possible. They had to be ready in case things escalated. Dickheads like the ones earlier were only one beer away from thinking they were the toughest blokes in London. Drunks never listened to good advice, so brute force was necessary. According to the new regs, physical intervention was a last resort. That wasn't the rule at Eden's. In Igor's book, the threat of violence equalled respect.

'Sounds like you could do with a drink.' Samson clicked his fingers to summon the barman. 'What's your poison, Mac?'

I didn't really want a drink. I wanted to get Daisy home. It was clear she was plastered and needed to sleep it off, but only a braver man than me said no to Samson. I'd been enjoying his eighteen-year-old single malt Highland Park earlier, but I knew how much a bottle of that cost, so I didn't order that in front of him. I wanted to leave here tonight with my balls still intact.

'I'll have a Dead Man's Fingers and Coke.'

The irony of what I just ordered wasn't lost on me. I knocked it back in a couple of swallows.

'Another one?' Samson asked.

'I'd better not. I should make sure Daisy gets home OK. I wouldn't like to put her in a cab like that.'

I glanced over to where she was crashed out on the table in the same position she'd been in when I first arrived.

'That's very noble of you.'

'It's got nothing to do with being noble, but I don't want some creep preying on her. Some of those cab drivers are dodgy as fuck.'

Cab drivers were the least of my concerns. But Arben's threat was hanging over me like a menacing shadow.

'Sounds like you've got a soft spot for her.' Samson looked annoyed.

'Nah. I'd do the same for any young woman. I wouldn't want it on my conscience if something happened to them after I let them go home on their own.'

I hadn't just said that for Samson's benefit. I meant every word. I was a sucker for a damsel in distress.

'I'd had such high hopes for her, but the little tart can't hold her booze.' Samson's lip curled.

I felt myself bristle, but I didn't react. Like Des, Samson wouldn't be impressed if he thought Daisy and I were getting up close and personal. Obviously, he was allowed to shag people who worked for him, but he didn't extend that invitation to the rest of us. Relationships between employees were off-limits.

'There's nothing remotely attractive about a bird off her face on booze or drugs for that matter. In fact, I'd go so far as to say it disgusts me. She's lucky I don't terminate her contract on the spot.'

Samson looked well and truly pissed off. Daisy was walking on thin ice, which surprised me. I'd thought Samson would be besotted with her. He had an eye for the ladies, and Daisy was absolutely stunning.

'You're not serious.'

Samson looked surprised that I'd spoken up, but I was the manager here, so I was entitled to an opinion.

'I'm deadly serious. Look at her. She's a fucking disgrace.'

Samson's features hardened as he glanced over at Daisy.

'Please don't do anything hasty. Since Lily and Daisy have started singing at Eden's, Tuesday nights are booming. It was the quietest night of the week for us, but they're really pulling in the punters and the takings are swelling.' I couldn't work Samson out. Before the twins signed their contract, the club was going down the pan.

I felt obliged to fight Daisy's corner. She hadn't been in that condition when Jermaine had called me to the door. A wave of guilt suddenly washed over me. If I hadn't left her on her own, she wouldn't have drunk so much. I'd told her to get another cocktail while she waited for me to come back.

'That's as may be, but look at the state of her. She couldn't pull a cork out of a bottle.' Samson's lip curled.

Daisy was bollocksed, but she must have been OK when Lily went home because, much as the two of them were constantly bickering, Lily wouldn't have gone and left her sister in a state like that. Twins were tethered together.

'What's got into you all of a sudden?' Travis asked. 'You're being a real little bitch. Are you having your period?'

Samson didn't look impressed that he was the butt of Travis's joke, especially when he let out a belly laugh.

'Proper comedian you are. Maybe we should give you a slot at Eden's. What do you think, MacKenzie? He could replace boozy Suzie over there.' Samson flicked his head in Daisy's direction.

Samson always got nasty when he'd had too much to drink, but I kept my mouth shut.

'I'd pay good money to see you get booed off stage,' Samson said.

'And I thought my missus was the moodiest cow going. One minute, she's the sweetest thing. The next, she'd have your balls in a vice. Proper little tiger she is. But you're in a different league altogether. You could wipe the floor with her.'

He was laughing so hard tears were running down Travis's cheeks.

'Is that right, you fucker?' Samson shook his head and then began laughing, too.

'Maybe I should set up a meet. Handbags at dawn?'

Travis slapped Samson on the back. He was the only person who would get away with talking to my boss like that.

'But seriously, mate, don't you dare pull the plug on those girls. Not before I have a chance to check them out for myself.' Travis smiled.

'Fair enough. That's my Christmas present to you, my friend,' Samson replied. 'Now get her out of my sight before I change my mind.'

49

DAISY

Christmas Day

My head felt like it was going to explode. I half opened my eyes and saw hazy sunlight slanting through unwashed windows. That was the moment I realised I wasn't in my own bed. I scrambled upright and pulled the quilt tightly around me. Where the hell was I? This wasn't my room. I searched the cobwebby corners of my mind, but I had no recollection of where I was or how I'd got here.

'Happy Christmas, sleepyhead.'

My eyes were still blurry with sleep, but I followed the direction of MacKenzie's voice. He was standing in the doorway with two steaming mugs in his hand. I was a seasoned party animal and couldn't remember the last time I'd woken up feeling as rough as this. From the taste in my mouth, I knew I'd been sick last night.

'What time is it?'

'Half two,' MacKenzie replied.

He walked towards me and put one of the mugs of coffee down on the bedside cabinet next to me. Then he lifted the other mug to his lips and took a sip.

A million thoughts started whirring around in my brain. Mum and Dad were going to kill me. They'd have already been to the cemetery by now. Missing the Christmas Day pilgrimage was an unforgivable offence in our household. But it was too late to worry about that now, so I pushed it to the back of my mind.

'You're going to have to help me out. I don't remember much about last night. How did I end up here?'

'You were in a bad way after the cocktails...'

'Oh God,' I said as the realisation hit me. 'No wonder I feel so rough. I think I drank my body weight in cosmopolitans.'

'I think you did. Maybe twice your body weight,' MacKenzie laughed.

I shook my head, embarrassed that I'd let myself get so drunk.

'Did anything happen between us?'

It was mortifying to have to ask, but I couldn't remember, and I'd rather know. I was still wearing my dress, but that didn't rule out the possibility that we'd had sex.

'Of course not! What do you take me for? You were barely conscious.'

From the indignation in MacKenzie's voice, it was obvious he'd taken offence.

'I wasn't accusing you of anything...'

On any other occasion, I would have been delighted to be waking up in MacKenzie's bed, but this wasn't how I wanted the first time to be.

'Fair enough.' MacKenzie looked wounded.

'I'm sorry I got so pissed.'

'Don't apologise, there's really no need. We've all done it at one time or another. Getting drunk at the Christmas party is a rite of passage.'

'Please tell me I didn't get off with the boss.'

As soon as the words left my mouth, a memory stirred from

deep within me. I hadn't snogged Samson, but he'd definitely taken advantage of my drunken state. Details were starting to come back to me. I remembered his weight as he pushed me against the basin in the ladies' toilets. My blood ran cold as a vision of him forcing his fingers inside me hit me straight in the face. I could barely hold myself up, let alone fight him off, but he'd carried on regardless, even though I'd begged him to stop. I wanted to tell MacKenzie, but I barely knew him. I was worried he might not believe me, and then it would make things awkward between us, so I decided to keep it to myself at least for the time being.

'I'm sorry I got called away, but it was all kicking off on the door, so I had to go and help out. I take it you had a good chat with Samson. What did you think of him?'

Blood rushed to my head. How was I going to answer that and not give the game away?

'I'm not really sure. My brain doesn't seem to be functioning properly. I seem to be suffering from short-term memory loss,' I laughed.

I'd decided to use the fact that I'd been pissed last night as an excuse so that I could skirt around his question. I didn't want to say the man needed locking up. He was a sex pest and a danger to women.

'His big puppy dog eyes usually have women going weak at the knees. They literally throw themselves at his feet.'

'Really?'

MacKenzie nodded. 'Hell, yeah. Samson's a big hit with the ladies. He bones every woman in sight.'

A sudden waft of stale vomit made me nauseous, and I had to swallow down the saliva that had formed in my mouth. The memory of last night hit me like a bolt of lightning. I could still feel the indents of Samson's fingers digging into my flesh. I was on the verge of telling MacKenzie what had happened when my words caught in my throat.

'He can be a dickhead when he's been drinking. Who am I trying to kid? The man's an arsehole. Full stop.'

I couldn't have agreed more, but MacKenzie slating Samson seemed to have come from nowhere.

'How come you're digging him out all of a sudden? Did Samson say something to you about me?'

I'd become ultra-defensive, which seemed to take MacKenzie by surprise.

'No, he never said a word, but I know what he's like. He's a complete tool to the men who work for him. Especially me, but he's usually as charming as charming can be where women are concerned.'

Charming? My mouth dropped open. I wouldn't have called him that. Lecherous. Pervert. Sleazebag. Those were a few words that sprung to mind. I couldn't talk about Samson right now. The memory of what he'd done to me last night was too fresh. Too raw. I didn't want to think about it.

'Showbusiness is a fickle business, so if your singing career doesn't take off, there's a lot of wealthy men out there who'd be more than happy to throw a few quid your way for a double date with you and Lily,' MacKenzie joked.

I didn't find that funny at all, given the circumstances.

'I'd better make tracks,' I said, throwing back the quilt and swinging my legs over the bed to put an end to the conversation. 'Can I use your bathroom, please?'

'Of course, it's the first door on the right,' MacKenzie replied.

As I got to my feet, I caught sight of the state of my dress. There was dried puke all down the front of it. Bloody typical. I couldn't even throw it in the washing machine. It was dry clean only. This could only happen to me. It was the most expensive thing in my wardrobe, and I'd ruined it the first time I'd worn it. Something like this never happened when you were wearing an old T-shirt and a pair of leggings. I let out a sigh. Oh well, it was only money.

I closed the bathroom door and stared in the mirror. I looked an absolute fright. The damage was worse than I'd thought. There would be no disguising the state I'd been in. The smell of vomit on my clothes would herald my arrival before I came into view. My make-up was all smudged, and my hair was matted. I was a mess. I needed a shower, but I didn't have anything clean to change into, so I'd just have to brave it. The sooner I got home and faced the music, the better.

'What are you up to today?' I asked, slipping on my beautiful shoes.

I glanced down at my feet and smiled. At least they'd survived the night.

'I'm going to my mum's. She's making lunch for me and my two brothers.'

'Oh, that's nice. I didn't know you had brothers. Older or younger?'

'Younger. It should be good. My mum's a great cook.' MacKenzie smiled.

'I'll be out of your hair in just a minute. I just need to call an Uber if that's OK.'

'There's no need. I can drop you off on my way.'

'I can't ask you to do that. You've done enough already. Sharing your bed with a woman covered in sick must have been hell on earth,' I said, to try and hide my embarrassment.

After my antics last night and the state I was in, most guys would have given me a wide berth. But rather than running for the hills, MacKenzie had looked after me in my hour of need. I'd been dreaming about waking up in his bed since I'd first clapped eyes on him and a golden opportunity to kickstart a relationship with him had presented itself on a plate to me. But yesterday I'd been too hammered and now I was too hung over to do anything about it. I was a complete idiot. I'd potentially ruined everything before it had a chance to get off the ground.

'It's honestly no trouble. I insist,' MacKenzie replied.

'Thanks. I really appreciate it,' I smiled, slipping on my fake fur coat and picking up my clutch bag.

'If you fancy coming over later, give me a bell,' MacKenzie said, keeping his eyes on the road.

'I'd like that.'

Maybe all was not lost.

As soon as MacKenzie pulled up at the kerb, I could see Dad's shadow twitching the curtains.

50

DES

'Daisy's back,' I called out, then stepped back from the front room window.

Tara and Lily were in the kitchen preparing the Christmas dinner while I was standing guard like a German Shepherd, waiting to see if she'd materialise. Daisy got out of the passenger seat of a black Mazda hatchback and sauntered up the path, still wearing the clothes she'd gone out in. Even from this distance, I could see she looked a mess.

Daisy had always rebelled against the rules. But things were getting worse the older she was getting. It wasn't just at home. Her attitude spilled over into her working life. Lily had always loved being the centre of attention on stage, but Daisy sank into her sister's shadow where performing was concerned. Tara and I had hoped we'd be able to draw her out as the years went by, but she never seemed comfortable being in the limelight. Tough shit. Needs must. She had an opportunity to make real money. Money that would keep the wolf from the door. Warren Jenkins was going to hang me out to dry if I didn't keep up the repayments. So she needed to knuckle down and get on with it.

Working at Eden's had given her a chance to really make something of herself, but she seemed more interested in drinking and staying out all night than embracing the opportunity. Tara and I couldn't work out what her problem was. It wasn't a confidence issue. She was brimming over with that. My daughter was too defiant for her own good.

'So nice of you to bother to grace us with your presence. Where the hell do you think you've been?' I let rip the minute Daisy opened the front door, so she stood in the doorway and didn't venture in any further.

'I couldn't get a cab, so I stayed over at a friend's.'

That was a perfectly reasonable explanation, but it was the brazenness of her tone that made me bristle.

'What friend?' I asked, planting my hands on my hips.

'Nobody you'd know.'

'Get in here before all the neighbours start gossiping.'

My mum would have called her a dirty stop-out.

'Who cares what they think? I don't.' Daisy glared at me. Her big blue eyes were smudged with last night's make-up.

'Well, I do, so stop making a show of yourself.'

I was boiling mad, and she wasn't doing anything to try and pacify me. She was just winding me up. And it didn't take a lot to make me blow my fuse. Daisy stood opposite me with her arms folded across her chest, staring into my face, challenging me. I'd hoped she would have taken a more submissive approach, but obedience wasn't part of Daisy's character.

'Are you deliberately trying to ruin everybody's Christmas?' I asked, breaking the silence.

'Of course not,' Daisy replied.

But there wasn't an ounce of sincerity in her voice.

'You've got no respect, have you? You didn't even bother to text us and tell us where you were. You could have been lying dead in a ditch for all we knew. Your mother was worried sick.'

'I find that very hard to believe. Mum, worried about me? Yeah, right,' Daisy said with attitude.

'Of course I was worried.' Tara's voice came from behind me.

I turned around to look at my wife. She was wearing a bright red wrap-over dress, which made the most of her figure. If I hadn't known she'd been slaving over a hot stove all morning, I'd never have guessed. Unlike my wayward daughter, she looked the epitome of glamour. Her glossy dark brown curls tumbled over her shoulders, and her make-up was flawless. Daisy could do worse than to take a leaf out of her mother's book.

'It's one thing staying out all night and not telling us where you are, but you know we always go to the cemetery on Christmas morning...' Tara let her sentence trail off, but when Daisy stayed silent, she began to speak again. 'We waited for you for over an hour. Dad kept phoning you, but you didn't bother picking up, so we went without you.'

It was good that Tara had spoken up. I was absolutely livid. I could feel my blood boiling, so I wasn't going to be able to deal with Daisy in a calm manner, and she knew that. I didn't want to give her the satisfaction of getting a rise out of me, but she had. I'd leapt down her throat the moment she'd walked through the door. The last thing I wanted was for there to be a family bust-up. Today of all days. But I couldn't help myself. Daisy rebelled at every opportunity, which made me lose my rag.

'I'm going to have a shower,' Daisy said without any explanation.

She looked pleased with herself. I saw red. I couldn't stand by and let her think she'd got one over on me.

'Aren't you going to apologise?' I shouted, putting my hands on my hips.

My face jutted towards Daisy's as she walked past me, totally unbothered by the trouble she'd caused. She paused on the bottom step, then turned around to face me.

'I'm sorry I didn't text you. I'm sorry I didn't call. I'm sorry I missed the visit to the cemetery. Happy now?'

An impenetrable layer of defiance coated my daughter's words. Fury blinded me. All I could see was red, so I lunged at Daisy, but she ducked out of my reach before I could grab hold of her.

'Please, Des, it's Christmas Day. Let's not start World War Three,' Tara said, throwing me a warning look.

I withdrew my arm and bit down on my lip to stop myself from saying or doing something I might regret. Daisy took that as her cue to leave. She turned around and walked up the stairs. The bathroom door closed and locked. A moment later, I heard the sound of running water.

I stood in the hallway, trying to calm myself down. My pulse was racing, and my heart was beating ten to the dozen. Tara and I often wondered why Daisy was so different to Lily. But truth be told, Daisy was just like the two of us. She was stubborn to the last. Lily was the one with the alien personality. She was so highly strung, and she didn't get that from either of us.

I often wished we weren't so alike and felt bad that Daisy bore the brunt of my temper. I knew I was hard on her, but I didn't know how to handle her. She exasperated me. Daisy's refusal to conform felt like a personal attack so I lashed out at her.

Twins were meant to be one of the great wonders of nature. A blessing, people said. But it didn't always feel like that. We'd chosen their names to show they shared a special bond. Two flowers instead of picking the same initial or something that rhymed. Tara thought that would be corny, and I agreed with her whole-heartedly.

Lily brought out my sympathetic side. I was sorry to say Daisy brought out the worst in me. I wished that wasn't the case. But I saw her backchat as a threat to my dignity, my pride. We were locked in a power struggle. And there was only ever going to be one winner. That was me.

Our girls were clever. Something else they didn't inherit from Tara and me. Daisy had the edge over Lily academically, but more often than not, Lily's grades were better because she was a grafter.

'Dinner's ready,' Tara called up the stairs.

At least she'd had the sense to stay out of the way until the food was on the table. Tara, Lily and I were already seated when Daisy breezed into the room, pulled out a chair and plonked herself down on it. She might have smelled a lot sweeter than before, but she hadn't lost the attitude.

Daisy was an absolute nightmare. Even though she was clearly in the wrong, she was still behaving as though she was being given a hard time for no good reason. She loved playing the victim. Daisy lived life on her terms and didn't feel the need to explain or justify her actions to others. But if you asked me, she wouldn't get very far behaving like that. I knew first hand that stubbornness could be a curse.

Daisy was make-up-free, and her long blonde hair was scraped into a ponytail. We always made an effort to wear something nice on Christmas Day. It was one of the few occasions we bothered to take family photos, but it had either slipped her mind, or she was doing it to prove a point. It would be hard, but I was going to ignore the fact that she was wearing skinny jeans and a hoodie while the rest of us were dressed up. If she'd done it to get a rise out of me, she was wasting her time. My eyes were firmly fixed on the roast potatoes, and that was where they were going to stay for the fore-seeable future.

I was useless in the kitchen, so my services hadn't been required. It was my job to keep Tara's wine glass topped up while she basted the turkey and prepped the veg. She'd been slaving away for hours with Lily by her side to pull this meal together. I wasn't about to ruin things by bickering with Daisy. If she wanted to look like a slob, that was her prerogative.

The atmosphere around the table was tense enough without me adding to it. The only sound was coming from knives and forks scraping across plates. I couldn't ever remember having a Christmas Day like this. I'd never understood why people didn't love it as much as I did, but I totally got it now. Our presents were sitting unopened under the tree, but nobody seemed to be in the mood to find out what was inside them. I knew I was partly to blame for the hostility in the room, but I couldn't have let Daisy off the hook without saying something. Otherwise, she'd think she could walk all over me.

Daisy put her knife and fork down on her plate. She'd barely eaten a mouthful. Rage erupted within me. I couldn't help myself. I'd bitten my tongue for long enough.

'Is that all you're going to eat?'

Daisy glared at me.

'Do you know how long your mum and sister spent preparing this food?'

I began drumming my fingers on the table, impatience getting the better of me, but Daisy's stare was unwavering.

'All you've done is push your dinner around your plate.' I looked over at Tara and shook my head.

'I'm not hungry,' Daisy finally replied.

'I'm not surprised. I'd say you've got the hangover from hell, judging by the state you were in when you walked through the door.'

'Jesus, Dad! Give it a rest for once. I'm twenty-three years old. If I want to get drunk and stay out all night, that's exactly what I'll do.'

Daisy pushed her chair back from the table and stood up.

'And I'm fifty-three, although you seem to think I came down in the last shower. It might surprise you to know I remember what it was like to be young. I hate to be the one to burst your bubble, but the invincibility you're feeling right now doesn't last.'

'Save the lecture for somebody who gives a shit,' Daisy said, stomping out of the room.

'Where do you think you're going?' I called after her, but seconds later, the front door slammed.

51

DAISY

The effort to stay silent had demanded intense concentration. Dad's nagging was relentless, and I was losing the will to live, so I turned on my heel and got out of the house as quickly as I could. My head was still banging from last night's booze without listening to him droning on and on. My attitude stank. I knew that. Everyone knew that. It was old news.

I had a strong preference for doing things my own way in my own time. Big deal. You would have thought by now he'd have realised that constantly getting on my back didn't work. But he couldn't help himself. He had to try and rein me in at every opportunity. I'd spent years being dominated by him. I was powerless, and that had shaped my personality.

My grandad used to say I was full of devilment. He was right. As a child, I'd had a naughty streak a mile wide. I was always in trouble both at home and at school. Grandad told Mum and Dad not to be too hard on me. He thought I was a little character and warned them not to try to break my spirit. Even though Lily was everyone's favourite, Grandad had a soft spot for me, which went a little way to redress the one-sidedness. He understood me like nobody else did. I adored him. Worshipped the ground he walked on. I was seventeen when he died and it broke my heart. I'd lost my biggest cheerleader. I suddenly felt bad that I hadn't gone to pay my respects this morning, but I'd make it up to Grandad. I'd go and visit him tomorrow instead.

It was already getting dark as I turned out of our road. I slowed my pace, walked over to the covered bus stop and sat down on the red plastic seat. I pulled my Marlboros out of my bag, took one out of the pack and lit it. I inhaled deeply. Bliss. That first hit of nicotine helped me to relax and handle the stress.

'There's nothing running today, love,' a guy walking a French Bulldog said.

'Thanks,' I replied.

I already knew that, but it was nice of him to say. I was just trying to kill some time as nothing was open unless I fancied checking out the aisles in the BP garage shop. MacKenzie had thrown out a loose invitation when he'd dropped me off, but he was having lunch with his mum and brothers, so he was busy for the time being, which wouldn't have been an issue if things had gone to plan. I'd been expecting to be at home until early evening but Dad had other ideas. He was like a dog with a bone. He was going to give me a hard time over anything and everything if I hadn't cut and run.

The wind was picking up, and I didn't have a jacket with me. I'd left the house in such a hurry I'd forgotten to grab mine. This wasn't how I thought I'd be spending Christmas Day. I pulled the drawstring tighter on the neck of my top, then lifted up the hood, tucking strands of my hair inside in an effort to keep warm. I suddenly felt Baltic. I wasn't sure how long I could stay out in these conditions. The last thing I wanted to do was go back to the house and be forced to eat humble pie. Dad would be insufferable if he thought he'd got one over on me. I took my mobile out of my pocket and scrolled through my list of contacts.

'Hi, MacKenzie, it's me.'

'Hi, Daisy. I was just thinking about you. What are you up to?'

'I've just had a massive run-in with my dad, so I had to get out of the house. Are you still at your mum's?'

'Yes, but I'm gonna be heading home soon if you want to come over.'

'I thought you'd never ask,' I laughed.

'I'll come and pick you up. Where are you?' MacKenzie asked.

'There's no need. I'd prefer to walk.' I needed to let off some steam.

'As long as you're sure. It's no trouble.'

'Honestly, the walk will do me good.'

MacKenzie sounded keen to meet up. I couldn't wait to see him, too. Pleasure welled up inside of me when I thought of him. It kept me awake at night. He had the gift of making a person feel as though they'd known him all their lives.

I'd only just begun walking when the heavens opened. The torrential rain was sheeting down. It was the same every year. Wet and windy. Why did we never get any of the white stuff? The picture-perfect Christmas card scene always had one magical ingredient. Snow. Snow. And more snow. But we very rarely saw any of it in London. A white Christmas was rarer than Dad admitting he was wrong.

Icy cold water sent shivers down my spine as it ran down my back. I kept my head down as I paced towards MacKenzie's flat. When I turned into the top of the road, through the gloom, I could see he was just pulling up outside his place.

'MacKenzie,' I called out, breaking into a run.

I'd only gone a few steps when I started wheezing, so I made a mental note to myself to cut down on the fags, or my sprinting days would be over. I should make a New Year's Resolution to take up clean living like my perfect twin. Yeah, right. As if that was going to happen! By the time I'd made it to his front door, I was drenched.

'You're soaked to the skin. We'd better get you out of those wet clothes before you catch your death,' MacKenzie said with a glint in his beautiful eyes.

Here's hoping, I thought as I followed him into his flat. Maybe a wet Christmas wasn't such a bad thing after all.

'Take a seat, and I'll get you a towel.'

MacKenzie gestured with a flick of the head to the first door on the right. I pushed down on the chrome handle as he disappeared down the hallway. His living room was minimal. A black L-shaped sofa lay against the far wall. Two square glass tables sat at either end. Black and white photos of cityscapes lined the walls which were painted charcoal grey, a couple of shades darker than the laminate flooring. A huge TV took up most of the wall space opposite the seating area. Windows lined the wall adjacent to the door and had a view of the street. Opposite those was a low-level black storage cabinet.

When MacKenzie came back from the bathroom carrying a large black towel, I was standing in front of the fabric sofa. Because my clothes were drenched, I didn't want to sit down.

'Here you go,' he said, handing it to me.

'Thanks.'

'Let me get you a drink. What do you fancy?'

'White wine if you've got it, please.'

'Coming right up,' MacKenzie replied.

Given the amount I'd sunk last night, it would have been more sensible to ask for a soft drink, but I had a hangover to feed, so more booze would either kill me or cure me.

I quickly pulled my hoodie over my head, then wrapped the large towel around me. I untied the laces from my Adidas plimsoles and kicked them off. I set to work peeling off my skinny jeans, not an easy thing to do as they were dripping wet and stuck to my skin. My socks were just as tricky, but by the time MacKenzie came back into the room, I'd managed to get them off. My underwear was soaked, too, but I'd left it on.

'Hair of the dog,' MacKenzie laughed, handing me the glass. 'Have a seat.'

'Thanks.'

I reached forward with my right hand to take the drink while clutching the towel to my chest with the other before I perched on the chair.

'Are you starting to warm up?' MacKenzie asked.

'A bit.'

I could see goose pimples on my arm as I raised the glass to my lips and took a large gulp. As the wine flowed down my throat, I let out an involuntary shudder. The cold liquid seemed to make my body temperature drop. I put the glass on the table to keep it away from my skin. Then, I wrapped my arms around myself.

'You're freezing.'

MacKenzie scooted along the sofa towards me and pulled me towards his chest. I didn't resist. He was like a human radiator, so I nuzzled into him. He responded by sliding his hand up and down my thigh.

'Should we take this into the bedroom?' MacKenzie had a glint in his eyes.

'I think we should.' I nodded.

MacKenzie stood up and took hold of my hand. He led me out of the living room, down the hall and into his bedroom. Once we were by the bed, he untucked the towel I had wrapped around me and let it fall to the floor. I was glad the room was dimly lit. I could feel his eyes roaming over me. Drinking in every detail of my body. My heart was pounding. I had butterflies in my stomach. I was nervous. Excited.

MacKenzie unclipped my bra and slipped it over my shoulders. Then he pulled his T-shirt over his head. First, his hands. Then his lips. Then, his tongue explored my body. He broke away and slipped off his jeans and boxer shorts. Opening the drawer of the bedside cabinet, he slipped on a condom and lay down on the bed. Pulling me on top of him, I felt his stomach tighten when I straddled him, hard as a board. Pushing my knickers out of the way, he eased himself inside. I arched my back like a cat as pleasure coursed through my veins until we lay side by side. Exhausted. Fulfilled. Content.

'That was the best Christmas present ever,' MacKenzie muttered into my neck, his fingers trailing across my bare stomach.

'Wasn't it just,' I replied.

We lay like that for hours, bathed in the afterglow of sex. I had no intention of going home tonight, but I decided to text my mum just so my dad wouldn't have anything to complain about when I next showed my face. I wasn't in any hurry to return to the family home. I was enjoying MacKenzie's company too much. I couldn't get enough of him. He was like a drug I was craving.

'Is it OK if I stay here tonight?'

'It's more than OK,' MacKenzie replied.

'I'm just going to text home and let them know I'm staying out. I can't handle two guilt trips in the same week.' I laughed.

I could only imagine how this was going to go down with my mum and dad. But causing trouble was something I did best. I was a rebel at heart and a non-conformist. I loved stirring the pot. Because my dad was never very affectionate, I craved men's attention, so I wasn't going to let him ruin the moment for me by cutting my time with MacKenzie short. I was too happy to care what my parents thought right now. The fallout would have to wait until I was ready to deal with it.

52

DAISY

Boxing Day

I'd been awake for a while watching MacKenzie's chest rise and fall. His ultra-long lashes cast shadows on his face as his eyelids twitched. He was lost in sleep. I shifted next to him, hoping the movement would disturb him, but he didn't stir, so I got up and went to use the bathroom. When I came back, MacKenzie was sitting up in bed, leaning against the headboard with a spliff in his mouth. He took a long drag on it, then held it out to me.

'No thanks,' I said.

Much as I enjoyed smoking weed, it was a bit early for me, and I was keen to get back under the covers. Even though we'd had sex last night, I felt really awkward standing in the middle of his room with nothing on.

'Come on, have some. It's really good gear. Marrakesh's finest,' MacKenzie beamed. He knew he was going to be able to talk me into it.

'Well, if you insist,' I said, taking the joint out of his hand once I was under the quilt.

My head was all over the place. The weed gave me a much stronger high than when I'd smoked after having eaten.

'I thought you'd done a runner when I woke up, and you weren't here.'

'You're not getting rid of me that easily,' I smiled before taking another hit.

I decided not to add, you might not be getting rid of me at all if it goes tits up when I go home and I need a place to escape to, because I didn't want to scare MacKenzie off. If I nurtured a relationship with him, moving into his flat would become a natural progression. Goodbye, Mum, Dad and Lily, it's been nice knowing you. Not!

'God, I'm dying of starvation. Fancy a bacon buttie?' MacKenzie asked.

'Only if you're offering to cook. I don't suppose I could borrow some clothes, could I?' I smiled.

MacKenzie got out of bed, picked up the stuff he was wearing last night and walked across the room.

'Will this do you?' he said, lifting his dressing gown off a hook on the back of the door.

'That's perfect,' I replied.

He threw it over to me and then put his clothes back on.

I slipped my arms into the sleeves, pulling the edges of the fabric around me. It was soft and snug, and I found myself burrowing my chin into the collar.

'It suits you,' MacKenzie said before walking out of the bedroom and down the hall.

He was putting rashers of bacon into a frying pan when I walked into the kitchen. 'You never told me what happened with your dad.' MacKenzie tore his attention away from the sizzling frying pan and directed it at me.

'He went nuts when I didn't come home on Christmas Eve.'

'You're a grown woman, so if you want to stay out all night, it's nobody else's business.'

MacKenzie flipped the bacon over, and my stomach rumbled in response as the mouthwatering smell filled the air around us.

'Exactly, but he was livid that I didn't phone or text them to let them know I was OK. I get where he's coming from; I should have told them, but I was absolutely bladdered, so phoning home was the last thing on my mind. I'd fully intended to apologise, but the minute I opened the front door, he'd had both barrels loaded. I hadn't even stepped over the threshold when he tore into me.'

MacKenzie listened as he buttered thick slices of white bread. Taking the bacon out of the pan, he held it in mid-air to let the fat drain off of it before he laid it on the bread. When all of the base was covered, he put the lid on top and handed me the plate.

'I guess if I had a daughter who looked like you, I'd be overprotective too.' MacKenzie smiled.

Overprotectiveness didn't come into it. Dad just liked giving me a hard time.

'Do you want ketchup?' MacKenzie asked.

'Yes, please.'

MacKenzie took a bottle out of the cupboard nearest the cooker, then walked over and put it down on a small circular glass table on the far side of the kitchen. He pulled out a chair and dropped onto it. I took a seat opposite him. We sat in silence. Thoughtful. Comfortable enough in each other's company for the pause in conversation not to be awkward as we began devouring our sandwiches.

'If it's any consolation, my old man was an arsehole, too. He was a parasite. He never worked a day in his life and ponced off everyone who came into contact with him. He was a complete piss head. A waste of space. But he did us all a favour when he fucked off with some tart he met down the pub.'

MacKenzie was the first one to speak. His words sounded bitter. It was clear there was no love lost between him and his dad. I couldn't agree more. I'd found a kindred spirit. We both had dads that were scroungers. Lily and I did all the work and Dad helped himself to the biggest share. It was outrageous.

'I never got a chance to ask, did you have a good time at the party?'

MacKenzie's question took me by surprise, and I almost choked on my buttie when a piece of crust went down the wrong way.

'Are you all right?'

MacKenzie looked concerned as I coughed my guts up.

'I'm fine,' I replied when I finally caught my breath. 'It was OK.' I decided to keep my answer as brief as possible.

'What did you think of the big boss?' MacKenzie wiped sauce from the corner of his mouth with the pad of his middle finger.

'Do you want my honest opinion?'

MacKenzie nodded.

'I think he's vile.'

MacKenzie threw his head back and laughed.

'You must be the only woman in London who thinks so. They literally fall at his feet. The ladies love him. They can't get enough of him. Trust me. That's why Samson likes to keep himself looking sharp. He has his hair trimmed every week and is partial to a regular facial and manicure. His idea of dressing down is wearing one of his expensive suits with a T-shirt and plimsoles.'

I couldn't imagine what the fascination was. The man was a groper. More than that. He was a molester. A total fucking creep. He needed castrating. I'd be happy to oblige with a rusty implement. My blood ran cold when I thought about what he'd done to me. He'd taken advantage of me in my drunken state, which was unforgivable.

I was tempted to confide in MacKenzie, but I couldn't seem to find the right words. I was worried that he wouldn't believe me. He'd just told me women threw themselves at Samson, so he didn't need to force himself on anyone. Why had he done it? What was going through his head? Maybe he was drunk, too. My guess was he'd done this before. It was like I owed him something. Samson would ultimately be instrumental in whether Lily and I succeeded in this business. He knew that, so he was exercising his power, which made me question how many other victims had suffered before me.

No wonder so many sexual assaults went unreported. I knew I should speak up. Samson had no right to treat me like a piece of meat. My feelings were valid. I had a right to express them. And I had a responsibility to others. If I stayed quiet, he'd get away with doing this again, but I knew I wouldn't go through with it. It was out of character for me to keep my mouth shut and every fibre of my being urged me to report the bastard. But I couldn't bring myself to tell anyone what happened because I didn't want to relive the trauma. The voice of the victim was so important. Unfortunately, my fear of Samson had silenced me.

'I'm sticking with my first impression. I wouldn't touch him with a barge pole. He gives me the ick,' I said after a long pause.

MacKenzie was staring into space. He'd drifted off somewhere and was no longer part of the conversation. He seemed preoccupied. Like his mind was on other things. I could see by the look on his face he wasn't listening.

'Is everything OK? MacKenzie?'

'Sorry, babe, I missed that. What did you say?' He gave me a distracted smile.

'It was nothing important.' I shook my head.

I didn't want to talk about Samson anyway, so it would be good to get off the subject.

'Don't be funny with me,' MacKenzie said before reaching for my hand.

'I'm not.'

No wonder he was being a bit distant. I shouldn't have landed on him on Christmas Day without an invitation. There was nothing worse than people you weren't expecting barging in at a moment's notice. I should have read the signs. Not ignored the clues. It wasn't my style to hang around if I wasn't welcome. I wasn't a needy person.

'You're working tonight, aren't you?' I gave MacKenzie a get-out clause. I didn't want him to feel awkward. It was bad manners for the host to have to ask the guest to leave, and it wouldn't be right to put him in that position. 'You look tired. I'll let you get some rest.'

Lady Bountiful, eat your heart out. Lily's halo effect must have been rubbing off on me. As I got up to leave, MacKenzie caught hold of my arm.

'Don't go. I'm sorry if I've been a bit quiet. It has nothing to do with you. I've just got a lot on my mind,' MacKenzie smiled, and it lit up his face. There was a slight hesitation before he continued. 'I'm dreading going into work later. It's Boxing Day, for fuck's sake. I'd much rather stay here and get drunk with you instead.'

That brought a smile to my face.

'Why don't you tell me more about yourself? What's it like being a twin?'

I wished I wasn't. Things might have been different between us if we'd been born years apart. As it stood, I couldn't stand the sight of Lily. My life would be much simpler if my perfect sister didn't exist.

'In a nutshell, it's tedious,' I replied. I didn't want to waste precious time talking about her, so I gave him a bland answer to quell his interest in the topic.

MacKenzie grinned. 'In what way?'

That wasn't the response I was hoping for.

'Total strangers think nothing of coming up to us on the street and asking us random stuff. The stupid things people want to know infuriates me. Mindless, illogical questions they have no right to expect answers to.'

'Really?' MacKenzie seemed surprised. 'Like what?'

'Oh, I don't know. People ask things like can you and Lily tell what the other one is thinking? As if? We're not aliens or telepathic.'

'You're not? How disappointing,' MacKenzie laughed.

'I mean, I could hazard a good guess, but unfortunately, I'm not a mind reader with a psychic antenna.'

'It must be really weird.' MacKenzie shook his head.

'It makes me wonder what the hell is wrong with people. They don't bother engaging their brains before they start to speak.'

'I can't imagine going up to somebody I didn't know and asking them anything other than directions.'

'That's because you're a normal, well-adjusted member of the human race,' I smiled.

'Thanks for the compliment, but I'm not sure I'm that well-adjusted,' MacKenzie laughed.

'Sometimes we get asked if we share boyfriends!'

'No way!' MacKenzie's eyes were wide with astonishment. 'Who asks you that? Guys, I bet.'

'Correct.'

'From the picture you're painting, it does sound pretty tedious.'

'I rest my case,' I smiled.

MacKenzie swivelled around in his chair and pulled open a drawer. He took out a silver case about the same size as a credit card and continued rummaging around inside until he found what he was looking for.

'Do you fancy some rocket fuel?' MacKenzie waved a small bag containing white powder in the air. 'It's great gear. I save the highest quality flake for myself. This coke is eighty per cent pure. The bargain basement stuff I flog is only thirty per cent.'

'Not for me, thanks.'

I hoped he didn't think less of me because I wasn't joining in.

I watched while MacKenzie opened the lid on the silver case; one half of it was a mirror. Inside were a razor blade, a tiny long-handled spoon and a metal straw. He scooped a small amount of the cocaine up and put it down on the mirrored surface. Then, he chopped it with the razor blade to get rid of any lumps, forming it into two short lines. He put one end of the straw into his nose and ran the other end along the line, hoovering up the white powder.

'Come on,' he said, holding the straw out towards me. His pupils were already dilated.

I really didn't want to get pressured into taking cocaine.

'You don't know what you're missing,' MacKenzie replied before the second line disappeared up his nostril.

I didn't want to be part of this. Seeing MacKenzie snorting coke wasn't sitting well with me. It was time for me to make a move.

53

MACKENZIE

I hoped Daisy hadn't realised I'd been tossing and turning all night. She hadn't mentioned anything, and every time I'd glanced over at her, she'd been in a deep sleep, so I think I got away with it. She'd definitely noticed I was distracted by something while we were eating breakfast. I'd tried to bluff my way out of it, but it was almost impossible to focus on anything other than Arben. The weight of his threat was suffocating. The man was like a vulture hovering above me ready to pick my bones clean.

I was feeling on edge and irritable. Time was running out for me. He wanted his money back today, and I didn't have all of it. I'd got thirty grand squirrelled away, but I was a long way short. Arben wasn't the type of man to listen to excuses, so I'd have to do whatever it took to pull the rest of the cash together.

Teenagers and general pub users tolerated low-grade cocaine because I sold it cheap at forty pounds a gram. But I needed some punters with pots of cash filling their pockets through the doors tonight. The higher quality gear I had went for sixty pounds a gram. If I could shift a rake of those baggies, I'd be in with a fighting chance.

I hadn't meant to frighten Daisy off when I pulled out the coke, but it was a blessing in disguise that she'd gone home. Now, I could let myself into the club before anyone else arrived. I wanted to be the only one on the premises while I got the gear ready to sell. I acknowledged the guilt and then let it evaporate into thin air.

There was very little markup on the gear I was selling. Arben had got me over a barrel when he'd sold it to me in the first place. He'd shown me incredible hospitality and come across as a nice, genuine guy who'd wanted to help me out, so I hadn't been expecting him to be this impatient. Business had slowed down pretty much as soon as I bought the coke from him. I should have realised that people would be skint in the run-up to Christmas. I wished I hadn't been so hasty now. I would have been able to get by on the little bit of Samson's stock I had left if I'd known my customer base was going to disappear, but it was too late now to have regrets. I'd made the deal, so I was committed to seeing it through. I had to make some dosh one way or another.

As soon as I'd shown Daisy out, I jumped in my car and headed for the club. The roads were virtually deserted. People who weren't heading for the sales were still tucked up in bed, sleeping off their Christmas Day hangovers. Lucky bastards.

The staff car park was empty, so I ditched my motor in the space closest to the building. The security cameras would clock me going through the entrance, but if anyone questioned why I was so early – it wasn't like me to be this keen – I'd just say we had a busy night ahead of us, so I wanted to make sure everything was set up in plenty of time.

The alarm started counting down when I opened the glass door, but it stopped as soon as I entered the four-digit code. I walked down the corridor and into my office, closing the door behind me. I left my scales and small plastic bags in one of the filing cabinets. The gear itself was locked away in the safe. It didn't matter how much I trusted my staff, it was common knowledge that people could be light-fingered when the chance of making money presented itself. If you didn't want to be taken advantage of, you shouldn't put temptation in people's way.

When I opened the safe to get the cocaine, I couldn't help noticing Christmas Eve's takings were still sitting inside. As the two large stacks of cash stared me in the face, a thought suddenly sprung into my head. It was Friday today, so the banks were closed for the next few days. If I used the cash to pay Arben, who would know? Samson hardly ever showed his face at Eden's. He liked being elusive, surrounding himself with an air of mystery. He didn't often visit the club, knowing he'd create a frenzy of excitement on the rare occasion he did turn up. Samson likes to be considered a rare commodity. He didn't want people taking his presence for granted. He'd been here on Christmas Eve, so it would be highly unlikely that he'd turn up twice in the same week.

Eden's was a small club which had a turnover of around fifty thousand pounds a month. But December alone pulled in three months' worth of revenue thanks to office parties and punters generally in the mood for a good old-fashioned piss-up. Even before I counted it, I knew I was looking at a sizable wedge. As my hand wrapped around the first bundle, I smiled. How ironic? I'd proved my theory was correct. Temptation was impossible to resist. It was as simple as that.

Obviously, I'd pay back every penny. I wouldn't dare steal from Samson. I wasn't that stupid. I just needed to borrow the cash that was sitting in the safe for a couple of days. Just until the banks reopened. By the time I was able to pay in, I'd have flogged more gear.

As it was Boxing Day, we'd booked two headliners. A rock band and a Michael Jackson tribute act. I wanted to have all bases covered to pull in as much dosh as possible. Eden's should be heaving when we opened the doors. I was confident I'd make Samson's dough back in no time.

I pulled out the second pile of notes and fed them both into the money counter sitting on the side of my desk. There was enough in takings to pay back Arben, so at least I could get him off my back while retaining all of my fingers. I put the cash into a small black holdall and placed it back in the safe. Now that I'd sorted out my finances, I needed to start preparing some baggies before the rest of the crew arrived. I'd have to shift half a kilo of coke to raise thirty grand. A vein in my temple started to throb. That was going to be a big ask. I was a good salesman, but was I that good?

54

DAISY

I didn't smoke weed on a regular basis, so having it before breakfast
was a first for me. I'd been in no rush to go home until MacKenzie
had topped up the high with a couple of lines of the white stuff.
When he'd started snorting coke, it was a step too far. I hadn't
known what to make of it. Was this his usual morning routine? I
hoped not. I'd be lying if I said it didn't bother me.

It was bad enough that MacKenzie was a user, but I was strug-
gling to get my head around the fact that he was also a dealer. He
seemed totally unconcerned that he was peddling class-A drugs.
The thought of what he might be involved in scared the shit out of
me. He seemed like a great guy, but he'd got himself mixed up in a
bad situation. I'd set my sights on developing a relationship with
him and if he had a drug problem it was going to be an issue. But
I'd have to keep a lid on my concerns or I'd put myself off him,
which would be a shame as right now he was the best option I had.
And I could almost taste freedom.

I knew MacKenzie enjoyed a drink and smoked both cigarettes
and weed, but I'd had no idea he took cocaine. I smoked and liked
weed, too, and loved the taste of alcohol, so we had that in

common. But that was where I drew the line. Pills of any description, cocaine and heroin were strictly off-limits. It was too early to say if this was going to be a deal breaker for us.

I started making up a list of pros and cons in my mind. Taking hard drugs was definitely a con. Being a dealer was another. But he had lots of things going for him. MacKenzie had a great personality, and he made me laugh without even trying. He had the nicest set of eyes I'd ever seen. He wasn't a balloon animal, pumped up on anabolic steroids, who spent every waking moment working out in the gym. I'd never seen what the fascination was for men with bulging muscles or ones who preened. Being with a man who was glued to the mirror or checked his reflection in shop windows was a big turn-off. He might not walk a straight line, but who doesn't love a bad boy? Why sing with the choir boys when you could dance with the devil himself? Not me, for one. I felt better about the situation already, as the list of pros far outnumbered the cons. What more could a girl ask for than that?

Mum and Dad had taken an instant dislike to MacKenzie, but it wasn't just me that was drawn to him. He was a big hit with the ladies. I'd seen with my own eyes the way women flirted with him when he was behind the bar. And they weren't just looking for a free drink either. He had real charm. Real charisma. I'd go so far as to say magnetism.

He might look a bit scruffy and rough around the edges, but that's what made him attractive. There was a huge difference between scruffy and dirty. MacKenzie was hot on his personal hygiene. I wouldn't be with him otherwise. The thought of letting a man put a pair of grubby paws on me would be enough to send me running out of the door. He didn't wear designer clothes, but he always smelled nice and had lovely, straight, normal teeth. Natural teeth. Not a veneer in sight. I couldn't think of anything worse than being with somebody with ultra-white gnashers. The type people came back from Turkey with. Anyone who hadn't had cosmetic dentistry was rare these days. It wasn't surprising as we lived in a world that demanded perfection.

I'd been dreading opening the front door, unsure how I was going to be received after my Christmas Day departure from the dinner table. I paused on the doorstep with my key poised in front of the lock, giving myself a last-minute pep talk, mentally preparing myself for getting back in the ring for another twelve rounds with Dad.

'Is that you, Daisy?' Mum called from the kitchen when the door closed behind me.

'Yes,' I replied.

I dragged myself down the hall and stuck my head around the door. Mum was at the sink washing up. The bottom half of her arms were submerged in froth-filled water. She looked over her shoulder and glanced at me before looking away.

'Lily and your dad are in the garage going through some songs for your next gig,' Mum said, skilfully avoiding yesterday's fallout, although her tone was far from friendly.

'OK, I'll just get changed, and I'll go and join them.'

Lily was belting out 'Sweet Dreams' when I opened the door of our makeshift studio. That wasn't part of our set. What was going on? Over the years, I'd asked Dad a hundred times if we could mix things up a bit with some songs we'd never sung before to break the monotony of doing the same show over and over. The routine was torture for me, but he wouldn't have it. He'd tell me people paid good money to hear those numbers, so we had to sing them. They paid our wages. I was an ungrateful brat for even suggesting we shake things up. I shouldn't be bored singing number ones. Those songs would put us on the map, and then he'd drone on about famous bands who'd started off the same way. It was hell on earth listening to him.

'We've decided to try adding in some new material,' Dad said.

I couldn't believe what I was hearing. Was Dad feeling all right? Maybe we should call the doctor.

'That's great,' I replied.

Anticipation began fizzing around my body. We'd been stuck on the hamster wheel for so long that the thought of doing something different was both exciting and terrifying.

There was no mention of yesterday's bust-up. That, in itself, was a miracle. But there was still a strange atmosphere in the room. The unspoken words hanging between Dad and I were causing tension, which was hard to ignore. But at least we weren't arguing.

I'd thrown myself into rehearsals, which I hoped would pave the way to a peaceful day. For once, Dad had no complaints about my performance, and we'd got through the whole set without a single gripe. Hallelujah! Praise the Lord! It seemed like we were on the same page, which was a rarity in itself. Wonders never ceased.

I didn't want to jinx things, so I'd taken myself off to my room after we'd run through the songs for Tuesday night. I was beginning to regret shutting myself away. I had nothing to distract myself from thoughts of MacKenzie and spent the whole afternoon clock-watching, checking my phone every two minutes to see if he'd been in touch, but there were no missed calls or text messages. Come to think of it, he hadn't tried to stop me from leaving. Far from it, he'd practically shown me the door. That was another con to add to the list.

55

LILY

I felt like I was floating on air. Daisy and Dad hadn't exchanged a single cross word during the session, and it had made an enormous difference. He'd backed off, and she hadn't made one mistake. Her voice had never sounded better. I often wondered if Daisy had taken up smoking as an act of self-sabotage. So far, she seemed to be getting away with it. Cigarettes weren't having any adverse effect on her voice, but Dad would go mental if he found out. I hoped for her sake he never did.

He hadn't said anything, but Dad must have noticed the huge improvement. Maybe he'd take that on board and would adopt a new approach, but somehow, I doubted it. It wasn't just where singing was concerned. Daisy bore the brunt of Mum and Dad's criticism. They were so hard on her. She tried to put a brave face on things and make out she wasn't bothered, but I think she struggled more than she cared to admit.

Daisy was the black sheep. The problem child. It had been like that for as long as I could remember. It was toxic. Uncomfortable. It wasn't character-building. It would destroy a person's self-confidence if they let it. But Daisy was stronger than that. She was the spirited one. The life and soul of the party. Scarlet lips were her trademark. She had the confidence to carry off the look.

I got away with a lot more than my sister. My mum and dad often swept my mistakes under the carpet. Daisy wasn't shown the same leniency and I felt bad for her. But that had its downside, too. I was expected to be good at everything. My parents' high expectations made me hyper-critical of myself.

Although we were identical to look at, we were wired differently. I'd studied Daisy on so many occasions. Seeing my expressions and range of emotions played out by somebody else was weird, but fascinating. I knew what I looked like when I was happy, sad, angry. The list went on. I even knew what I looked like when I was fast asleep.

There was something different about today's rehearsal. Dad always insisted we sang the same set even though Daisy kept nagging him to let us break up the monotony with other material. He refused point-blank to add new songs in case she messed them up. I think he'd only asked me to sing 'Sweet Dreams' to get back at her because she'd ruined our Christmas. He knew it was one of her favourites.

I considered it an honour to perform to a crowd, so I was ready to give it my all every single time. When I went on stage, and the beam of light fell across it, I came alive. There was no better feeling in the world than looking out at the sea of faces smiling back at me. It was indescribable.

From my perspective, making people happy was a privilege. The audience's rousing reaction at the start of a song gave me the energy to sing it like it was the first time. Hearing people cheering and clapping and calling out for more was the best feeling in the world, something I'd never grow tired of experiencing.

We were living the dream. Things didn't get much better than this. If Dad and Daisy could maintain the ceasefire, we were going to have a bright future ahead of us. The sky was the limit. Bring it on. I was ready for stardom. This was what I'd been born to do. My destiny was calling.

56

MACKENZIE

Samson didn't want people bringing their own drugs into Eden's. He'd stopped short of putting up a sign stating only drugs bought on the premises could be consumed within its walls, but he took a hard line on anyone found breaking the rules. As a result, Eden's was never swamped with resident dealers. They never got past Igor, so over the years, they'd given up trying. He'd introduced airport-style searches, which meant it was really hard to get drugs over the threshold.

We showed an outward display of zero tolerance but turned a blind eye to drug use and supply inside as long as we were the source. People didn't just want to get drunk on a night out. They wanted to get high. The only dealing allowed within the club was by me. I sold in plain sight, none of that taking people into a dark corner. They ordered the gear along with their drinks. Job done. It worked like a charm.

I was trying to front it out, but I was a nervous wreck waiting for Arben's guys to get here. We hadn't arranged a time. They'd come when it suited them. I needed to be available, so I'd arranged cover on the bar. I didn't want to be stuck pulling pints when they finally got here.

Every dickhead in London had turned up at Eden's tonight. It was like a zoo on the dance floor. Judging by the state of the punters, they must have been on the beer since breakfast. Even though all my guys were on duty, it felt like we were very thin on the ground.

With big crowds, trouble was never far away. It loomed over the place like a dark cloud. I was glad I was free to lend a hand. The golden rule was never to take your eye off the ball. I was on high alert. If there was one thing I needed to look out for, other than fights and brawls, it was vomit. I was an expert at spotting the signs. A bit of staggering preceded the person adopting a stance of feet slightly apart, hands hanging down by their sides, before the floodgates opened.

Experience meant I could usually always tell who was driving the drama. The key was identifying the source of the problem and putting the person out of the joint before anything kicked off. That was where my guys came in. It was their job to keep the nice customers safe and the troublemakers out.

Being Boxing Day, the party was in full swing from pretty early on. The club hosting the live acts didn't open until nine, but the bar maintained regular hours, so the drinks were flowing. I'd been keeping an eye on a group of young lads who'd had one too many. They were getting a bit lairy and mouthy with each other. If I let things progress and they started getting physical, Igor and the guys would have a much bigger job on their hands.

We all had walkie-talkies with an earpiece and microphone attachment so we could hear each other over the racket. I pushed the talk button positioned on a wire close to my mouth.

'I'm going to need some assistance. Three lads are a bit worse for wear, and they need to be shown the door,' I said.

'We're on our way,' Igor replied.

Caleb reached the guys first.

'Come on lads, give it a rest. You're acting like a bunch of clowns,' he said, wading in between them.

Igor was a man of few words, which was why he let other door staff do the talking down while he watched their backs. He was good at reading people's body language to see if trouble was brewing. At the first sign of it, he'd intervene before any punches were thrown.

One of the guys took umbrage to his intrusion, and Caleb narrowly missed being glassed. It was time to go hands-on. No more talking, just moving. If the softly, softly approach failed and sheer force was called for, the huge Pole was the man for the job. As the guy took a swing at Caleb, Igor sprang into action. He covered his bald head with his arm to protect himself from being hit as he moved in close, inside punching range, but he was a mean fucker who could handle himself physically. Igor wouldn't think twice about kicking the shit out of somebody if they threatened one of his team. He was old school and didn't take too much notice of the new rules and regulations. He liked to fight fire with fire.

Igor got the guy in a clinch, then began moving him through the crowd towards the door. No match for my doorman, the fool thought he was big and mighty because he was fuelled by drink. The nicest punter can change into a different person once they've got too much alcohol inside them. Then, the threat of violence was never far away. We saw it all the time. You had to be a good scrapper to do this job.

The guy was trying to protest, but Igor was ignoring him. He just kept him moving. Caleb had tried sweet-talking the drunk into settling down. Neutralising brawls was the bread and butter of his role. But he hadn't listened, so now physical persuasion was required. He was doing his best to break free, but Igor had a firm grip on him, so he wasn't going anywhere. Caleb was escorting the two other lads out. They were going peacefully and not putting up any resistance. I brought up the rear. I knew it was all under control, but I wanted to see Igor fling the bloke out for the entertainment factor. He was a great leader and that filtered all the way down the line. When the shit hit the fan, my team watched each other's backs. They were a close brotherhood. Igor had created the strongest army with no weak links.

Caleb got up in the guy's face at the front entrance while Igor held him in a lock. 'You were warned to rein it in, but you ignored my request, so now I'm telling you to step away from the premises and don't come back.' He waited for a response, but the guy said nothing. 'If you choose to ignore me again, my friend here will beat the shit out of you.'

Caleb gestured with a sweep of his far from dainty hand to Igor.

'Do you understand?' Caleb asked.

The man was too drunk to form the words to answer, so Igor turfed him out onto the street, giving him a powerful shove for good measure to send him on his way. The guy staggered around the pavement before finally finding his feet. Then he started rocking backwards and forwards. I was sure he was about to become better acquainted with the floor, but he somehow managed to stay upright.

'Listen, lads, take him home before I call the police,' Caleb told the guy's friends.

'As if that's going to happen,' I said under my breath.

It looked like the guys were taking notice. I watched them walk over to the drunk, and the three of them disappeared into the distance. That technique usually worked every time. But I had no intention of involving the cops. Igor would deal with the fucker in his own way if he was stupid enough to come back, and by the time he was finished with him, the guy would be begging to spend a night in the cells.

I couldn't blame Igor. When things kicked off, did you fight, or did you talk? Words were never enough in some situations. That was where Igor came into his own. He'd wade in and show no fear. But he always made sure he was out of the CCTV's range before he let loose. I didn't have a problem with it. The beatings were always justified. Some people never listened to reason, and it was the only way he could get the message across.

'Great work, fellas,' I said to Igor and Caleb.

Then I went back inside and slipped down to my office for a sneaky drink. After that fiasco, I'd definitely earned it. I pulled out a bottle of dark rum and a glass and poured myself a hefty measure. As I started to swallow the large mouthful, I caught sight of Jermaine. He looked anxious when he stuck his head around the door. I knew what he was going to say before the words left his mouth.

'Sorry to disturb you, Mac, but Arben's guys are waiting for you in reception.'

'Can you bring them through, please?' I asked before knocking back the contents of the glass and refilling it.

Jermaine nodded before disappearing out of the door.

If I was quick, I should just about have time for some more Dutch courage. God knew I needed it. These men were big-time gangsters, and if it all went Pete Tong, they'd put me in a shallow grave without giving it a second thought.

I'd ditched the bottle and glass and was sitting behind the desk when Jermaine led the four guys into my room a few minutes later.

'It's busy out there, so I'd better get back,' he said, leaving me alone.

I knew that was true, but he hadn't seemed keen to stick around. Who could blame him? He was just a kid, and these guys meant business. It was probably a blessing that he'd shot through, as I didn't want anyone to witness the transaction I was about to make. The problem was, now I was completely at their mercy with no backup in sight. I was a lover, not a fighter, so I didn't rate my chances against the Adidas Army. It was just as well I wasn't planning to antagonise them.

'You know why we're here?' one of Arben's men said.

I nodded. 'Here you go,' I said, handing over the small black bag containing the money I'd taken out of the safe.

'No offence, MacKenzie, but you don't mind if I count it, do you?' the lead guy said.

'Of course not. I fully expected you to,' I replied. I didn't trust them either.

Getting up from my chair, I walked over to the shelves and took down the electronic money counter.

'It'll be quicker if you use this.'

And more accurate, too, I thought, although I kept that to myself. I didn't want to offend him by suggesting he might not be honest.

'I prefer to do things the old-fashioned way,' he grinned. 'May I?' he gestured to my chair, then sat himself down before I had a chance to reply.

Talk about making yourself comfortable. That hadn't been part of my plan. I wanted to see the back of them. The sooner I got them out of my office, the better, but I'd just have to bide my time and let him do what he had to do. Even though I knew all of it was there, I felt myself break out into a cold sweat. My pulse galloped in my wrist as he painstakingly leafed through every single note.

'Arben will be pleased. You've proved yourself to be trustworthy. But my friend here is gutted. He was looking forward to practising his carvery skills.'

The man flicked his head towards the guy standing nearest to him, who responded by pulling back the side of his Adidas puffer jacket. As I spotted the glint of metal coming off the knife sticking out of the waistband of his dark wash jeans, it sent my Adam's apple bobbing up and down while I tried to swallow down my fear. I had to hold my nerve. This wasn't the time to lose it.

'I'm so sorry to disappoint you,' I said to make light of the situation.

'Maybe I'll get lucky next time,' he replied before running his index finger across his throat.

My joke had fallen flat. This fucker meant business, I thought as he stared at me with cold, killer's eyes.

'Now, if you'll excuse me, gentlemen. The place is heaving, so I need to get back to work. Let me show you out.'

I led the way along the corridor without waiting for them to reply. Then I stood in the foyer watching them go while breathing a sigh of relief when a scuffle broke out at the front of the queue. Igor was never off duty. Being in charge of the door was a lifestyle, not a job. He was constantly watching people, trying to predict their next moves.

'I thought I told you to take this muppet home,' Caleb said.

'I don't know what you're talking about, mate. I've never seen you before,' the guy replied.

'So I've got you mixed up with somebody else, have I?'

Caleb put his hands on his hips and took a step closer to the guy.

'Yes,' he replied, nodding his head up and down.

Who was he trying to kid? They were the three blokes we'd thrown out earlier, but they'd turned up wearing baseball caps, thinking we wouldn't see through the pathetic attempt to disguise themselves. The lengths some people went to blew my mind. Samson was very selective about who we let in. If we'd turfed a punter out, they'd definitely be refused entry if they came back on the same night.

'Move along now, fellas,' Caleb said.

He blocked their path as Igor ushered a group of four scantily clad women into the foyer so that Leroy could check their ID.

'Hey, how come those slappers are allowed in and we're not?'

Bouncers were the judge and jury in a situation like this. They decided who was coming in or not. It was as simple as that.

One of the women spun around on her sky-scraper heels and glared at the mouthy guy.

'Who do you think you're calling a slapper?' she shouted.

The well-built, hefty woman was more than a match for her scrawny opponent. She looked like she could snap the guy in two, no problem. I didn't rate his chances if she got her hands on him, but I'd love to watch the fight.

'I suggest you apologise to the ladies right now,' Caleb said, realising that it was about to kick off in the foyer.

'Fuck that,' the mouthy guy replied.

As the woman went to swing for him, Caleb grabbed him by the back of the jacket and dragged him across the pavement. The last thing we needed was a bloodbath on our hands.

'Settle down, love, he's not coming in,' Jermaine said to the woman before pacing after Caleb, who was being followed by the man's two friends.

When one of my staff was involved in an altercation, we often swapped them out of the equation to let the dust settle.

'I'll handle this,' Jermaine said to Caleb.

Caleb let go of the guy and took several paces back but continued to watch from a close distance in case he needed to step in again.

'Your mate's had too much to drink. Do me a favour and take

him home so he can sleep it off,' Jermaine said to the mouthy guy's friends.

'Let me tell you something; you're going to wish you'd never been born if you come back here again tonight.' Caleb called after them as they weaved their way along the street away from Eden's.

Let's hope they listened this time. Caleb didn't make idle threats. I glanced over at Igor. He was watching the queue like a hawk looking for prey, so I felt comfortable leaving him to it. I needed to get my arse out on the floor so that I could shift some gear and recoup Samson's money.

There had been so much trouble tonight. The last thing I needed was to attract the unwanted attention of the police or, worse still, Samson. If he turned up now, he'd make mincemeat out of me. Pressure was building on all sides. I couldn't take much more of it.

57

DAISY

Saturday 27 December

I hadn't seen MacKenzie since I'd left his flat yesterday. So far, I'd resisted the urge to text him, but it was lunchtime now, and I still hadn't heard from him. I knew I shouldn't jump to conclusions. There was bound to be a logical explanation. Two live acts had been performing, so Eden's would have been rammed. I'd been hoping he'd find the time to give me a call last night, but he was probably up to his neck in it. MacKenzie wouldn't have finished work until the early hours of the morning and was more than likely still asleep. All of that made perfect sense. Logic told me I was reading too much into it. So why did I have a horrible feeling in the pit of my stomach? It was never a good idea to ignore your instincts, was it?

MacKenzie had tried to hide it, but he'd seemed a bit strange yesterday. Distracted by something. As soon as he realised I'd noticed, he started making an effort to sound interested in what I was saying, but the conversation between us was different than before, more forced. Dare I say, fake.

MacKenzie wasn't invested. I seemed to have lost my appeal in record time, which was a shame. I liked him more than ever. Wasn't that typical? Guys that gave me the ick, I had to beat off with a stick, but the ones I was attracted to ran a mile. I supposed that was what happened when you had a soft spot for bad boys. I needed to learn to avoid the 'love them and leave them' variety like the plague.

The more I mulled it over, the more certain I was that he was avoiding me. MacKenzie had been acting really weird since we'd slept together. I was kicking myself for jumping into bed with him too soon. But I was besotted with him. I hadn't realised the feeling wasn't mutual. It just went to show what a lousy judge of character I was. Thank God our fling was a closely guarded secret, or I'd be a laughing stock. Lily knew we'd kissed, but she didn't know we'd taken things to the next level, which was just as well. She would get some mileage out of this if she found out. She could give Dad a run for his money in the nagging department.

I had to try to stay busy to keep my mind off things, but every time I tried to distract myself, thoughts of MacKenzie kept entering my head. I was fed up of waiting. It was time to take matters into my own hands. I was a modern woman and felt comfortable making the first move. There was no law stating the man needed to message you first. A lot of men found women who used their initiative a turn-on. I hoped, for my sake, MacKenzie was one of them.

How's it going? Do you fancy meeting up?

I typed and then hit send before I had a chance to change my mind.

58

MACKENZIE

I heard my phone ping just as I was about to pull away from the kerb, so I picked it up from the passenger's seat and brought the screen to life. The message was from Daisy. Under normal circumstances, I would have jumped at the chance to meet up. I could think of worse ways to spend the afternoon. There was nothing better than a good shag to reduce a man's stress levels. Daisy was a great girl with a cracking body; slender but with curves in all the right places. What a shame I didn't have time to see her right now. And I was going to be busy for some time to come. Well, at least until I shifted a considerable chunk of Arben's gear. My balls would be blue by then.

I could still picture her when she'd walked in wearing that skirt that barely covered her arse, showing off a set of legs that went up to her armpits. I'd been desperate to get my hands on her, and she'd lived up to my expectations. I shook my head to dislodge the image, but it wouldn't go away. It was refusing to budge, stuck on play and going around and around on a loop.

I put the phone down on the seat and started the engine. I had to focus on the job in hand and not allow myself to get distracted.

couldn't afford to get caught up in back-and-forth messages right now. Time was of the essence, so I'd reply to her later. It wasn't a big deal. She'd understand; whether I liked it or not, work had to come first sometimes.

Customers had been thin on the ground last night. I'd been hoping they'd have wads of Christmas money lining their pockets, but there'd been no evidence of it. I'd mingled with the punters until the early hours, looking for some dance floor transactions. Nobody was biting. So I'd been working around the clock to try and flog as much cocaine as I could. It had been years since I'd done any street dealing. It was far more risky driving around London with a supply of coke in the car than selling it behind the bar or in the club. I was leaving myself open to get nicked, but desperate times called for desperate measures.

Where the hell was everyone? I'd been cruising around Ferndale Street in Brixton, which was meant to be a hotbed for drugs, for over half an hour, but the place was deserted. The only person I passed was a dude wearing a parka, who was more than likely another dealer, not a user. Business was non-existent, so I gave up pretty quickly. Hopefully, I'd have better luck at Eden's tonight. I couldn't ever remember a time that I'd sold so little. The market was saturated with cut-price coke. I couldn't give the stuff away.

I had a lot on the line and was too scared to think about what would happen to me if I didn't put the money back before Samson noticed. Nobody crossed him and lived to tell the tale. I knew that for a fact.

59

DAISY

The day came and went, and I still hadn't heard a peep from MacKenzie. He hadn't even given me a lame excuse as to why he couldn't meet up. He'd just left me hanging. Not cool. What a dickhead!

I'd taken myself up to my room with a bottle of Pinot Grigio and a glass so that I could relax in peace for the evening while avoiding the rest of my family. There was still a bit of an atmosphere in the house. I needed time to think and wasn't in the mood for company or making polite conversation. I'd done enough treading on eggshells to last me a lifetime.

MacKenzie had a lot to answer for; he was occupying my every thought. I couldn't decide what to do for the best. It would be so awkward seeing him on Tuesday if he hadn't made contact before then. But it was only Saturday, so I could well be jumping the gun by thinking he'd lost interest. The not knowing was the worst bit. If he wasn't interested, I'd rather he just had the balls to say so.

The wine was going down a treat, but by the time I was three quarters of the way through the bottle, a completely different scenario had started forming in my head. I just hoped he didn't pull the plug on our act over this. I'd never hear the end of it if he terminated our contract. My life wouldn't be worth living if that happened. Mum would be livid. Dad would be furious. Lily would be devastated.

Lily had always maintained that no singer should ever take the gift of performing lightly or for granted. Until we'd signed with Eden's, for me, it had been like pulling teeth. Being forced to work, so that my dad could skim off most of the money to bail himself out of debt, sucked. I'd have preferred to be on a date with Fred West than performing at our previous gigs. It had been a burden. Dad constantly reminded me to buck myself up; I had a job to do, and I did it, but I hated every minute of it. And then MacKenzie entered the scene and changed my outlook. I never thought I'd hear myself say it, but I loved singing at the club and would be gutted if it came to an end.

Lily took her performance seriously. Before and during a gig, she kept her vocal cords hydrated with mineral water. I preferred white wine. She also believed in looking after herself from the inside out. Lily loved healthy eating; goji berries and curly kale were two of her favourite things. She never missed having at least five a day, fuelling her body with food that supported her well-being. What a load of crap! I was a takeaway junkie and was doing just fine on my diet of fast food. She was always trying to get me to change my eating and drinking habits, but Lily did enough clean living for both of us. Life was too short to waste time reading the packaging to check for the saturated fat and salt content.

Lily and I were due to perform on the thirtieth. For the first time since we'd started working at Eden's, I didn't want to go. I might have to pretend to be ill, struck down by a mystery virus. Dad wouldn't buy that. I'd need to be on my deathbed to get out of taking my place on stage. The show had to go on no matter what. I'd send MacKenzie one more message and see what happened. I didn't want him to misinterpret what I was asking, so I was going to get straight to the point. I wasn't known for my tact and diplomacy. I'd be direct. Frank. Blunt. It was the only way in a situation like this.

Why are you airing me? Have I done something to piss you off?

I pressed send and then stared at my phone, waiting for a sign that MacKenzie had seen my message, hoping he was typing a reply. But nothing happened. I decided to reread the message I'd sent to check it had been delivered, but when I tried to focus on the words, the letters began swimming in front of my eyes. After waiting longer than I should have, I put my phone down on the bedside table.

I was exhausted, but my mind was still whirring. Sleep wasn't going to come easy tonight, so I decided to polish off the rest of the bottle of wine for medicinal purposes, reasoning it would help me drift off. I turned off the light and then snuggled under the covers, hoping to go out for the count the minute my head hit the pillow, but the alcohol wasn't having the desired effect.

I'd been tossing and turning for hours, checking my phone every two minutes to see if MacKenzie had replied well into the early hours of the morning. The longer it took him to respond, the more angry and wound up I was getting. Who the fuck did he think he was, treating me like this? How long did it take to pick up the phone and drop a quick reply? Minutes. No, seconds.

I was in two minds as to whether to send him another message telling him exactly what I thought of him. I managed to stop myself in the nick of time before my tipsy brain got carried away with itself. Why did alcohol always lower my inhibitions and make me do really stupid things? Thanks to the bottle of wine I'd sunk, my brain couldn't tell the difference between a good decision and a bad one. Step away from the phone before you end up doing something you're going to regret, I told myself. For once, I hoped I took my own advice.

Tuesday night was going to be hell, but I'd have to brazen it out. I couldn't afford to bail, or I'd lose face, and I didn't want to give him the satisfaction of thinking I was bothered. If this was how MacKenzie was going to treat me, I'd had a lucky escape. Dodged a bullet. It was his loss, not mine. I'd wear the sexiest outfit I could find in my wardrobe. The shorter, the better, so he could get a good look at my legs and see what he was missing. Fuck him. If he'd thought I was an ice maiden before, he was in for a rude awakening.

60

MACKENZIE

Sunday 28 December

I'd just finished serving a customer when Samson stormed up to the bar with a face like thunder. Just when I'd thought things couldn't get any worse than they already were.

'In my office, now,' he demanded without bothering to exchange pleasantries.

My balls had started tingling at the sight of him. He was absolutely livid.

Samson stood in the doorway, his nostrils flaring, waiting for me to catch up. I'd been dragging my heels, trying to buy myself some time so that I could come up with an excuse. I wasn't in any hurry to listen to the bollocking I knew was coming my way. I'd barely stepped over the threshold when he slammed the door shut behind me. His impatience was plain to see.

'Perhaps you'd like to tell me where my fucking money's gone,' Samson roared.

His eyes were blazing. As he stood in front of me, waiting for my answer, I could see him grinding his teeth. I never expected him to find out that the cash was missing before I'd had a chance to replace it, so he'd caught me off guard. I'd been so busy trying to flog the gear I'd forgotten to sort out an alibi for myself. I'd have to come up with a feasible explanation as I couldn't tell him the truth.

'I'm still trying to get to the bottom of what's happened.'

That was the best response I could come up with off the top of my head.

'So you knew, and you didn't fucking tell me. Why not?' Samson narrowed his eyes and glared at me.

I was beginning to wish I'd denied all knowledge now. My hands were sweaty, and my mouth had dried up. It was as though every drop of moisture had drained out of my body in an instant. It was hard to think straight as fear took hold of me. My life was on the line.

'I didn't want to worry you until I knew the details.'

'When did you realise the takings were short?' Samson put his hands on his hips and kept his eyes trained on me.

'Yesterday evening.'

'So let me get this straight; the money from Christmas Eve was in the safe when you came in on Boxing Day.'

'Yes.'

'But when you opened up yesterday, some fucker had helped themselves to it. Is that what you're saying?'

'Yes.'

'You're the only person who knows the combination.' Samson wasn't trying to hide the fact he suspected me, which made my pulse rate soar.

'Not the only person; you know it as well.'

'Don't be such a fucking smart arse. Why would I steal my own money?'

I was kicking myself for saying that now. I'd managed to rile him up even more. I should have covered my tracks better and pretended the club was broken into. Staged a robbery or something. The biggest mistake I'd made was thinking Samson wouldn't be back at Eden's any time soon. I'd allowed myself to be sloppy. And now I was going to suffer.

'It's not impossible to crack a safe, though, is it?' I blurted out. It was the best thing I could come up with under pressure.

'No, but that doesn't make any sense. If you were going to go to the trouble of breaking into a safe, you'd take all of the money and not just some of it, wouldn't you?'

Fuck! I'd dug myself into a hole, and Samson was like a crazed Jack Russell trying to root me out.

'Do you seriously expect me to believe the crap you're spouting out?'

Samson's eyes bored into mine, which made the pulse at the side of my neck start to throb.

'This must have been an inside job, and you're looking as guilty as fuck from where I'm standing. Help yourself to a little Christmas bonus, did you?'

Panic started rising in my chest, but I couldn't let it show.

'I can assure you I didn't touch your money, and none of my guys would have done either. I can vouch for all of them. They're one hundred per cent trustworthy.'

'So what's happened to the takings then? One of your lot must have stolen them. They didn't disappear into thin air.'

'My guys didn't touch the cash.' That was the first true thing I'd said to Samson this evening. 'As I mentioned earlier, I'm trying to find out what happened.'

'Well, try harder.' A nerve twitched in the side of Samson's jaw as he got right up in my face.

'Any crook worth their salt would know the banks have been closed for days, so the Christmas takings would be in the safe until tomorrow.'

I could see by the look on his face that Samson wasn't buying my explanation.

'Have you checked the CCTV?' Samson asked.

'Of course.'

'And?'

Samson's impatience was palpable. I could sense he was one step away from grabbing me by the throat and shaking the answers out of me.

'The cameras on the back entrance have malfunctioned, so they haven't recorded anything.'

That was complete bullshit. I'd well and truly fucked up. I'd have to make sure I wiped the tapes as soon as Samson stopped chewing me up and spat me out. He'd tear me limb from limb if he found out I was lying.

'I take it you've checked the doors. Was there any sign of a break-in?'

'Not that I could see, but there is a broken window in the cellar. I guess somebody could have got through that.'

A newborn mouse wouldn't have fitted through the tiny piece of broken fan light. I'd be a dead man if Samson asked to see it.

The crap was rolling off my tongue at a rate of knots. One lie seemed to feed another. It was a risky strategy, but I couldn't think of an alternative. Samson's grip was tightening with every minute that passed. Fear was a powerful driving force and it was making me do reckless things.

'When did the window break?'

I threw my hands up in front of me. 'I noticed it on Boxing Day.'

Samson's face turned red and then purple. 'For fuck's sake, MacKenzie! Are you completely incompetent? Why hasn't it been fixed?'

'Everything's closed for Christmas. I'll get somebody to have a look at it tomorrow.'

'You're supposed to be the manager, and you didn't think it was a priority to make sure all the cameras were functioning when you went home for the evening and left all that money sitting in the safe.'

'They were working when I checked them. They must have malfunctioned during the night, or maybe the thief tampered with them.'

I was on a roll, but Samson was a hard man to convince.

'This all sounds a bit too convenient if you ask me. There's a broken window in the cellar, and the cameras covering that area just happened not to be recording when the Christmas takings were filling the safe.'

He was right. My story did seem a bit hard to swallow, but I'd just pulled it out of my arse.

'You've got all the answers, haven't you? Apart from the one to the million-dollar question. Where's my fucking cash?'

Samson lunged forward and grabbed hold of a fistful of my T-shirt. My heart started hammering in my chest and I nearly lost control of my bowels.

'I honestly have no idea.'

Samson held me in front of him while his eyes scanned my face. Then he pushed me backwards.

'I don't believe you. But I'll tell you this, whether you stole my money or not, you're in charge of the club, so that makes you responsible for any losses. I want every penny of it back by the close of play on Wednesday.'

'You can't expect me to pay the money back. I had nothing to do with this.'

I shook my head, unable to believe what Samson had just said.

'You're in a position of authority, so you're ultimately respon-sible for anything that goes missing from the premises. I'm not going to be out of pocket.'

I felt a bead of sweat slowly trickle down my back.

'Jesus Christ. I wish you'd told me that before I'd accepted the job.'

'Aww, my heart bleeds for you. Why don't you take me to the employment tribunal?' Samson smiled.

'There's no way I can come up with that sort of money by then. You're going to need to give me more time.'

Talk about déjà vu. My head felt like it was about to explode. Threats were coming at me from every angle. As soon as I dealt with one, another one was there to replace it. I didn't know who I was more scared of upsetting: Samson or the Albanians. They were equally dangerous.

'I don't need to give you anything. You need to give me back the money you stole before the time runs out, or there'll be a price to pay. Now get out of my office, you fucking snake. I don't want to see your ugly mug unless you're about to hand me a big wad of cash. Understand?'

61

DAISY

Tuesday 30 December

Mum and Dad had made last-minute plans to go away with some of their friends to see in the New Year, which was an unexpected blessing. If MacKenzie and I ended up having a massive argument at least they wouldn't be at the club to witness it. I hoped it wouldn't come to that. I'd like to think I could come out of this mess retaining a tiny shred of dignity. But his rejection stung, so if he didn't handle this sensitively, my inner fishwife would come barrelling out. I'd be powerless to stop it.

I'd spent all afternoon getting ready to make sure I looked my best. I'd chosen a low-cut, red, figure-hugging top to go with my ultra-short, black leather mini skirt and pointed-toe black stilettos that tied around my ankles in a series of criss-cross straps. I'd decided to cover all bases, making sure he had a view of the top and the bottom so he'd be in no doubt about what he'd let slip through his fingers. One man's loss was another man's gain. Childish behaviour, I know, but in my opinion, necessary. MacKen zie's future girlfriends would thank me for taking this stand for the sisterhood.

As usual, we'd arrived at Eden's way before we'd needed to. Thank you for prolonging the agony, Lily. She'd glared at me with a sour look on her face when I poured myself a large glass of white wine, but she had the good sense not to say anything. I was psyched up and ready to do battle, so she could probably feel the anger radiating off me, which had nothing to do with any secret twin code. My fury was bubbling under the surface, and I was having trouble hiding it.

I was primed and ready to give MacKenzie the cold shoulder, but the cowardly fucker was keeping himself well out of the way. I'd secretly hoped he'd be waiting in the foyer with a huge bunch of flowers begging for my forgiveness, but he was nowhere to be seen. After wiping away the drops of condensation that had settled on the glass with the pad of my thumb, I made a promise to myself. I wasn't going to waste another minute thinking about him. I could take a hint. The dickhead didn't need to spell it out to me in capital letters. I was another notch on his bedpost. Not something I was proud of, but I wasn't going to dwell on it either.

Our set had gone brilliantly. There was a great crowd on the floor tonight. Their energy was infectious, and I was buzzing by the time we hung up our mics and headed for the dressing room. I opened the fridge, took out the chilled bottle of Pinot Grigio and topped up the glass I'd left on the counter from earlier, filling it right up to the brim.

'Are you sure you can't get a bit more in there?' Lily stared at me as she looked into the mirror.

'For God's sake, Lily, give it a rest,' I snapped.

The last thing I needed was her nagging me over my alcohol consumption. I never told her to let herself go and live a little instead of being so anal all the time. Interesting how she'd managed to hold her tongue before our performance. She was calculated. I'd give her that.

I picked up the glass and took a large gulp to avoid spilling it while carrying it over to the sofa. Plonking myself down, I watched Lily in my peripheral vision, giving me the side eye. I never understood why she didn't wait until we got home to take her make-up off. When I'd questioned her, she'd mentioned some rubbish about the foundation clogging her pores if she didn't remove it immediately. What a load of bollocks! I regularly went to sleep wearing a full face of slap, and my skin looked no different to hers. I couldn't take the eyeballing any longer, so I got to my feet.

'I'm going for a smoke.'

Lily swivelled around on the stool before she told me not to be too long.

'You don't need to wait for me. I'll get a cab,' were the last words I said to her.

Moments later, I sensed my life was about to change forever when Lily was bundled into the back of a car and driven away into the night. The situation was far from normal. Something must be seriously wrong at Eden's for this to have happened. I was beginning to wonder if it was the respectable establishment it claimed to be. MacKenzie openly dealt drugs and Samson and his music mogul friend Travis had a seediness about them. Who knew what was really going on behind the scenes?

I still couldn't believe Lily was gone. Trying to work out why somebody would snatch her was making my brain ache. There wasn't a clear motive and the kidnappers hadn't left any clues behind. The first thought that entered my head was that the men must have taken her by mistake. I didn't care what MacKenzie said, Lily wasn't involved in anything dodgy. I knew that for a fact.

MacKenzie's response was weird when I'd told him about Lily, which had made me uncomfortable. I'd suddenly felt concerned for my own safety, so I'd gone back to the dressing room, picked up my phone, coat and bag along with Lily's, and then called an Uber.

MacKenzie's attitude towards me had changed since Boxing Day. I'd put that down to the bender he'd been on and the fact that he felt awkward after we'd slept together. But why was Igor lying to me? He was covering up for somebody. I just needed to work out who.

Lily was in big trouble. If I didn't do something to help her, she could end up losing her life. Guilt stabbed at my conscience. I'd been such a bitch to her and had wished bad things would happen to her countless times. Now that the shit had hit the fan, I realised I didn't want her to come to any harm and would do anything in my power to find her and bring her home. I'd be putting myself in danger, but I owed it to her. I'd put her through hell over the years. It was time to make amends.

62

LILY

It all happened so quickly. I didn't have time to think, let alone react. One minute, I'd been taking my make-up off, and the next, I was dragged out of the club and bundled into a car. My eyes darted around and settled on the dimly lit passageway at the side of the club. The sight of Daisy gave me a small glimmer of hope. I had to stay calm and not let fear get the better of me. My sister would raise the alarm, and all of this would be over soon.

A knot twisted in my stomach as the car turned left onto Grove Lane and began heading towards Camberwell Green. We passed The Oval and Vauxhall Park before the driver sped along Nine Elms Lane. I'd been trying to pay attention to the route he'd taken as I hadn't been blindfolded, but by the time he turned into an industrial estate, I'd lost my bearings.

I'd battled to hold them in, but tears rolled down my cheeks when the driver stopped the car outside a detached modern unit at the edge of the plot. It was in a secluded position, well away from the other lock-ups, nestled between two sets of railway lines, which stretched far into the distance.

The man on my right opened the back passenger door and

stepped out onto the forecourt. Then he leaned in and pulled me out. I tried to resist, but it made no difference. The guy in the front passenger seat got out of the car and began walking towards the white corrugated iron building. The man restraining me dragged me along behind him. I began shaking like a leaf as I watched him operate the black electric roller shutter door. When he switched on the overhead lights, I was almost blinded by the glare bouncing off the shiny white floor. The walls were white, too. Black metal beams ran up the opposite wall and across the ceiling about a metre apart. Once we were inside the cavernous double height room, the lead man tore the gaffer tape off my mouth and pulled out the gag. I gasped for air, swallowing lungful after lungful, trying to ignore the throbbing skin around my mouth.

'If you start screaming or making a racket, it's going back on.'

I jumped when the man spoke so suddenly in a deep, threatening voice. His speech appeared slurred, as though he was drunk, but I knew that wasn't the case. The world seemed to be moving in slow motion. What was going on? I didn't know who had taken me or, more importantly, why. My heart pounded wildly in my chest as the desperate urge to survive kicked in. Then, a wave of nausea washed over me. The taste of fear on my tongue left me feeling lightheaded.

'What are you going to do to me?' I asked, having found the strength to speak up.

'Now that would be telling,' he replied with a menacing look on his face.

His words sent a shiver down my spine. My mind travelled to the scary place where murders occurred. Twenty-three was too young to die. I refused to let myself think about that in case I fell to pieces. I couldn't afford to let that happen. So, I pushed the dark thoughts out of my mind.

'The boss will be here soon. You might as well sit down and

make yourself comfortable,' the man said, gesturing to a petrol-blue velvet sofa at the back of the room.

Waiting to see what was about to unfold was terrifying. But I did as instructed. Compliance was the name of the game if I wanted to get out of this unscathed. After I sank into the soft surface, I cast my eyes around the room. Several doors led off the central space and there was a mezzanine level above where I was sitting, reached by a black metal staircase. There were no windows but sections of the ceiling were made of glass panels. It was modern. Minimal. Immaculate. Everything was either black or white. The warehouse clearly wasn't used for industrial purposes. Nonetheless, the surroundings had an ominous feel to them.

I'd hoped focusing on mundane details might help to quell my rising panic. It wasn't working. I could feel my legs trembling. I just hoped it wasn't noticeable. I glanced down at my hands resting in my lap. My wrists were aching from being bound. Every tiny movement was excruciating as the rigid plastic cuffs dug into my skin. I'd like to say I was confident that Daisy would come to my rescue and save the day. Save me from whoever had kidnapped me. But that would be a lie. She hated my guts, so she wasn't likely to ride into battle for me no matter how much I wanted her to.

63

MACKENZIE

New Year's Eve

My head had barely touched the pillow when my mobile pinged. I reached over to the bedside table and picked it up, reading the message with bleary eyes.

> Counterfeit notes are not an acceptable form of currency. There will be consequences.

What the fuck? I'd counted the money myself, and so had Arben's guy, for that matter. Neither of us had noticed anything dodgy, and now that it was no longer in my possession, I had no way of proving the cash was genuine. This had to be a misunderstanding unless Arben was trying to pull a fast one and double-cross me. I wouldn't put it past the slimy git, but it would be a suicidal move to accuse Arben of lying.

I felt my blood run cold as I read the message again. My nerves were jangling. I needed something to calm me down. I got out of bed and made my way to the kitchen. After turning on the light, I went over to the fridge and took out a cold can of Stella. I glanced up at the clock hanging above the cooker. It was five to seven. It was a bit early to be on the sauce, even by my standards. But desperate times called for desperate measures. I opened the ring pull without giving it another thought, gulping down the alcohol so fast some of it spilt down my chin.

The booze hadn't even taken the edge off. So I took a bag of coke and my silver case out of the drawer, laying them down on the table. Using the little spoon, I scooped up a small amount of the rocket fuel and chopped it on the mirror with the razor blade before arranging it into two lines. I snorted it through the straw, rubbing the tiny amount of residue left behind into my gums. Waste not, want not. Moments later, my heartbeat speeded up. The buzz wasn't far behind, which drove the anxiety out of my body. Now that my confidence had returned and I was on top of my game, I'd be able to think straight and work out a strategy for dealing with the Albanians.

There was no way I could show my face at Eden's tonight. The Adidas Army were bound to make an appearance. And I valued my fingers too much to have a run-in with that mad bastard wielding his knife. He'd been itching to dish out some punishment the last time we'd met, so he'd be unstoppable now that Arben was giving him the green light.

My thoughts turned to Daisy. Arben had threatened to sell her to the highest bidder. I didn't want to imagine the kind of depraved things that would happen to her. As I tried to dislodge the sickening thought, another one came barrelling towards me. Was Arben behind Lily's kidnapping? I felt myself break out into a cold sweat as the Stella started sloshing around in my stomach. If he was, she was really going to suffer. All because of me. Oh, fuck. Poor Lily. I shook the idea from my mind. I couldn't allow myself to get bogged down in guilt, or it would cloud my judgement.

I'd have to phone Igor later and pretend to be struck down by a mystery illness. It didn't matter what I said was wrong with me as long as I mentioned the words highly contagious. Samson would go mental when he found out I'd gone AWOL on one of the busiest nights of the year. But there was no way I could turn up for my shift. I didn't have the money I owed him or a death wish, and I wouldn't bring trouble to Eden's door. My guys would have their work cut out tonight without me adding to it.

The only saving grace was that Arben didn't know where I lived, and I had every intention of keeping it like that. The way I saw it, I had two choices. I either had to lie low in my flat or get the hell out of here. I mulled over the equally undesirable alternatives for a nanosecond. Cutting and running seemed like the best option by far.

64

DAISY

I'd spent a restless night racking my brain, trying to work out who'd taken Lily. She wasn't the sort of person to have enemies. Everybody loved her, and there was no way she was mixed up in anything dodgy. Why would MacKenzie even think that unless he was trying to take the focus off himself? Whatever the case, I was sure he knew more than he was letting on.

I was tossing and turning under the quilt, trying to make sense of what happened last night, going around in circles, but none of the pieces of the puzzle seemed to fit, when I heard a car pull up outside the house. As the two car doors closed, I glued myself to the mattress and huddled under the duvet. Had the people who'd taken Lily come to get me now? Footsteps on the garden path sent my heart racing. I was on the verge of tears by the time I heard a key turn in the lock.

'Lily. Daisy. We're home.'

Dad's voice came thundering up the stairs and sent a fresh wave of panic crashing towards me. Just when I'd thought things couldn't possibly get any worse, Mum and Dad had unexpectedly come home. I should have been relieved that the kidnappers weren't breaking through the front door. But this was a different kind of catastrophe.

What the hell were they doing here? They weren't due back until New Year's Day. Fuck. Fuck. Fuck. What was I going to do? I couldn't tell them Lily was missing and that I'd taken MacKenzie's advice and hadn't called the police. They'd lose their shit.

'Lily,' Dad shouted, then paused for a moment. 'Daisy,' he called, then paused again.

I had to think of something fast, but my head was scrambled. Then, an idea suddenly came to me. I flew out of bed, tiptoed across the room and inched the door open as quietly as I could. Lily's bedroom door was open, so I reached around and grabbed her white dressing gown that was covered in bright pink hearts from the hook and slipped it on over my pyjama shorts and vest. Then I legged it down the stairs and went into the kitchen. I wasn't at all sure that this was going to work, but I didn't have another option.

'How come you're back so early? Is everything all right?' I asked, trying to hide my breathlessness.

Mum was sitting at the table looking like death warmed up when I walked into the room.

'Hello, love,' Dad said when he caught sight of me.

He was standing next to the fridge, filling a glass with mineral water.

'I'm sorry, I hope I didn't wake you. I'd forgotten you had a late night,' he continued.

Wake me? I'd barely slept a wink, but I kept that to myself. If I was going to be able to pull this off, the less interaction I had, the better. So far, so good. Dad never showed me this much concern or called me love, so the plan must be working. He would usually have been able to tell Lily and me apart without any trouble, but because I was wearing Lily's dressing gown, he'd automatically presumed that was who he was talking to. Pretending to be Lily to buy myself some time might just work after all.

'What's going on?' I asked, then cleared my throat. My voice was croaky from performing last night.

'Didn't you get my text?' Dad asked as a frown settled on his face.

I shook my head.

'I thought it was strange when you didn't reply. I messaged you about midnight to say Mum was really poorly. She started feeling sick almost as soon as we arrived and spent all evening with her head down the toilet. It's some kind of vomiting bug,' Dad said.

'Oh no. You poor thing,' I said, welling up, just as Lily would have, doing my best concerned daughter act.

Don't get me wrong, I didn't wish my mum ill, but Lily would have been far more bothered by the news than I was, and I needed to keep my performance as authentic as possible to keep the pretence going.

'There's nothing worse than a vomiting bug.'

I threw Mum my best sympathetic smile as I channelled my inner Lily and continued to react the way she would have.

Mum gave me a cursory glance by way of acknowledgement. But it was clear she wasn't with it because she was feeling so rough. To be fair, she looked terrible. She had dark circles below her eyes and hadn't said a word since she'd got here.

'Bloody typical, isn't it? We were really looking forward to catching up with our friends. But there was no point in being away if we were going to be holed up in the hotel. Mum just wanted her own bed, and I don't blame her one bit,' Dad said, placing the glass of water down in front of her. 'We'll go away another time to make up for it. How are you feeling?'

Mum shook her head. 'Terrible,' was the only thing she managed to say.

Dad was fussing around Mum like a blue-arsed fly. It was an absolute blessing that he was preoccupied with looking after her.

'Where's Daisy?'

When Dad asked me that question, I felt like jumping for joy, but I had to restrain myself.

'She stayed over at a friend's last night,' I replied.

'I bet she did. I can't say I'm surprised that the minute our backs were turned she went off gallivanting.'

Dad had a very short memory. He seemed to have forgotten that I did whatever I wanted, whether their backs were turned or not. It took every ounce of determination I had not to take the bait. If I did, I'd blow my cover, so instead, I had to let that thought disappear into the ether and concentrate on playing my role to perfection.

'How was last night's gig?'

A change of course to our conversation couldn't have come at a better moment.

'It went really well.'

'Did Daisy sing OK without me there to crack the whip?'

What a fucking cheek. Dad's comment made me see red, and I felt myself bristle, but I had to swallow down my anger.

'Yes, she was fine.'

I was more than fine. I was on fire, but I couldn't go overboard, or Dad would smell a rat. I needed to get off the subject before my temper made an unwelcome appearance.

'You look awful, Mum. Why don't you go to bed?' I suggested, going off on a tangent.

Mum couldn't quite manage a smile, but she gave me a half-hearted nod as she pulled herself up from the table. She was as weak as a kitten. She ran her hand along the white tiled wall as she made her way towards the kitchen door.

'Don't you think you should help her? She looks a bit unsteady on her feet,' I pointed out.

'Good idea, love,' Dad said before scampering after her.

Who knew Dad could be so pleasant? That was a turn-up for the books. Once they were out of the room, I made myself scarce. I'd got away with the charade up until now, but I didn't want to tempt fate.

Mum looked exhausted and needed to sleep, so Dad would be at a loose end. I had no intention of babysitting him. I had to find Lily, and that wasn't going to happen if I was sitting across the table making polite conversation with him. So much for having the house to myself.

The more time we spent in each other's company, the greater the chance he'd catch me out. I was amazed I'd got away with it. I'd had a lucky break. Mum being ill had provided a very welcome distraction as Dad's attention was focused on making sure his Queen had everything she needed. It was endearing to witness his devotion. What the hell was wrong with me? I was going soft. That would never do.

65

DAISY

I grabbed a pair of Lily's trackies and one of her sweatshirts from the ironing pile. Taking them into the downstairs toilet, I got changed into them. Then I lifted her coat and handbag off the hook, slipped on her Ugg boots and disappeared out of the front door before Dad reappeared. I needed to plan, and that wouldn't happen if he was breathing down my neck.

When I stepped outside, I shuddered. It was bitterly cold, and a fine drizzle, the kind that made your hair double in size, was falling, so I needed to find somewhere to take refuge from the elements. Quickly. Before I froze to death. As I paced along, the dank air was thick with traffic fumes. I almost coughed up a lung when a van's diesel engine engulfed me in a plume. Once this was all over, I'd have to give up the fags.

The familiar blue and white sign of Greggs wasn't far away. My eyes fixed on it as it grew closer. I pushed open the door. The heat and delicious aroma dragged me in from the pavement. I could almost taste the bacon roll and flat white before I'd ordered it. Once I'd been served, I sat down at a table furthest away from the window. I didn't want to be distracted by people-watching.

The way MacKenzie had reacted to Lily being snatched had made me suspicious he was involved. Although, logic told me Samson had to be behind this. Igor would never have let anybody into the club after closing unless he was following the boss's orders. But why would Samson want to kidnap Lily? Was this his way of taking revenge on me for Christmas Eve? I couldn't imagine he'd be that petty. MacKenzie reckoned women threw themselves at him every day of the week. And I believed that. Embarrassing as it was, some females thought it was acceptable to offer themselves up on a plate to a powerful man with money as though they were some kind of commodity. After he'd molested me in the toilet, he'd said women like me were ten a penny. A shiver ran down my spine as the memory lodged in my brain. I knew first-hand what he was capable of, so if he was holding Lily she was in real danger. I'd have to act fast before something terrible happened. I'd never been close to my sister but I'd never forgive myself if she came to harm because I'd rejected the head honcho's advances.

I had to confront Samson. If I took him by surprise, I might be able to catch him off guard. Glancing at my watch, I realised it was eight o'clock in the morning. I didn't feel brave enough to knock on his door this early. It would have to wait until later. Sorry, Lily. In the meantime, I'd have to find out where he lived or get a contact number for him. Neither of those things were going to be easy. I knew MacKenzie wouldn't give them to me, so I'd have to find out for myself.

I started surfing the web on my phone using Samson Fox's name, and after a while, I stumbled across an article in House Beautiful featuring a makeover he'd done on his seven-bedroom, six-bathroom mansion in Sutton Lane, close to Battersea Park. The article was four years old, but I bet he still lived there. Nobody went to the trouble of redecorating an enormous property like that if they were planning to move in the near future. That was excellent news. According to Google maps, it was about fifty minutes from here on the train.

The thought of visiting Samson didn't appeal to me at all, but if I didn't help my sister escape from her kidnapper's clutches, who was going to save her?

66

MACKENZIE

I'd been trying to decide on the best course of action when my phone pinged as a text came through. I'd been expecting it to be another threatening one from Arben as he turned up the heat, but that wasn't the case. I felt the colour drain from my face when read the message.

> Did you really think I wouldn't find out about your deal with Arben?

As Samson's words registered in my brain, they exploded like fireworks. The letters scrambled together and scattered my thoughts. Oh, Jesus. Now, I was well and truly fucked! There was no time for weighing up options; I needed to get my arse into gear. The clock was ticking like the fuse on a bomb waiting to go off. I was under pressure. The fear of what would happen if I didn't do something made my stomach flip. It was do or die.

I paced out of the room and along the hallway. I couldn't get to the sacred kitchen drawer soon enough for my liking. My trembling fingers fumbled to open the bag and the silver case. After snorted down the coke, I pulled out a chair and waited for the hit. Even two lines of rocket fuel didn't give my confidence the boost it needed to see a way out of this mess. Having one villain after me was bad enough, but now that another one had jumped on board, I had a horrible feeling the last of my nine lives were up.

I'd had my fair share of scrapes and run-ins with both the law and the lawless over the years. But this was a greater threat than anything I'd faced before. The Albanians were cut-throat by nature, and Samson was one of the meanest fuckers I'd ever encountered. The world and his wife were on my back, demanding their pound of flesh. Only I could manage to piss off two rival gangsters at the same time. Samson and Arben were baying for my blood. I wasn't about to hang around here waiting to see which one got to me first.

My old boss, Roscoe Allen, had left London a few years back in search of early retirement and a quiet life by the sea. Nah, not really. He was still very much operational, albeit on a new patch. Heading down to Kent seemed like an excellent prospect if you asked me.

Roscoe had been the main player around Brixton until Samson had muscled in on his territory. He'd accepted defeat gracefully, but the score had been left unsettled. Roscoe had asked me to go with him, but I'd turned him down. I was a London boy, born and bred, and I couldn't picture myself living anywhere else at the time, but those white cliffs were looking very tempting right about now. I had no intention of being caught. Staying under the radar was the way forward.

I'd throw some clothes and a few bits in a bag and get on the road asap. Samson knew where I lived, so this would be the first place he'd come looking. I'd give Roscoe a call en route. I didn't want to turn up on his doorstep like a bad penny. I was pretty sure he'd welcome me with open arms. Why wouldn't he? We'd parted on good terms, and he hated Samson with a passion, so I was hoping I could count on him for protection.

Daisy was in a vulnerable position. Arben and Samson would want revenge, so she may well have a price on her head. The chances were one of them was behind Lily's disappearance. And if they were, it was my fault. I was seriously worried she was going to come to harm.

I briefly considered inviting Daisy to come with me, but she'd be like an albatross hanging around my neck. Roscoe was more likely to take me in as a single bloke than if I was part of a couple. If he agreed to put a roof over my head, he wasn't going to put me up for nothing. I'd have to work to pay my way. I didn't want Daisy to get involved in dealing, so she'd be dead wood. Brutal as it sounded, she'd be a hindrance, not a help.

I was a prize bellend. I'd tried to look out for the twins right from the get-go, but instead of keeping them safe they were both now in danger because of me. I was gutted. I hadn't intentionally dragged them into this. But the situation had spiralled out of control and I was powerless to stop it from escalating.

67

Just as I was about to leave Greggs to take the train to Battersea Park, I remembered Lily's car was still in Eden's staff car park. Thank God Dad was too preoccupied with Mum not to have noticed it wasn't outside the house, or I'd have had some explaining to do.

I rummaged through her handbag to make sure the key was inside before braving the elements again. I was sorry to say nothing had improved since I'd taken refuge in my favourite spot. I'd intended to walk, but if I took the bus, I'd be there in five minutes, which would shave off ten minutes and, more importantly, save me from getting frostbite. As I emerged from the shop, I could see a number forty in the distance, so I legged it to the empty bus stop and stuck out my arm.

Once I was sitting behind the wheel, I typed Sutton Lane into the search bar on Waze and hit view routes. The South Circular was the quickest. I hated that road, but I'd just have to suck it up and get on with it. At least there wasn't a lot of traffic around today.

I turned off the A3220 and onto Sutton Lane. I didn't know which number Samson lived at. But I was confident I'd recognise the house from the photos. It was very distinctive. It had off-white walls, a grey Mansard roof and dormer windows which made it look like a French manor house.

I cruised slowly from one end of the road to the other, leaning towards the windscreen, but I couldn't see the impressive house anywhere. It wasn't as though you could miss a huge mansion like that. I couldn't help thinking it didn't belong on a road like this.

After reading the article, I'd been expecting multi-million-pound properties set back from wide tree-lined pavements, but it was like the poor lived on one side and the rich on the other. Left versus right. It was really strange. I don't think I'd ever seen a road like it before. At the top of the road, a modern, flat-roofed, red brick building faced a grand period property with a front garden full of huge exotic palms that could rival the ones at Kew Gardens. Its next-door neighbour was an impressive detached Edwardian villa. Further along, four-storey stucco-fronted Georgian properties rubbed shoulders with loft-converted Victorian semis. In contrast, tower blocks spread along most of the right-hand side of the road. I loved the fact that none of the houses were the same, but I knew which side of the street I'd want to live on.

When I came to a T-junction, I was beginning to wonder if I'd gone to the wrong Sutton Lane. It wouldn't be the first time I'd got the name right, but the wrong location. I decided to turn the car around and take one last look. If I was in the right place, the house had to be on the side of the road with the elegant homes. I inched Lily's Fiat 500 along until I came to the first house on the street, the property with the palms. I hadn't noticed to begin with because I'd been expecting to be able to see Samson's place from the road, but there was a huge metal gate between that house and the Edwardian one. Maybe it was behind that.

I pulled into the driveway and stopped the car outside the electric gate. There was an intercom installed on the right-hand side, so

I unwound the window and pressed the buzzer. As I waited for a response, I couldn't shake the sense of impending doom. It was hovering over me like a black cloud.

The screen came to life, and a woman in her fifties appeared on it, which took me by surprise. I'd been expecting to hear a voice, not engage in a video call. I should have known Samson would go the extra mile. Flash bastard.

'Can I help you?' the woman asked.

'I'm here to see Samson Fox,' I replied.

When she asked, 'Is he expecting you?' I knew I had the right house.

'No, but I need to speak to him urgently.'

'Who should I say is calling?'

'Daisy Kennedy.'

'One moment, please.'

I was beginning to think she'd forgotten when the solid electric gate slowly slid to one side. It wasn't the wrought iron type with railings to allow passers-by a sneaky glimpse of the property. It was solid. Impenetrable. Worryingly so. The thought of being behind it with Samson almost stopped me in my tracks, but I'd come this far, so I wouldn't back out now.

I drove Lily's car along the tarmac towards the detached monster of a house which was surrounded by high walls and set within enormous, manicured grounds. The sprawling property had the seclusion of a country house and was so far back from the road, you would walk right past the entrance if you didn't know it was here. Who would have thought a plot of this size would be hiding behind a very ordinary, albeit enormous, metal gate? Its position was unique in a relatively built-up part of London. So private, yet so central.

When I stopped outside the house, Samson's housekeeper was standing in the doorway, dressed in a black short-sleeved dress with a white starched collar and a white apron tied around her thickened waist. A ball of nerves bounced around my stomach as I walked up to her.

'Please come in,' she said, offering me a warm smile.

The entrance hall was enormous, with marble floors and a sweeping staircase. In the centre, a glass octagonal dome flooded the space with light. Leading off the hall were several doors on either side.

'If you'd like to follow me, please?'

The housekeeper led me into the first room on the right. It had high ceilings and was an interior design masterpiece; everything was either white, silver or shades of blue. My attention was drawn through the large windows facing me, which offered a view of the extensive gardens. Evergreens, exotic palms of every shape and size and an enormous holly bush laden with bright red berries were peppered between formal flower beds. The grounds were breath taking, even in the depths of winter. They could give any of London's Royal Parks a run for their money. A paved seating area was on the far right and a two-storey house stood behind that. I guessed it was either guest accommodation or used by staff.

'Mr Fox will be with you shortly. Can I get you some tea or coffee?'

'No thanks,' I replied.

I could hear his footsteps before he came into view.

'I don't remember inviting you around?'

My heart started galloping in my chest as we stood opposite each other, locked in eye contact. Samson was wearing a plush navy dressing gown and a pair of sliders. It was clear I'd got him out of bed. He didn't look happy. I'd go so far as to say he was livid.

'Where's Lily?' I asked, getting straight to the point.

Samson looked taken aback by my directness. My stomach flipped when he stepped into my personal space.

'How the fuck should I know?'

His voice was so loud it almost loosened my teeth. And his morning breath was stale. Repulsive. I had to stop myself from flinching when it hit me full force in the face. I was beginning to wish I'd taken a more gentle approach now. It was never a good idea to poke a bear, was it?

'Last night, three guys bundled her into a car outside Eden's. She was bound and gagged,' I said. There was no point in back-peddling.

'What's that got to do with me?'

Now, it was my turn to be surprised. His lack of empathy was astounding.

'It has everything to do with you. It's your club, and she's your employee...'

'I'd lose the attitude if I were you,' Samson threatened, taking a step towards me.

'Is everything OK, boss?' A huge guy dressed in a dark suit and tie stepped into the room.

Samson nodded, and the man retreated.

'Why did you kidnap my sister?' I turned the palms of my hands out.

'Stop flipping your tits! I suggest you rein it in, right now.' Samson's lip curled as he jabbed his index finger in my face. 'You turn up on my doorstep and accuse me of taking Lily without a shred of evidence. Where's your proof of my involvement?'

I could see Samson's heavy step back into the room out of the corner of my eye.

'There's no way Igor would have let the men in unless he was following orders,' I replied, trying not to squirm as I realised how flaky that sounded.

Samson laughed in my face.

'That's it? That's all you've got on me? You're pathetic. You should look closer to home before you start throwing wild accusations around. I've got a good mind to let Gary teach you a lesson you won't forget in a hurry.' Samson gestured with a flick of his head to the bodyguard filling the doorway.

The dark-haired man had a boxer's nose, and the way his square jaw jutted forward made him look like he was primed and ready to fight.

'What do you mean I should look closer to home?' I asked, tearing my eyes away from the hired muscle as I brushed Samson's threat to one side.

'If I had to make an educated guess, I'd say MacKenzie's behind the kidnapping. I'm sure I don't need to tell you he's the manager at the club. Well, he used to be, anyway. Don't you think Igor would follow his orders, too?'

Samson looked so smug, which made me feel like a complete fool. I hadn't wanted to believe MacKenzie was involved, but he'd been acting shady around me since he'd got into my pants. Now, it was time to face facts. To say I was gutted was an understatement. I'd trusted him. Saw a future with him. And he'd let me down in the worst way possible. I'd sensed he was hiding something from me, but I had no idea it had anything to do with Lily. No wonder he didn't want the police involved. Somebody had called him just after she'd been taken. I'd hung around outside his office, but I couldn't work out who he'd been talking to, as I could only hear one side of the conversation. As I tried to make sense of it all, something Samson had said suddenly slapped me around the face.

'Sorry, did you say MacKenzie *used* to be the manager?'

I'd warned him about selling drugs at Eden's, but he'd taken no notice of me.

Samson nodded. 'Igor just told me MacKenzie's quit his job without giving notice. He's left me high and dry, which is unacceptable. I sent one of my guys over to his flat to ram that message home, but the fucker's shot through.'

It wouldn't have surprised me if MacKenzie had been fired. What shocked me was that he'd left his job without saying a word to me. He was turning into more of an arsehole with every minute that passed.

'What makes you think he's got anything to do with Lily going missing?' I asked the question, but I was dreading hearing the answer.

'He owes money to the Albanian mafia. They run a prostitution ring. I'm sure you can work out the rest...' Samson let his sentence trail off.

My breath caught in my throat as a memory hit me between the eyes. MacKenzie had said something about show business being fickle and implied that Lily and I could make our living out of wealthy men, but I'd thought it was an insensitive joke.

'My guess is that MacKenzie has taken Lily to use her as a bargaining tool. He's up to his neck in debt, and a beautiful blue-eyed blonde fetches a lot of money, particularly in the Middle Eastern market. The pimp who buys her will want to get his money's worth. Lily can expect to service ten to fifteen clients a day.' Samson smiled.

My blood ran cold as Samson's words registered. He was a creep, and I suddenly felt uncomfortable. It was time to go.

'I shouldn't have come barging into your house uninvited. I think I owe you an apology...'

I offered him a weak smile, but he threw me a scowl in return. A ticking clock on the mantelpiece filled the silence between us. Counting down the time before one of us was forced to speak.

'You owe me a bit more than that.'

And just like that, it was Christmas Eve, and I was back in the ladies' toilets. I needed to respond, but every drop of moisture had left my mouth. My words stayed static on my tongue. Before I knew what was happening, Gary grabbed hold of my arms and pulled them behind my back with one hand while holding a knife against my throat with the other.

'Maybe I should let Gary alter your appearance to teach you a lesson.'

'Please don't.'

The back of the blade scraped my skin as I spoke. My body began to tremble as the enormity of what I'd walked into hit home. I was way out of my depth. My stubbornness had made me resilient, so I'd waded in without properly thinking through who I was taking on. Even though I hated to admit it, I was no match for Samson. I could feel the sting of tears and had to fight to keep them at bay.

'Gary's very handy with a knife. He could carve something right in the middle of your face. Then every time you look in the mirror, it will remind you what happens when you piss the wrong people off. What do you think, Gary?'

'I'd be happy to, but it's your call, boss,' Gary replied.

'I'm really sorry. I know I've messed up. Please don't hurt me.'

It was humiliating to beg, but there was no other way.

'It does seem a shame to disfigure such beautiful features...' Samson ran his index finger down my cheek, and my body broke out in goose pimples.

'I was out of order. Please let me make it up to you.'

Me and my big mouth. Why the hell did I say that?

'I was going to track that scrawny fucker down myself. I'm a big fan of blood sports and love hunting prey, especially the human variety. But it's a time-consuming business, and I'm hosting a party tonight. So if you want to get back into my good books, you could flush out MacKenzie to save me the trouble,' Samson said.

It wasn't as though I was in a position to refuse.

'OK.'

I was more than a bit relieved that he hadn't suggested a sexual favour.

'You've probably noticed I'm not your biggest fan. You have no idea how close you came to losing your slot at Eden's.'

I felt my mouth drop open, but I said nothing.

'You're a tramp. I hate women who can't hold their drink. After your little display at my Christmas party, if it hadn't been for MacKenzie fighting your corner, I'd have slung you out of the door. Now, are you still prepared to flush out your knight in shining armour?' Samson looked pleased with himself.

'Yes.'

I didn't hesitate to answer. Even though he'd stuck up for me, serving up MacKenzie would be a pleasure. He'd turned out to be a total prick. Our fledgling relationship was dead in the water. Getting Lily back and saving my own skin were far more important.

'So much for loyalty.' Samson laughed.

He was getting so much pleasure from belittling me but I had to hold my tongue. It would be a suicidal move to react.

'Don't fuck this up, or I'll personally do a job on that pretty little face of yours.' Samson looked down his nose at me before his lips lifted into a smile.

68

DAISY

I'd had a lucky escape; I didn't think I was going to get out of the house in one piece. I was certain Samson was going to let Gary loose with that knife or torture me in some other way. I'd been terrified he'd demand I have sex with him or, at the very least, give him a blow job. But he hadn't laid a finger on me. Having said that, freedom still seemed like a long way off.

I kept looking in the rearview mirror as I drove along Samson's driveway in case he was coming after me. The gate, separating me from the outside world, rolled back at a snail's pace as I sat behind the wheel with sweating palms, hoping it would hurry up. The second there was enough space to manoeuvre the Fiat through, I put the car into gear and shot through the opening.

Me and my big mouth. How the hell was I going to track MacKenzie down? I didn't have the faintest clue where he might be. But Samson's threat was looming over me, so I had to keep my word. Failure wasn't an option. I needed to come up with a plan quickly, but my head was spinning, so I drove the short distance to Battersea Park. A walk might help me to think straight. There was nothing like a blast of fresh air to liven up the senses.

After wandering around while racking my brains for what seemed like an eternity, I stopped to admire the view of the Chelsea Embankment. After a while, I turned away and was gazing up at the Peace Pagoda when a memory came hurtling towards me at the speed of light. I remembered MacKenzie mentioning his old boss. I was pretty sure he'd said he ran a pub in Dover, but I couldn't think what it was called. I took my phone out of my pocket and googled pubs in the area. As soon as I saw The Castle, I recognised the name.

I might be about to go on a wild goose chase, but I didn't have a better idea, so it was as good a place as any to start. I loaded the address into Waze. It was two hours and ten minutes away. Fuck. That was a long way to go on a hunch.

As I walked towards the car, my mind was in turmoil. I'd be lying if I said I wasn't worried about my safety. If MacKenzie was mixed up with a prostitution ring, I didn't want to end up in the same position as Lily. I knew the way men's depraved minds worked where twins were concerned. Tracking him down could be a dangerous move. I had to weigh up the balance between helping my sister and getting myself into trouble. It wasn't an easy decision to make, especially when you threw Samson's threat into the equation. I couldn't decide what to do for the best.

69

MACKENZIE

Driving to Dover had been a smart move. My old boss, Roscoe, hadn't let me down. When I'd told him that Samson was making me pay back the money that was stolen out of the safe over Christmas, so I'd had to shoot through, not only did he offer me a job with accommodation on the spot, but he offered his protection, too.

I'd only arrived a couple of hours ago, but he'd already put me to work behind the bar. I wasn't complaining, there wasn't a single customer in sight. But an empty boozer was a double-edged sword. With nothing to do, the time was dragging. My guess was people were saving themselves until later. New Year's Eve was one of the busiest nights of the year. So I should enjoy the calm before the storm.

I'd been familiarising myself with the stock's layout when a text came through on my phone. I opened the message from a withheld number, and an image of Lily tied to a chair with her mouth taped stared back at me. She looked terrified. I got such a shock I almost dropped the handset. My finger hovered over the play button for several seconds. I wasn't sure I wanted to see the footage, but I eventually pressed it. Lily's large eyes seemed bigger than usual as she looked at the camera. I bit down on my lip while I watched the ten-second clip. Lily was in a nondescript room, and the sound had been muted, so I had no idea where she was or who had taken her. A fresh wave of panic came hurtling towards me as I digested the fact that the kidnapper knew my personal mobile number.

I didn't hear her come in until I glanced up from my phone. I jumped out of my skin when I realised she was standing on the other side of the bar, watching my every move.

'Hi, MacKenzie.'

I felt like I'd seen a ghost.

'Hi, Daisy. What are you doing here?'

Thoughts were racing through my head at a million miles an hour. How did she know where to find me?

'You don't look very pleased to see me,' Daisy laughed.

'Of course I am. You've just taken me by surprise, that's all.'

I gave her a beaming smile as the lie rolled off my tongue.

'What brings you to Kent?' I asked, as she hadn't answered my question.

'I could ask you the same thing. Nice of you to tell me you were leaving.'

The look on Daisy's face told me she wasn't impressed that I hadn't said goodbye.

'It was a last-minute decision...' I let my sentence trail off. I didn't want to go into details.

'I won't keep you. I can see you're rushed off your feet.' Daisy cast her eyes around the empty bar before she turned her attention back to me. 'I was hoping you might be able to shed some light on Lily's kidnappers.'

Daisy fixed her piercing blue eyes on me, and my balls started to tingle.

Had she seen me watching the video? She couldn't have done. I was holding the phone too close.

'So she hasn't turned up then.'

Denial was about to become my best friend.

'You know she hasn't. Where is she?' Daisy asked, narrowing her eyes.

I was taken aback by her directness. This was going to be harder than I'd thought. My heart was hammering in my chest.

'How would I know?'

'It's so obvious you're lying.'

Convincing Daisy I was innocent wasn't working, so I tried a different approach.

'Excuse me?' I did my best to sound outraged.

'Just tell me what you've done with her.'

Daisy's interrogation wasn't showing any sign of coming to an end.

'I haven't done anything with her. You said you saw three guys bundle her into the back of a car...'

'How much did you get for her?' Daisy looked daggers at me.

'What the fuck are you talking about?'

'Samson told me all about the money you owe to the Albanian mafia, and he said you were going to sell Lily into prostitution to clear the debt.'

My head started banging. I should have realised Samson was behind this.

'And you believed him? Did you really think I'd be capable of doing something like that? Jesus, Daisy.' I shook my head.

'I don't know what to believe! I'm clutching at straws. But something bad has happened to my sister. I know that for a fact.'

Daisy's beautiful face looked troubled, and I genuinely felt bad for her.

'I'm sure the Albanians have taken her, but I don't know how to find them. I desperately need your help.'

'Listen, Daisy, if I could, I would, but I swear to you, I have no idea how to get hold of them.'

'I feel so helpless. What should I do?'

Daisy fixed me with pleading eyes.

'I know it's hard, but you'll have to sit tight for the time being. If Lily has been kidnapped, the people who've got her are going to want a ransom paid before they release her.'

That wasn't strictly true. If the Albanians had taken her, she'd be on a one-way ticket to the sex trade. There wouldn't be any negotiating with her family. The deal would already have been done, but I wasn't going to tell Daisy that, or I'd never get rid of her.

'How am I meant to pay a ransom? I haven't got any money!' Daisy threw her hands up in the air.

'It just so happens, I know a man who has! You're not going to like this, but Samson has more cash than he knows what to do with, and he should take some responsibility. Lily was snatched while she was on Eden's premises. If I were you, I'd ask for his help. He's very obliging where attractive women are concerned. And the Albanians will be wary of him. Samson's a powerful man.'

Daisy seemed to buy the rubbish I'd fed her. Even so, I still breathed a sigh of relief when she walked out the door.

70

DAISY

There'd been a strange atmosphere when I'd walked into The Castle. MacKenzie was glued to his phone, and he'd jumped out of his skin when he realised I was there. Turning up unannounced didn't always guarantee a warm welcome, but the look on his face said it all. He was almost repelled by my presence. From the indignation in MacKenzie's voice when I'd grilled him about Lily, it was obvious he'd taken offence at my comments.

I'd channelled my inner Gestapo to try and draw information out of him, but he wasn't giving anything away. I'd reached a dead end. There was no sign of Lily. MacKenzie was either telling the truth, or he'd already exchanged her to clear the debt. Time was slipping through my fingers. The sooner I phoned Samson, the sooner this would be over. I wouldn't dare double-cross him, or I'd end up with a price on my head.

I took my mobile out of my pocket as soon as I left the pub. I started walking along the promenade, but the seagulls were squawking so loudly overhead that I had to turn right and head towards the town centre to get away from the noise.

'Hi Samson, it's Daisy,' I said when he answered the call. 'I've found MacKenzie.'

'Really? That was quick.' Samson sounded shocked.

'I told you I'd find him.'

Confidence was the key here.

'So where's the scrawny little runt hiding out? Up a chimney?' Samson chuckled.

'He's in Dover,' I replied. My tone was flat. I couldn't bring myself to laugh at his joke. 'I'll text you the address.'

'Stay where you are. Gary's on his way,' Samson replied before ending the call.

I was in for a long wait unless Gary was about to change into a red cape and blue Lycra suit and fly here like Superman. It had taken me over two hours to get to Kent from Samson's house. It wasn't exactly a day at the seaside weather. It was blowing a gale, and the English Channel was the colour of mud. Even Dover Castle looked ominous. It appeared to hover over the town, looming out of wispy grey clouds. It was way too windy to risk a walk along the iconic White Cliffs. And for obvious reasons, I couldn't go back inside the pub, even though it was warm and cosy, so I'd have to take refuge in the car instead.

With time on my hands, my thoughts went into overdrive. I'd kept my word to Samson and tracked down MacKenzie, but I was no closer to finding out who'd taken Lily. Although, everything was pointing towards the Albanians. I had no idea how to contact them, and even if I could track them down, I wasn't brave enough to take them on. It would be a suicidal move for me, and it wouldn't help Lily. It was a no-win situation. I felt off-kilter. A sense of unease had wrapped itself around me.

The cold was seeping into my bones as I waited for Gary to arrive. Just as I was losing the will to live, a Range Rover with blacked-out windows pulled up next to me. A heartbeat later, Gary got out of the driver's door. I scrambled to pull back the handle with numb fingers.

'Where's MacKenzie?' Gary asked.

I was tempted to say, 'Kiss my arse.' But I thought better of it.

'He's in the pub,' I replied.

Gary pushed his enormous shoulders back and paced towards the door. I scampered along after him. Not that I'd be any help, but I wanted to see the guy I'd once put on a pedestal, who was more than likely responsible for my sister's disappearance, brought into line.

I stood back as Gary burst through the doors. My heart started pounding when I realised the place was deserted. Maybe MacKenzie was changing a barrel or had gone on a break while no customers were around.

'Where the fuck is he?' Gary's eyes blazed as he grabbed me by the throat.

Pain shot through my body as my windpipe constricted. I couldn't have answered him even if I'd wanted to. I looked into his face, contorted by rage, with pleading eyes. Gary released his grip on my neck and slammed his massive fist onto the bar. His hand was clenched so tightly that his knuckles had turned white. The force made the bottles rattle in the optics.

'He must be here somewhere. I've been outside the whole time.'

Gary started rampaging through the pub, trying to find MacKenzie. For my own safety, I stayed near the door so I could run if I needed to. My heartbeat went into overdrive when I saw Gary round the corner with his fists clenched. He was almost frothing at the mouth, focused on tracking his prey. Who needed an XL Bully when you had Gary on your team?

Gary reached me in three steps and fixed his hand around my throat again. My lungs burned as I gasped for air. The more I struggled, the more he tightened the pressure. Gary's steely eyes were cold as they bored into mine.

'The fucker's given us the slip. Samson's not going to be happy.'

Gary's words bounced around in my brain as he pulsated his grip. I felt lightheaded. Faint. But he was relentless. In the absence of MacKenzie, he was taking his anger out on me, and I was powerless to stop him.

'Right, you're coming with me.' Gary sprayed me with saliva as he got right up in my face.

I tried to dig my heels in, but Gary dragged me out of the pub and tossed me onto the backseat of the car before locking the doors. Confronting Samson had been a huge mistake. I should have known it wouldn't achieve anything. And by agreeing to do his dirty work, I'd made things ten times worse. I was shitting myself. He was definitely going to make me suffer.

71

DAISY

It was dark by the time we'd made it back to London. Some New Year's Eve this turned out to be. I couldn't remember a worse one, and I had a few disastrous offerings to choose from. In my experience, it was either the best night ever or the worst. There was no middle ground.

Gary turned into Sutton Lane and stopped the Range Rover outside the metal gate. Dread started to rise up within me as it slid open. By the time I caught sight of Samson pacing backwards and forwards on his tarmacked drive, my heart was hammering in my chest. His huge house was lit up like Buckingham Palace, so I could see his expression clearly. He wasn't happy. More than that. He was boiling mad. Fuming.

I started shaking like a leaf. I was in way over my head. I liked to think I could talk the talk, but it was clear I couldn't walk the walk. Playing with the big boys was harder than it looked. I couldn't match their strength. Gary had thrown me around like a rag doll. If I wanted to live to see another day, I'd have to engage my brain and pull myself together. And not let fear paralyse me.

As soon as the car came to a stop, Samson pulled open the back door. He leaned in and grabbed me by the arm. I could smell the alcohol on his breath and tried to stay out of his reach, but he made contact with me and hauled me towards the door. I'd tried to resist, but I was hurting myself in the process. Samson overpowered me and frogmarched me into the house.

'You had one job to do, and you fucked it up. The golden rule is, you never take your eye off the ball. But you let that little fucker slip through your fingers, so now you're toast,' Samson bellowed into my face, pulling me up onto my tiptoes by the lapels of Lily's coat.

'You told me to find him, not bring him back to London. I kept my part of the deal,' I said.

It was the first thing that came into my head, and I'd thought it was a good response until Samson's fist made contact with my face. Pain shot through my cheek as my head snapped back like the punch ball on a stand collecting dust in our garage. My mouth was always getting me into trouble.

'Stop fucking winding me up, you bitch.' Samson's eyes were blazing.

I could feel my lip trembling, but I refused to cry. It was time to dig deep.

'I've got a good mind to finish you off. You're a fucking waste of space. I have zero tolerance for people not following through on an agreement. I'm a man of principle, and I never go back on my word.'

'I found him once. I can find him again,' I said.

The side of my face was starting to swell, so my voice appeared strange. Samson glared at me. The only sound was the clock on the mantelpiece ticking. I could feel my cheek throbbing in time with it. Before he could answer, a text came through on my phone. It was vibrating in my pocket.

'Who the fuck's messaging you?' Samson's face contorted with rage.

'I don't know.' I had to hold back the tears that were threatening to flow.

'Don't you think you should find out? It might be MacKenzie.'

I doubted that very much, but I didn't want to piss Samson off more than I already had, so I delved my hand into Lily's coat pocket, pulled out my mobile and opened the message. I could see Lily beaming at me. I couldn't stop my tears from rolling down my cheeks.

'What the fuck are you crying about, you stupid bitch?' Samson roared.

'It's Lily,' I sobbed, turning the handset towards him so that he could see the footage before I hit play. 'I just wanted to let you know that I'm alive and well.'

I was annoyed at myself for letting the floodgates open, but was so relieved, my emotions got the better of me.

'Well, well, well. MacKenzie must have thought better of handing her over to the Albanians because if they'd got their hands on her, she wouldn't be walking away now,' Samson replied. 'It's ironic, really. Lily's free, but you're up to your neck in shit.'

Even though I hadn't managed to bring MacKenzie back, Lily was safe, so some good had come out of the situation. I couldn't believe I'd contemplated abandoning her. What was wrong with me? How could my jealousy run that deeply? Leaving my sister to fend for herself was an appalling idea, whichever angle I looked at it. I was ashamed of myself. But beating myself up over it wasn't going to help me now. I had my own battle to face.

'I know I've fucked up, and I'm really sorry about that. But if you give me a second chance, I promise I'll lure MacKenzie back so you can settle the score.'

I'd gone against my natural instincts and taken a submissive role. I'd never aspired to be a doormat, but I was prepared to give it a go to try and smooth things over. Samson considered himself an Alpha male. King of the jungle. And men like that viewed women as the second sex, and although it went against everything I believed in, I had to play smart. We'd got off to a bad start, so he wasn't invested in my well-being. I meant nothing to him. He wouldn't think twice about disposing of me. I was surplus to requirements. If a bit of sucking up meant I got to walk away unscathed, then so be it. Bring it on. Subservience was the only tool I had in my arsenal. I was going to have to go back to basics.

'What do you think, Gary? Should we see if sugar tits can reel him in?' Samson laughed.

I was riled up by his offensive comment, but I had to keep my expression neutral while in the company of a couple of cavemen armed with imaginary clubs.

'It's your call, boss,' the square-jawed knucklehead replied.

'She might just be able to do it. Mac definitely had the hots for her,' Samson said as his eyes roamed over every inch of my body.

I felt like a piece of meat. It was humiliating. Degrading. But necessary. Just keep your cool, I told myself. Losing it now could be a fatal move.

'Mac said you were the kind of woman who gave a man an instant hard-on. He must have been easily aroused. I can't say I'm getting that reaction.' Samson looked down at his crotch before rearranging his balls. 'How about you, Gary? Is anything stirring?'

Samson's face stretched into a broad smile. He was enjoying every minute of the verbal torture. Trying to break me down with his words. Reduce me to tears. But I had a thick skin. And a temper. I was boiling mad and wanted to lash out at him. That wasn't an option, so I stood in front of him with a dejected look on my face, which seemed to do the trick. Thinking he was upsetting me gave him an immense amount of pleasure.

'Nope. I can't say that there is,' Gary replied.

The feeling was mutual. I didn't find either of them remotely attractive either.

'MacKenzie was gagging for you and never stopped singing your praises. But there's no accounting for taste.'

I only just managed to stop myself from rolling my eyes. Samson was like a broken record. A grown man with the mentality of a five-year-old. He didn't rate me. I got the message loud and clear.

'If that's the case, surely I'm your best chance of flushing him out,' I said, hoping to focus Samson's attention back on MacKenzie.

'Decisions, decisions. Will you live, or will you die?'

I was having trouble concentrating, distracted by the sound of Samson's words rushing around my head. I had to force myself to find my voice.

'I know you don't like me, but killing me seems like an extreme reaction.'

Speaking up was a judgement call. I didn't know whether it would help or not, but the situation was so dire it couldn't really get any worse.

'I've killed for less,' Samson replied.

A sob escaped from my lips. I couldn't help it. I was shitting myself. I had a really bad feeling about this. Samson's eyes bored into mine. My fate was in his hands. All I could do was try and swallow down my rising panic while he mulled things over. He was taking forever. Prolonging the agony. Not knowing what was going to happen to me was torture.

'You know what, I'm feeling generous, so I'll exchange your life for MacKenzie's.'

'Thank you,' I said, as relief washed over me. This wasn't the time to forget my manners.

'Don't let him slip through your fingers again,' Samson replied.

'I won't.'

'Gary's going to be sticking to you like glue to make sure you don't,' Samson grinned.

72

DAISY

The pressure I was under was fucking with my brain, and I was struggling to think straight, but there was too much riding on this to let MacKenzie get one over on me. As far as he was concerned, he'd fobbed me off with a load of old flannel and sent me packing so he wouldn't be expecting me to come back again.

It was a long shot, but I had a hunch MacKenzie would still be at the pub in Dover. It wasn't as though he had many options, and there was no way he'd be stupid enough to come back to London with Samson and the Albanians ready to tear him limb from limb. I reckoned he was hiding in plain sight. It was so obvious he wouldn't expect me to think of it.

I hadn't seen MacKenzie leave The Castle, but that didn't mean he hadn't slipped out the back door. As far as he was concerned, I was on my way back to the Big Smoke. He didn't know I'd been killing time waiting for Gary to arrive. I'd spent a lot of time scrolling through my phone so he'd have had plenty of opportunities to go out without me noticing.

The fact that MacKenzie wasn't inside The Castle when Gary arrived didn't mean he was on to us. He could have been on a break or running errands, for all I knew. I wasn't overjoyed about travelling to Kent for the second time in one day, especially with Gary. But it had to be worth a try. I didn't know where else to look, and my gut was telling me it was the right thing to do.

The pub was heaving, so Gary and I slipped inside unnoticed. Just as I'd suspected, MacKenzie was standing behind the bar as large as life. I looked up at Gary and smiled. He stayed stony-faced, keeping his eyes focused on the prey. We edged our way through the crowd to the far side of the pub, then slipped out of a side entrance and walked along the corridor, before stopping outside a door marked private. From the position of it, it had to lead to the bar.

I pulled the handle towards me and let my XL Bully off the lead. He went straight for the target. MacKenzie yelped when his arm was wrenched up behind his back. A second later, Gary spun him around to face me.

'Happy New Year!' I smiled.

The look on MacKenzie's face said it all. I couldn't wait to phone Samson and give him the good news.

ACKNOWLEDGEMENTS

Thank you to my lovely editor, Emily Ruston, for all your brilliant suggestions and for helping me strengthen the story. This was the first time we've worked together. It was an absolute pleasure, and I'm really looking forward to working on the rest of the series with you!

Thanks to all the dream team who've worked so hard on this book. A special mention should go to Amanda Ridout, Nia Beynon, Jenna Houston, Debra Newhouse, David Boxell, Colin Thomas, Ben Wilson, Gemma Lawrence and Chris Simmons.

Thanks to Caroline Ridding and everyone at Boldwood Books for making me feel so welcome and supported.

As always, thank you to the amazing readers. Without you, none of this would be possible. I hope you enjoy the book!

ABOUT THE AUTHOR

Stephanie Harte is the bestselling gang-lit author of seven crime novels set in London's East End. Previously published by Head of Zeus, she lives in North West London.

Sign up to Stephanie Harte's mailing list for news, competitions and updates on future books.

Visit Stephanie's website: www.stephanieharte.com

Follow Stephanie on social media here:

 facebook.com/stephanieharteauthor

 x.com/@StephanieHarte3

 instagram.com/stephanieharteauthor

PEAKY READERS

GANG LOYALTIES. DARK SECRETS.
BLOODY REVENGE.

A READER COMMUNITY FOR
GANGLAND CRIME THRILLER FANS!

DISCOVER PAGE-TURNING NOVELS
FROM YOUR FAVOURITE AUTHORS
AND MEET NEW FRIENDS.

JOIN OUR BOOK CLUB
FACEBOOK GROUP

BIT.LY/PEAKYREADERSFB

SIGN UP TO OUR
NEWSLETTER

BIT.LY/PEAKYREADERSNEWS

Boldwood

Boldwood Books is an award-winning fiction publishing company seeking out the best stories from around the world.

Find out more at www.boldwoodbooks.com

Join our reader community for brilliant books, competitions and offers!

Follow us
@BoldwoodBooks
@TheBoldBookClub

Sign up to our weekly
deals newsletter

https://bit.ly/BoldwoodBNewsletter

Printed in Great Britain
by Amazon

40623751R00178